Unforgettable Dreams

Also By Nikki A Lamers

The Unforgettable Series

The Unforgettable Summer (#1)

Unforgettable Nights (#2)

Unforgettable Dreams (#3)

Unforgettable Memories (#4)

The Unforgettable One (#5)

Unforgettable Mistakes (#6)

Home Duet

Dreams Lost and Found (#1)

Finding Home (#2)

Spin-off From The Unforgettable Series

Breaking Cycles (Coming In 2023)

Unforgettable Dreams

The Unforgettable Series #3

By Nikki A Lamers

Copyright

Second Edition

Cover Design by Jessica Scott, Uniquely Tailored

Frey Dreams an Imprint of Nikki A Lamers

ISBN 978-1-951185-19-0 (paperback)

ISBN 978-1-951185-18-3 (eBook)

Table of Contents

Chapter 1

Sara

I slam my cell phone down on my bed frustrated as all hell. I cringe at the sound of laughter coming from the front of the two-bedroom apartment I share with my roommate and best friend Liz. I close my eyes and take a couple deep breaths to calm my anxiety so I can step out of my room to face her and her boyfriend Blake.

I love Liz and Blake, but he is always so caring and attentive to her it makes me sick. Don't get me wrong, I'm thrilled for my best friend. If anyone deserves to be happy it's her, but sometimes it's too damn hard to watch two people so in love when I know I'll never have someone who will treat me the way he treats her. It sucks always trying to paste on a radiant face when I'm hurting.

"Sara, I'm home." Liz yells with way too much enthusiasm for my current mood. "Are you home?"

Straightening my shoulders, I answer with fake cheer, "I'm in here." Gritting my teeth, I try to think about something other than the disaster of a phone call I just had with my ex-boyfriend. He just won't leave me alone. I just don't get it. It's been more than a couple years. I thought for sure he'd forget about me by now. "I'll be right out," I call back praying she won't come in here while I try to pull myself together. I stand up and look at myself in the mirror. I'm wearing dark blue slim fit jeans and a thin fitted red sweater with tall black lined leather boots. I push away the unwanted tears from my pale cheeks, figuring my outfit is fine for a frigid January day in Maine.

I continue looking at myself in disgust. I have flat blonde hair and hazel eyes. I think my boring eyes make me look different from other blonde girls and not in a good way. I'm so plain standing next to anyone else, although I can fake it like the best of 'em. I'm only five-feet, three-inches and about one hundred and fifteen pounds, which I think is too much for a girl as short as me with my frame. Liz always tells me how pretty I am, but that's what best friends are for, making you feel good, even if what they say isn't true.

Although when it comes to my best friend, it is true. She's gorgeous. She's a few inches taller than me and has beautiful brown wavy hair and green eyes. Besides the fact that she is the sweetest person I have ever met in my life. When it comes to best friends, I'm definitely more than fortunate.

I take a deep breath and plaster on my smile before turning towards the door to throw it open. It flies so fast it slams against the wall inside my room, making Liz jump a mile. I smirk at her, already feeling slightly better. I force out a small laugh, "Oops, sorry, guess I don't know my own strength."

Liz's boyfriend Blake chuckles. She hits him playfully in the gut making him laugh even harder. In all honesty, it's not really fair for me to call it a gut. He has incredible abs along with his tall thin and toned body, but I prefer to think gut when it's attached to my best friend's gorgeous sandy brown haired and chocolate brown-eyed boyfriend. They really are perfect together as well as sickeningly happy. I wouldn't want it any other way, but that doesn't mean I don't ever feel jealous of Liz and her relationship. Who wouldn't want to be that blissful? Liz turns towards me and asks sweetly, "Are you ready to go?"

I scrunch up my face in confusion. "Go where?"

Liz laughs, "Did you forget already? I just spoke to you like a half hour ago and you said to come and pick you up."

"Oh yeah, I um got a phone call and I guess it distracted me," I sigh, stumbling over my explanation. "Let me just grab my coat and wallet," I tell her and turn back towards my room before Liz can decipher my distraction. She knows a little about my ex since we all went to the same school, but he graduated the year before us. She thinks we broke up because I decided to go to a different school, and we would be too far apart. Although that may be true, if I could have picked a school farther away from him, I would have. I don't ever want her to know the whole truth. I'm too embarrassed.

I walk back out with my navy down coat on and wallet in hand. Liz's eyes are filled with unwanted sympathy as she questions, "Brad call again?"

Heaving a sigh, I nod in confirmation, giving her a small smile. Since I ran into him a few weeks ago on New Year's Eve while he was home for Christmas break, he hasn't stopped pestering me. I honestly have no idea what to do. Instead of saying that though, I shrug it off claiming, "It's fine. Let's just forget about him and go get some burgers." I practically drag her out the door with Blake following close behind.

Within minutes we are at a pub with the best burgers in town. This place is a bar that serves incredible greasy food with a completely laid-back atmosphere. Perfect for a town with so many college students. The walls and tables are all wood with both photographs and artwork of local places and artists. We sit at a high-top table near the bar and I smile genuinely across the table at my best friend. "Thank you for bringing me with you guys on your date. I don't get to see enough of you lately." I smirk gesturing towards Blake. "This guy has been monopolizing all of your time."

9

Liz blushes and glances over at her boyfriend who grins back, looking at her adoringly. "I'm sorry," she apologizes.

I quickly shake my head interrupting her, "Don't be. I'm thrilled to see you so happy. You deserve it," I insist, grinning. "Just remember to let me tag along with you guys once in a while and don't forget about our girl time and I'm good," I promise. I quickly add, "As long as he keeps treating you right," glancing pointedly at Blake.

He chuckles and insists, "You know I will."

The waitress comes over and we all order cheeseburgers, fries and beers to go with it. My mouth waters just thinking about it. I can't wait. When the waitress walks away, my eyes drift around the bar to see if I recognize anyone. They don't make it too far, though when they land on the bartender. "Oh, holy mother of..." I trail off and unabashedly stare at the sexiest man I've ever seen in my life!

Liz asks, "What?" I point towards the beautiful man standing behind the bar. Blake just smirks and shakes his head, looking away. "Ooo, he's cute. Why don't you go talk to him?"

I shake my head in refusal. "Are you crazy? I can't go talk to him, he's...umm wow." Besides, I think to myself, there's only one reason a guy like him would ever talk to a girl like me.

Liz laughs while I just stare. As the two of them talk with each other, I let my eyes slide over this man. He's probably around six feet with really short dark brown hair and blue eyes that shine so bright I can tell the color from here. He's wearing a tight black t-shirt with the pub's logo on it making his arms and chest look massive, but not too bulky, just firm.

I watch him as he wipes his hands on a towel and then tosses it down under the bar before leaning in towards a couple college girls with a sexy grin that would make anyone melt. The girls blatantly flirt with him while he takes their order. He laughs at whatever they're saying to him, causing me to go weak as the deep sound carries over towards our table. I'm ready to fall to the floor when I notice a dimple in his right cheek. He eventually nods his head at the two girls and steps away to make their drinks. I groan quietly, hoping Liz doesn't hear my audible reaction to him. She'll push me even more to go talk to him.

Liz laughs, "You sure you're okay there, Sara?" I look back at her in confusion. "Your mouth is hanging open and I could swear drool is coming out of it," she teases. Blake chuckles softly and I shake my head, trying to clear it. I close my mouth and narrow my eyes at her. I lean back, about to defend myself, but I'm thankfully interrupted when our waitress sets down our burgers and fries in front of us. I love the quick service here.

I turn away from my friends and pick up my burger to happily sink my teeth into it at the same time as Liz and we both moan in appreciation. Blake's eyes noticeably flare up as he stares at Liz. I can't hold it in and start laughing hysterically; finally releasing some of the tension I've been feeling.

I'm almost done with everything on my plate when my eyes shift back over to the bar. I spot the hot bartender leaning up against a wooden post in the middle of the bar near the cash register. His arms are crossed in front of him as he appears to survey the area now that things have temporarily slowed down for him. When his eyes come closer to approaching our table, I can feel my nerves begin to flutter, but I can't look away. His eyes reach me, and he immediately stops his perusal.

My stomach turns and heat slowly spreads throughout my entire body. When I know my face has turned completely red, his lips slowly curve up into a sexy smirk. My heart pounds so hard, I have trouble catching my breath. He raises his eyebrows like he's challenging me, to what I'm not sure.

Our waitress slides into my view right next to him and hip checks him. When his gaze turns to her and she gives him a playful smile, I tear my eyes away from him and back to my friends. He's probably wondering why some strange girl was staring at him or maybe just shocked at how much I ate. I'm sure he's used to female attention, but not by someone like me.

I quickly push my plate away, feeling a little disgusted by my appetite. My stomach continues to turn, filled with both grease and my chaotic nerves. "Ahh, I think I ate too much!" I complain, placing my hands on my stomach.

Liz laughs and concurs, "Oh my gosh, me too!"

Blake leans in and grabs a handful of fries off Liz's plate. "Not me," he states, smirking.

Liz giggles and shakes her head at him. "I have no idea how you eat so much and stay so ridiculously thin!"

His smile never leaves his face as he answers, "Good genes and fun extracurricular activities." Then he places a kiss on Liz's lips, turning her face instantly red.

I force a smile and mumble, "I need to use the bathroom. I'll be back." My stomach is tying itself in knots from the food, my friends, the conversation and honestly, the man behind the bar. I race into the stall and lock the door. I barely make it before I quietly get sick, purging nearly my entire meal. I take a deep breath and wipe my mouth with toilet paper. Before I step out to the sink, I flush the toilet. I take a few deep breaths, trying to calm myself down while I wash my hands. To clean myself up, I reach for a couple of paper towels. I dig through my purse, finding a mint and tossing it in my mouth to get rid of the horrible taste before taking a quick look in the mirror.

When I feel like I look like myself again, I stand up straight and walk out the door, crashing right into a hard chest. "Oh, I'm sorry," I stammer as I try to stop myself from stumbling. Two strong arms grab me at the waist to help steady me.

"Whoa there, sweetheart. In a hurry?" the man asks with a low grumble, sending shivers down my spine. I look up to answer him and I'm left speechless when I see those same sparkling blue eyes of the bartender staring back at me. His eyes look a little darker blue up close, or maybe it's the lighting. "Are you alright?" he asks, his voice full of concern as I unabashedly stare at him for another few seconds, not saying a word.

I finally realize my hands are on his hard, sexy chest and I awkwardly pull myself away. "Um, yeah, um, I'm okay. I just, um, thank you," I stumble over my words, feeling like an idiot. "I'm sorry, I just, um, thank you."

His lips quirk up in a gorgeous smile, taking my breath away. He chuckles lightly and I feel my face turning red, knowing I'm struggling from keeping my eyes glued to his mouth and that sexy ass smile and dimple that goes along with it I wanna' lick. "Are you sure you're okay?" he prods, arching his eyebrow in question.

I nod in affirmation. "Um, yeah. Thank you again," I mumble breathily as I step away from him, feeling a loss the moment his arms fall away from my sides. I force myself to turn and quickly make my way back to Liz and Blake. They're huddling so close together, I pray I'm not about to interrupt something when I step up to them.

I purposely flop noisily back down on my stool, causing both their heads to immediately snap up in my direction. I know Liz is studying me to make sure I'm alright since I took so long. "Are you ok?" she questions. I stop myself from laughing when she confirms my thoughts and only smiles faintly at her with a nod. "Hey, aren't those your friends Kara and Dana?" she inquires, pointing to the other side of the dance floor or the small area clear of tables and chairs.

I turn towards the direction she's pointing and smile. "Yeah, I should go say hi. I haven't seen them in quite a while." I look back over to Liz and prompt, "Wanna' go with me?"

Liz shakes her head with a smile and urges, "No, that's okay, you go ahead."

I nod my head, agreeing, "Okay. I'll be right back." I stride quickly over to see what their plans are for tonight. I don't think I can handle any more of the Blake and Liz love fest tonight. They can have their privacy and I can let myself relax a little.

Halfway across the dance floor, Kara and Dana both yell out, "Sara!"

"Hey, guys! What are you doing here?"

"Same as you. We're out for drinks and dancing tonight," Kara claims.

Shaking my head in denial, I mumble, "No, I came to eat and have a drink with Liz and Blake."

"Third wheeling it tonight?" Dana questions, arching her eyebrows in surprise. "Want to hang out with us?"

I instantly and gratefully answer, "Yes! I'll just let Liz know," I inform them before walking back over to Liz and Blake.

"Okay. How will you get home later, though? Do you want me to come pick you up?" she offers thoughtfully.

"Nah, that's okay. We'll take a cab later. I promise." I smile genuinely. "Thank you."

"Okay, then we'll see you later!" She leans in and gives me a hug, "Be careful, have fun and call if you need me to come back," she warns.

"Okay, mom," I smirk. Blake laughs, shaking his head and wraps his arm around Liz's shoulders as she rolls her eyes. "Thanks for dinner, guys," I add appreciatively.

"You're welcome," Blake answers. "Let us know if you need anything," he adds. I feel my heart warm as he again confirms how right he is for Liz.

14

I smile and wave goodbye before turning towards Kara and Dana with a grin. It's time to unwind and get my ex, Brad, and all my other BS out of my head.

Chapter 2

Sara

After a few beers, I finally begin to relax. Dana drags Kara and me out to dance, and I can't help but get lost in the music. I love to dance! I roll my hips to the beat, spinning my body around. When I'm facing the bar, I can't help but notice the gorgeous bartender watching me with a slight smirk, causing my heart to clench. He has two other people helping him behind the bar now, since it's a bigger crowd. When my eyes land on him, I slowly smile and continue to dance to Uptown Funk by Mark Ronson, putting on a show just for him.

By the time the song is over and Maroon 5 comes on, I'm feeling confident again and much happier. I laugh when he winks at me, and I turn back towards my friends. I know it's not right, but sometimes flirting when I know nothing will ever happen makes me feel better about myself. It helps me keep the dream that maybe one day someone will want me for more, even if my dreams are all I'll ever have.

Dana dances with some short, dark-haired guy, but she seems very content. I turn away from her towards Kara just as two tall, athletic looking guys come over and begin dancing with us. Kara smiles at one of them and I swallow hard, not really wanting any of these guys to get too close. Don't get me wrong, they are good-looking guys, but after talking to Brad tonight, I don't think I can handle a strange guy getting too close.

Both of them attempt to introduce themselves to us, but I can't hear them over the music and I'm not about to get closer to try when I really don't want to know. I think Kara reciprocates, sharing both of our names. My guess is confirmed when the guy with blonde hair sidles over to me with a look that makes me feel dirty. It's a look that only confirms Brad is right. I cringe as he yells in my ear, "You're an amazing dancer, Sara!"

I give him a stiff smile and try to swallow down my anxiety. He takes another step towards me, causing me to reflexively take a step back. As he steps into me, I instantly shake my head no before I turn towards the bar to flee, feeling the panic inside my chest. He pulls me back towards him and grips me tightly, digging his fingers painfully into my sides. He presses his hips into me, "Come on baby, don't be a tease. I've been watching you dancing for me all night. Our hips will move perfectly together on and off the dance floor." I think I'm going to throw up again as I push my lips together and try to push away from this complete asshole. I don't get very far when suddenly, I feel hands on me as he goes flying across the dance floor into the arms of security.

I'm stunned as I look up into those same blue eyes, now filled with concern taking my breath away. "Are you okay?" he asks, searching my face for the answer. I attempt to swallow away the tears, feeling completely vulnerable in this man's arms. Without an answer, he turns to the bouncer and demands, "Throw that asshole out of here." The bouncer nods firmly and leads the guy out the front door.

I realize I'm shaking but I don't want to lose it out here. Taking a deep breath, I try to pull out of his arms, but he barely loosens his hold, attempting to give me the space I need and still take care of me. He turns to my friends and whispers something to them before pointing to the back of the bar. I watch as they both nod, eyes wide, before he guides me in the same direction. Grateful, I let him lead me away.

We reach a door that says, "Employees Only" and he pushes it open to a small lounge. The room is mostly white, with one wall covered in graffiti. The only furniture includes a table and chairs along with a worn black leather couch.

Two vending machines filled with food and drinks along with silver lockers line the back wall.

"You're shaking," he observes. "Sit down and rest. I'll grab you some water," he states while he guides me to the couch. He steps up to the vending machine, and he hits something on the back of the machine before he pushes the button for a bottle of water. He reaches down to grab the bottle, then ambles over to me, opening it before handing it to me. I take a slow sip, but quickly set it down because I can barely hold it up to my mouth without spilling or dropping it.

He lowers himself onto the couch right next to me. I try to calm my nerves for a completely different reason as I take in all the warmth coming off his body. Noticing my trembling again, he reaches up, placing his hand on my back and soothingly rubs it in circles. After a few minutes, his fingers touch my chin, and he gently tilts my eyes up to meet his. "Are you okay?" he repeats, his voice full of concern.

I nod my head, eventually finding my voice. "Nothing really happened. You got there so quickly," I answer in disbelief. "How did you know?"

He shrugs like it was no big deal. "I saw the look of panic on your face. I wasn't about to let anyone touch you," he replies firmly. His response makes me wonder if it was because of my panic or...no, there is no or. Nobody would want me for more than what that asshole out on the dance floor wanted me for. No one except the man I hate.

I swallow down my feelings of disgust and struggle to hold back the tears. But then this beautiful man trying to comfort me does something unexpected and pushes me right over the edge. He wraps me up gently in his powerful arms. I hold my breath as my one last attempt to hold it all in. When he gives me a light squeeze and kisses me on the top of my head, I choke out the sob I can no longer keep in. I lean into this man, this stranger, giving me the strongest feeling of comfort I can remember. I don't ever want to let go. He continues to rub my back in slow circles and kiss the top of my head, telling me it's going to be okay until my tears eventually subside.

As I calm down, I feel an overwhelming sense of embarrassment. I push away from his chest just enough to wipe the tears away. "Um, I'm sorry," I mumble, keeping my head down so I don't have to see what I'm sure is pity lurking in those striking blue eyes.

He chuckles softly in disbelief before I feel his fingers underneath my chin, guiding me towards his gaze. When our eyes meet, I gasp at the power his eyes alone hold on me. "You have nothing to be sorry for." He continues to hold my chin still as he looks me over, like he's searching for answers. "I'm Jason, by the way," he introduces himself, smiling. My heart drops into my stomach before lodging itself in my throat. He then adds, "Jason Emory."

"Sara Miller," I barely whisper.

"Are you okay, Sara Miller?" he prods sweetly. He makes the sound of my boring name sound sensual. How the hell does he do that?

"I will be," I affirm, offering him a slight nod. I hate that I lost it over some idiot in a bar. I need to be stronger than that! "Thank you, Jason," I murmur gratefully as I stare shamelessly at his magnificent features. Yes, this man is beautiful with light stubble lining his strong jaw and soft looking skin around his eyes.

He nods marginally. "If you ever need anything, please let me know." I'm barely able to make a small noise in answer as his eyes lock onto my lips. He leans ever so slowly towards me and deliberately licks his lips before lightly brushing them against mine. I feel a jolt sending tingles from my lips throughout my whole body, causing my heart to go into overdrive. He pulls back to look in my eyes, like he's asking for permission, before gently pressing his mouth to mine in a soft and sensual kiss, leaving me nearly breathless.

He pulls back and barely gasps, "Beautiful," before the click of the door opening causes me to startle and jump away from him. He sighs regretfully and glances towards the door to see the waitress who served us earlier. "What do you need, April?" he prompts, sounding annoyed.

She grimaces when she sees the two of us. She gives me a small glare before focusing on Jason. "It's really busy. The guys need you out there and asked me to come and get you."

He groans and nods his agreement. "I'll be right there." She looks like she wants to say something else but changes her mind and retreats to the bar. "I'm sorry. I guess I have to go. Would you like to stay in here a while, or I can help you find your friends?" I just stare at him, not answering, wondering what the hell just happened. With my silence, he continues giving me other options, "Or I can help you find a cab home, or I can drive you home. I'll be done around three am." He pauses before adding, "It's just a ride home."

I glance at the clock and notice it's only one a.m. but knowing I can't deal with anyone in a bar for the rest of the night, I figure I should take a cab home. I don't need this guy to think he's going to be taking me home at the end of the night, even though he said it's just a ride. "I guess I should find a cab. There's no way I'm going back out there tonight," I admit.

He grimaces slightly. "I'll call you a cab and I can let your friends know." I nod my head in agreement, still breathless from his kiss. He stands and offers me his hand to help me up. I cautiously take it and he pulls me up. I feel a little dizzy and lose my footing. He reaches for my other arm and steadies me. "You okay to go now? You can wait and I'll come back for you in a few minutes."

I shake my head, insisting, "No, that's okay. I'll be fine. I think I just need to go home." I take a deep breath and proclaim, "Thank you." He smiles and slowly turns to leave, still holding my hand, so I trail along behind him. As soon as we step out of the employee lounge, I feel my anxiety increase and let Jason tug me close to him. I'm almost shocked it calms my nerves, but I let it go anyway. We stop at the bar, but he doesn't let go of my hand as he leans over to talk to one of the other bartenders. The guy glances at me before looking back at Jason and nodding his head.

He then tugs me over towards my friends and whispers in Kara's ear. She looks down at our hands and then smirks at me before waving goodbye. He steps over to the table we were at earlier and grabs my coat with my wallet slightly sticking out of the pocket and turns to walk towards the exit. I can't help but stare at him with curiosity, trying to figure out how he knew that was mine. He just looks at me with a genuine smile and shrugs, melting my insides yet again.

He tugs me to the exit and steps outside with me before helping me put my coat on. He runs his hands from my shoulders and down my arms before stepping in front of me. "You should really have gloves on. It's freezing."

"Really?" I ask with a smirk, looking him up and down, standing out here in a t-shirt and jeans. "I'll have to remember that for next time."

He studies me before adding, "You might want to check your wallet too. Sticking out of your coat pocket hanging off a chair is not the best place to just leave it, even in Maine."

I can tell he's fighting a smile as the corners of his lips keep twitching. I can't help but answer playfully, "Okay, Dad."

He laughs and I relax, giving him my full smile. "I think I prefer Jason," he grumbles. My breath catches in my throat as he holds my gaze.

Just then, a cab pulls into the parking lot. I feel a little disappointed and I softly mumble, "That was fast."

Jason grins and steps closer to me. "If you need anything at all, you know where to find me." Then he lowers his head and sweetly presses his lips to the corner of my mouth before stepping away. He opens the back door of the cab and leans in to say something to the driver before stepping back. "Get home safe, Sara," he adds, holding the door for me.

I whisper, "Thank you, Jason." I attempt to swallow the lump in my throat and take a steadying breath. I finally tear my eyes away from his and reluctantly step into the cab before my eyes instinctually return to him. When I'm all the way in, he gives my hand one more squeeze before he releases it and shuts the door for me.

I tell the driver my address and settle back in the seat for the short drive. I suddenly feel cold and confused as we pull away. We quickly get to my apartment and when I reach forward to pay him, he waves me off. "Your boyfriend took care of you. You're all set."

"Th…Thank you," I stutter a reply in shock. I step out of the cab and run quickly to my door. I quietly make my way to my room, so I don't bother Liz and Blake if he's here. I drop my coat and wallet on the floor next to my dresser before I collapse on my bed with a sigh, closing my eyes.

I have all these unanswered questions in my head. I'm so confused about what happened tonight. I've never had a more incredible kiss in my life, and yet he barely even kissed me. I wonder what it would be like to really be kissed by him. But I know I won't ever get the chance. I groan and my chest tightens with the thought. Why didn't Jason ask for my number? Was I not even good enough for that? But would I have really given it to him if he did? My mind drifts to Brad and what he'd probably say, "A guy like that just wants you for a quick fuck. Think about how you were dancing in there." I cringe thinking about it, but then again, it's true. Why would a guy like Jason want me?

Chapter 3

Jason

I run my hands over my short hair and grip the back of my neck, lacing my fingers together. As I gaze up at the dark sky, thoughts of her go through my head. I do not know what came over me tonight, but I had the strongest need to protect that girl. I couldn't take my eyes off her from the minute she walked through the door with her friends earlier. She was so fucking gorgeous! When she came out of the bathroom and crashed into me, looking like she'd been crying or maybe gotten sick, that's when it hit me. I not only can't take my eyes off her, I need to make sure she's ok. I must protect this girl with all that is in me.

When she was dancing, I think I almost lost my fucking mind! I couldn't do anything but watch her sexy body move. Until the look on her face nearly choked me when that asshole wouldn't leave her alone...I couldn't move fast enough. I shudder, thinking of the panic in her eyes. The way she broke down in my arms, I could swear there was more to it than just the asshole from tonight. But I don't know this girl. I don't really have a right to ask her. She felt so damn good wrapped in my arms; I didn't want to let her go. Eventually, I couldn't stand it a second longer and I just had to taste her. Fuck, she tasted good. "Sara," I think, "where the hell did you come from?" I ask myself reverently.

I drop my arms down to my sides with a sigh, knowing I have to get back into the bar before the other guys want to kick my ass for taking so long. I reach for the door to step back inside when the two drunk college girls that sat at the bar flirting with me all night stumble out the door laughing and fall right into me. "Oh, you're still here!" one

23

of them exclaims, shoving out her chest. I try not to visibly roll my eyes.

I give them a tight smile. "Still here," I confirm, about to step past them when one reaches out and grabs my arm. I stop and raise my eyebrows in question when she rubs my bicep. When she doesn't get the hint, I peel her fingers off. I don't really have the energy to deal with these chicks. They've been throwing themselves at me all night.

"What time do you get done working? We could stick around and wait for you, have our own fun," the other one suggests, grinning at me with what she probably thinks is a seductive look. Instead, I grumble under my breath, "You've got to be fucking kidding me!"

I don't know if it's because of this Sara girl I can't get out of my head right now, or because I've had enough of the one-night stands, but I can't even look at these girls with anything but disgust right now. "I'm good," I proclaim. I shrug my shoulders, stepping by them with their mouths hanging open. "Have a good night," I call over my shoulder before the door slams shut behind me.

"Asshole!" I hear muffled through the door.

I step behind the bar and Joey smirks at me. "Who's the girl?" I shrug, not answering. "Did you get her number?" he prods. I freeze, grinding my teeth with a feeling of loss in my gut. I drop my head in defeat. What the hell is wrong with me? I hear laughter erupt behind me and I turn to glare at Joey. "She turned you down, huh?" I sigh and shake my head in defeat. Of course, her last name has to be fucking Miller! Such a popular name that it makes finding her nearly impossible unless she comes looking for me or just comes back. I sigh, "It's gonna' be a long damn night."

When the bar is cleaned up and we're finally able to kick everyone out, all I want to do is get back to my new apartment and sleep. I head to the back of the bar to grab my coat, wallet, and keys out of my locker in the employee lounge. I slam it shut and turn right into April. I give her a tired smile and go to step around her. "Have a good night, April."

"Jason, wait." She reaches out to stop me.

I turn towards her with a sigh. "Yeah?"

"I saw that we both have Tuesday off and I was wondering if you wanted to go out? We could do dinner and maybe some dancing?" she proposes stepping into me and placing her hand lightly on my chest.

I hold back the groan I want to let out and put my hand on her arm, hoping to relax her before I reject her. This isn't the same as the two girls outside. I have to be careful. "Listen, April, I appreciate the invitation, but I have a lot of shit going on with my family and I'm just not looking to date right now," I answer with a partial truth.

"Really?" she prompts with raised eyebrows. "Well, if you're looking for a little fun, I could be that girl too," she offers, smirking.

I shake my head. "No, you can't, April. You're a good girl. Don't do that. And that's not what I want, anyway." I don't understand why girls do that to themselves, not that I have never taken anyone up on that offer. I'm just done with being that guy.

April pouts and narrows her eyes at me before answering. "Well, that's sure what it looked like when I caught you in here kissing one of the customers!"

I grind my teeth together in frustration. Now she's just pissing me off. "Maybe I was wrong about you being a good girl, but it doesn't matter. Nothing is going to happen with us, April. No dates and no fucking," I spit out bluntly, making sure to be clear with her. "Have a good night." I step out of the employee room and slam the door, done with this conversation.

"Asshole!" she screams through the door.

"That's not the first time I've been called that," I mumble and shake my head as I keep walking out the back door of the bar to my truck. I have a black Ford F-150 and I absolutely love it. My youngest brother, Christian, has the same truck in white. I'd say it's a family thing, but my other younger brother, Matt, has a dark red Chevy Silverado. Then again, Christian and I were always more alike. He just always fought to be different while I kept following in my father's footsteps, as expected.

I jump in my truck and start it up with Darius Rucker's "I Hope They Get to Me in Time" blasting through my speakers, making me cringe. I turn the radio off and back out while my mind drifts to my little sister, Theresa, after hearing that song. She's the reason I moved closer to my family again. I've been done with college at West Point for quite a while now, anyway. I'll never forget when Christian called me and told me a car had hit our sister and I was too far away to do shit. I've honestly never been more scared than I was that day. I love my little sister and all three of us boys will do anything to protect her. I went to Boston where she was in the hospital as fast as I could, but it wasn't quick enough. I need to be close to home.

She's gone through so much to recover since the accident, but she's doing much better now. She's still in Boston going through intensive therapy. As soon as she's done with the major therapy, though, we're moving her back here somewhere to be closer to all of us. As soon as I found out, I made my own plans to move to Maine. It hasn't been home for my family forever, but it has been for a while and I sure as hell am going to make sure I'm there for her with whatever she needs. I'll live here to be near my family even if I don't do anything with my life but work at a bar. Family is always worth it.

Matt still lives in Texas, but the rest of us all live relatively close to one another in Maine. My parents are on a lake only a little over an hour from me, while Christian lives about five minutes from my new apartment. We all know there's no way in hell he's going anywhere with his fiancée, Bree living right up the street. Bree's a great girl. She's beautiful, sweet, smart and perfect for Christian, and he's honestly a miserable asshole when she's not around. I know my parents are hoping once Theresa's here full time, maybe Matt will come to his senses and move up here too, but I guess only time will tell. He just finished college and although he quickly found a good job, he could easily find something closer than Texas.

I pull up to the back of my apartment building and hop out of my truck. I have a one-bedroom studio apartment right above a local bakery. It's perfect for me for now and makes it easy to grab breakfast in the mornings, especially with the fantastic smells that encompass my entire apartment every morning. The couple who owns it also owns my apartment and live in the larger apartment right above me. They have been in the building forever, from what I've heard. They're always good to me, saying they like taking care of me because they miss having their own kids around.

I unlock and open my front door before I slowly climb the stairs up to my apartment. I toss my keys into an empty dish on the kitchen counter, right in front of me to the left. Then, I drape my coat over the back of one of my mismatched painted stools since I don't have a front closet. I grab a bottle of water out of the fridge and lean back against the slate Formica counter, staring past the dark green cabinets into my small living room. I have enough room for a couch and two small armchairs, a coffee table and a small black entertainment center. My TV takes up almost the entire brick wall, but that's just because this place is tiny. At least I could mount it. I can't live without my TV to watch football. I love all sports, but I used to play football. It definitely tops the cake for me. When we were younger, we moved all over the country for my dad's job, including a few different areas in New England, which is why I've always liked the Patriots. It's nice to live somewhere in New England again where I'm not the only one rooting for them.

Opposite the stairs are two doors, one for my bedroom and one for the bathroom, both equally small, but it works. I figure I have what I need, and I just couldn't live with someone I didn't know again, let alone go through the entire process of trying to find a decent roommate. Moving in with my parents was not even an option. There's no way I could live with my dad again. He puts enough pressure on me as it is. Living with him after all these years would be a nightmare.

Fuck no.

After downing the bottle of water, I head to my room. On one side of the room, I have a box spring and mattress covered with a blue, red and green thick plaid quilt and a small blue nightstand sitting right next to the bed. On the other wall is an old dark blue painted dresser with my black laundry basket in the corner. I kick off my boots and toss them into the bottom of my small closet before pulling off my socks. I quickly strip my shirt and jeans, tossing all my dirty clothes towards my laundry basket. Keeping things picked up is one of those habits that's incredibly hard to lose after going to school at West Point. I guess you could say I like things to be neat and clean most of the time. My brothers and sister think it's hilarious to mess with me when it comes to that shit. It's annoying.

I drop onto my bed with just my boxer briefs on, exhausted and ready to crash. I realize it won't be as easy as I thought when I close my eyes and immediately see Sara's gorgeous hazel eyes staring back at me. I've never seen eyes more incredible. It's almost like they have a bit of everything, a little blue and green with specks of brown and gold…absolutely amazing. But there was something else in her eyes I wanted to ask her about but knew I couldn't yet. Hopefully, whatever I saw that seems to haunt her was a one-time thing. I hate the thought of her hurting. I want to know more about that girl, but how the hell am I supposed to do that when I don't even know where to find her?

Thinking about her makes me want to grab on to her beautiful blonde head and pull her full red lips to mine and devour her. I couldn't believe she let me kiss her. Her lips were so incredibly soft, but I'm glad I took it while I had the chance. I shake my head and laugh at myself in frustration while I readjust to make myself more comfortable. I wish I were still the kind of guy who could do one-night stands. Then maybe I'd have taken one of the girls tonight up on their offer and I wouldn't be laying here like a horny asshole dreaming about a girl I may never see again. But after the last time I had a one-night stand, I just can't go there ever again. It's not fucking worth it!

I jump off my bed, knowing there's no way in hell I'm going to relax right now. I figure I need to take a shower and wash the smell of the bar off me anyway before I crash. I hate smelling like a mesh of alcohol, smoke and perfume by the end of the night. Maybe after I'm clean, I'll feel a little better and be able to get some sleep. I just need to decide if it's going to be a hot or cold shower.

Just then, thoughts of Sara dancing run through my head and my dick decides for me.

Chapter 4

Sara

I'm sipping a cup of coffee still trying to get my head on straight when Liz comes through the front door startling me. I jump almost spilling the hot liquid in my lap. "You scared the crap out of me!" I gasp. "Where were you? I thought you were sleeping in your room," I question still trying to calm my nerves. I guess I'm more on edge than I thought, especially after not really sleeping very well again.

She chuckles, shaking her head in amusement. "You're pretty jumpy this morning." With no reaction from me she continues answering my question, "Blake and I went to breakfast this morning before he went home. He has to head back to Boston for a couple days to see his sisters and I have to work at the café so I can't go with him. I thought we mentioned that last night?" she prods. I just shrug my shoulders in response and her smile broadens. "I guess that must've been about the time you couldn't take your eyes off the hot bartender and weren't paying attention to anything we said," she claims, smirking. At that, I blush making her laugh.

"So, when are you working?" I inquire, nonchalant, my poor attempt at an obvious subject change.

Liz eyes me warily before she lets it slide for now. "I'm working the early morning shift for the next four days," she informs me, grimacing. "I guess they're trying to take advantage of my free time until classes start up again next week. I hate having to get up so early, but I guess it's better than having to work nights there, let alone the weekends. That's when all the drunken idiots come in who forget about tipping and that it's not okay to get all handsy. Now that's when it really sucks," she huffs her complaint. "I'm thankful so many people aren't back until this weekend. It gives me seniority, so I don't have to work the nights or weekends for at least one more week. I know I'll get more once everyone is back, but my schedule gets better every year."

"Yeah, but there aren't a lot of college students that are willing to work early morning shifts anywhere. Not unless they don't have a choice, so I'm sure those aren't exactly the prime shifts either," I add.

She grimaces. "Thanks for that," she grumbles. "So how was the rest of your night? Did you talk to the hot bartender?" she probes wiggling her eyebrows. I knew she would come back to that.

I roll my eyes and chuckle lightly. "Would you stop calling him that? He has a name, you know."

"Which is?" she prompts.

I can't stop my lips from curving upwards when I whisper, "Jason," from behind my coffee cup.

Liz's answering squeal makes me jump. "I knew you would talk to him! He couldn't take his eyes off you all night."

"How would you know?" I ask. "You had your back to him most of the night."

"So, what's he like? Are you going to see him again?" she asks excitedly, ignoring my comment.

My smile instantly turns into a frown with her questions. It makes me think about the fact that he kissed me and never even asked for my phone number. I'm just another girl at the bar to him that needed saving. He probably does shit like that all the time. I cringe at the thought. I didn't want to picture him with anyone else even though our kiss most likely meant nothing to him. I take in a deep breath imagining his lips on mine, pretending it meant as much to him as it did to me. I exhale slowly trying to rid myself of the dull ache in my chest, wishing I were good enough for more from a guy like him.

31

I realize Liz must notice my reaction and berate myself for getting so down in front of her. I know better than that. She quickly tries to change the subject again, understanding my mood. Unfortunately, she picks the only topic I hate more than anything in the world. "So, what the hell did Brad want last night? Why is he calling you?" she probes with a scowl.

I know I'm not getting out of this one though, so I guess I'll share just enough to satisfy Liz's curiosity. "He wants me back. What else?" I prod bitterly, pursing my lips with disgust.

"It's been years since you guys broke up. I honestly don't get it, Sara. I know he fucked up and all when you guys broke up because anyone would be lucky to have you, but why doesn't he stop?" she inquires in bewilderment.

I sigh and try to think about what to tell her, not wanting Liz to know how pathetic I really am. I begin fidgeting and stare out the window across the living room when I answer her. "Even when we broke up, he said we could go our separate ways for now, but we would end up back together one day. In fact, that day he told me he would be the one marrying me," I concede my heart full of sadness. That would be great and all if I loved him, but I've never hated anyone more in my life. I want him as far away from me as possible, even if what he says is true. I'd rather be alone for the rest of my life than married to him.

Liz shakes her head. "If you were still in love with him that would be incredibly romantic." I sigh and nod stiffly staring into my coffee so I don't have to look at her. "Do you still have any feelings for him, Sara?" she prompts. My eyes widen, snapping up to her with shock. She immediately attempts to explain her question, "It's just that you're usually so happy, but when it comes to him you get so upset whenever he even comes up in conversation or when he calls or even when you see something that reminds you of him in some way. Then when we ran into him on New Year's Eve, you were dancing with him by the end of the night, and you even let him kiss you. It seems to me like there's still some feelings there. He didn't just give you a little peck either," she adds, trailing off. "You've been really down ever since. You're definitely not your usual happy self. And it seems obvious to me that he's still in love with you," she whispers and watches me, hesitantly. I stare at her with my mouth hanging slightly open, fighting to hold the tears at bay. I guess I'm worse at hiding my feelings than I thought, but Liz has definitely come to the wrong conclusion. "It's okay to take him back if that's what you want to do."

I vehemently shake my head. "No," I reply struggling not to scream it. "I don't ever want to get back together with him." I swallow the lump in my throat and continue attempting to sound calm, "On New Year's we had been drinking and I saw him after I had a few drinks. I know that's no excuse, but...He just said some things that got to me that night." I pause and shake my head again, attempting to erase the memories from my mind. "I don't want him back and I definitely don't want to marry him some day," I barely croak.

I feel her gaze on me, assessing me, trying to understand me and only wanting to show she cares. After a few moments, Liz must sense I'm done talking about Brad when she nods her head and changes the subject again. "So do you want to do something today?" she prompts.

I sigh with relief, grateful to be at the end of that particular conversation. I respond to her question with a genuine smile, "Sure, what do you have in mind?"

She shrugs her shoulders and suggests, "We could do some shopping and I'll even let you help pick out some things for me. I know how much you love to dress me," she teases me referring to when we were younger. I used to always try to get her to wear particular clothes. I loved playing dress up with her.

I give her another small smile. "That sounds like fun!" I admit.

We spend the rest of the day shopping at the outlets, but we only come home with a couple outfits each. I beg Liz to do a mini fashion show with me like we used to do, but I have to add a ton of tacky accessories to make it more fun. We're both laughing hysterically by the end of the night. It's definitely the perfect kind of therapy for me.

When we're finally able to pick ourselves up off the floor, we order ourselves a pepperoni pizza. While we wait for it to arrive, we both change into sweats and grab pillows, blankets, plates, napkins and drinks. The doorbell rings just as we're sitting down, and Liz runs to answer the door to grab the pizza for us. We sit on the floor in the living room eating our pizza and the conversation turns more serious again. I lean over and wrap my arms around my best friend. "Thanks Liz, I really needed a day like today."

She pulls back and smiles at me. "I needed it too. It's been a long time since we've had just a girls' day."

"Yeah, your boyfriend is a pain in the ass," I tease. "He sure has been keeping you pretty busy lately. Hopefully doing lots of good things!" I proclaim emphatically wiggling my eyebrows.

"Sara," Liz warns, blushing a deep shade of red.

"I'll take that as confirmation," I laugh and smirk at her. She turns an even darker shade of red opening and closing her mouth like a fish. She definitely wants to respond, but can't seem to get the words out. "I'm kidding, Liz! Well, not really." I howl with laughter at her embarrassment, trying to keep pizza from shooting out of my mouth. She finally joins in shaking her head. "Seriously, Liz, I'm glad you guys are so happy together," I express sincerely.

"Thanks. You'll have that soon too, I just know it," she claims. "Maybe even a certain bartender," she probes playfully. I grimace and shake my head lightly. I know he doesn't want me, not the way Liz and Blake want each other. He's too gorgeous, strong, and sweet for someone like me.

She sighs at my reaction and thankfully changes the subject for me, "Hey, Bree wanted me to ask you if you would come to their engagement party. Christian's parents are throwing it for them at their lake house on Saturday. They wanted to have it before classes started back up, but they wanted to wait until after the holidays too."

"I'm surprised Bree wants to have an engagement party," I admit. "From what I've gotten to know about her, that doesn't sound like her."

"Yeah, it's something Christian's parents really want to do for them, and her dad is going to be in town, so it's this weekend or not at all." I nod in understanding. "It's going to be small. Just a few friends and family and I don't even know if all of Christian's family will be there, but they really want you to come. You up for it?"

"Yeah, sure, I can do that. I really like them," I add.

"You can ride up with Blake and me if that's okay with you. Then you can either sleep on the pull-out couch with Amy at Bree's house or Christian's parents said they have extra rooms at their house too." She must notice my panicked expression when she adds, "We'll just play it by ear. I will make sure you're comfortable no matter what. If you want, we can even drive home that night."

I shake my head and mumble, "We'll figure it out. I'm not going to make you guys drive back here, especially when I know Blake hates driving so far in the dark when it's icy." Since he was in a bad car accident with his family when he was younger, I really don't blame him. Unfortunately, it caused permanent damage to his younger sister Aubrey who now lives in an adult home near Boston. If that had happened to me, I think I'd be the same way. "I'll be fine," I emphasize. I frown continuing, "I don't know how I feel about sharing a bed with Amy though." Liz laughs and I add with a smile, "Hopefully I like Christian's family," making her laugh even harder.

35

"It will be so much fun. It's absolutely beautiful up there!"

"I remember the pictures from when you went up there with Blake. I'm looking forward to seeing it for myself," I admit. "Too bad it will be covered in snow this time and the lake will be frozen."

"Yeah, I didn't even think about that! Last time we were there we were out on the water and listening to the loons," she adds smiling reverently at the memory.

"Please tell Bree, thank you for inviting me and I'll be there," I request.

"Cool. So, do you want to have a Legally Blonde marathon?" she proposes.

"Are you sure?" I ask. "I know you have to get up pretty early tomorrow morning for work."

"Yeah, I'm sure. When I get home from work tomorrow, I have nothing to do but sleep. We can worry about going to pick up books for the new semester on Tuesday when I get done with work," she suggests. "But today is about hanging out with my best friend."

I give her a genuine smile knowing I couldn't ask for a better friend. "Perfect! I'll get the ice cream." I jump up and run to the kitchen excited about getting out of here this weekend. I'm sure it will help take my mind off of boys, or one boy in particular, at least I think.

Chapter 5

Sara

"I can't believe this week went so fast!" I exclaim.

"That's just because classes start back up next week," Blake suggests.

"I thought the week kind of dragged personally," Liz admits.

"That's just because you didn't have me around," Blake smirks and reaches for Liz with one hand, keeping the other on the steering wheel. She blushes poking him in the ribs while I laugh. "Hey, no messing with the driver!" Blake proclaims playfully. Liz's hand quickly snaps back and although he was teasing her, he notices Liz's nervous reaction. He quickly reaches for her hand intertwining their fingers, comforting her, while staring at the road in front of him. I can't help but feel the ache return to my chest, wishing I had what they have.

"So, how much longer until we're there?" I ask shakily trying to calm my nerves.

"Actually, it's right up here," Blake announces, nodding his head to the right.

I look out my window as we turn right down a long driveway covered in snow. We pull up to a large white farmhouse with a huge wrap around front porch sitting off to the left of the driveway. "Wow!" I exclaim as my mouth drops open in awe. "That's incredible." There are pine trees scattered everywhere except near the house itself, with a few other kinds of bare trees dispersed throughout them. I'm assuming the glistening white beyond must be the lake, at least somewhere, but it's hard to tell where it begins from here with the snow.

"Yeah, it is," Liz concurs. "It's beautiful inside too," she mumbles, pausing. "Is it just me, or does the snow make it look even bigger than it did in the summer?" she asks in wonder.

Blake laughs. "It's not just you. I believe it does too." Blake opens his jeep and pops the trunk. I immediately feel the cold air blast in giving me a sudden chill. "Come on, I'll grab the presents and you two just go on inside. We'll figure out the bags later when we know where everyone is sleeping," Blake suggests. "Is that okay? I'm freezing!"

Liz yells, "Great!" as she starts speed walking towards the front door. I slowly follow her, taking in as much as I can while I go. When I reach the wooden front porch steps, Liz is already at the top ringing the bell. There are a couple of wooden Adirondack chairs on my left with a small table and on the other side a wooden porch swing. "During the summer they had a lot more furniture out here," Liz observes right before the front door swings open and Christian's large frame appears in the doorway his blue eyes sparkling. His light brown hair still has some blonde highlights even in the winter. He's gorgeous, but only has eyes for Bree. I'm happy for them, but knowing I'll never have something like that still hurts. It seems to be all around me.

"Hey, guys," he barely gets out before Bree practically crashes into him placing herself under his arm with a squeal. He just laughs looking at her adoringly and kisses her on the top of her head.

"I'm so glad you guys are here! But get inside, it's freezing!" Bree exclaims.

"You look great, Bree," I express and Liz nods in agreement. She does, she's a beautiful girl. She's a few inches taller than me with wavy chestnut brown hair and flawless pale skin.

"Thanks," she smiles giddily back at us. "You guys too."

We hang our coats up on a large coat rack just inside the door to our left and remove our boots, so we don't trail in all the mud and snow. Blake sets the presents down and immediately embraces Bree tightly before shaking Christian's hand. He follows suit, taking his coat and boots off as well. He picks the presents back up before he asks, "Where can I set these?"

Christian nods his head in the opposite direction. "My mom is in the kitchen," he declares and starts walking in that direction with the rest of us in tow. We walk into a large open kitchen with a huge oak dining table on the other side of the counter. "Whatever I tell you will probably be wrong," he mumbles right as we walk into the room and then winks at his mom.

"Christian James!" she scolds with a smile stepping away from the kitchen counter. His mom is a beautiful woman. She's about five feet, eight inches and thin with pale skin, blonde hair, and green eyes. She shakes her head, drying her hands on a small towel before placing it on the counter. "You can just set those on the table," she nods towards the presents as she steps up next to Christian.

"Mom, you've met Blake, and this is his girlfriend, Liz and her friend, Sara," Christian introduces us and she walks over embracing each of us with a welcoming hug.

"It's good to see you Blake and it's so nice to finally meet all of you. We were disappointed to hear we missed the two of you when you were here over the summer, but I'm glad you enjoyed yourselves. And Sara, Bree has told us so much about you too." I blush with her comment, but I don't really know why. She seems so sweet.

"My dad, Bree's dad and one of my brothers are outside working on one of the snowmobiles. They'll be in a bit," Christian informs us.

Bree laughs and shakes her head, mumbling sarcastically, "Yeah, I'm sure my dad is really helping them."

39

She glances at me and admits with a smile, "He's not really good at that kind of thing."

"And Amy…" Christian begins with a slight cringe but stops abruptly the moment she bounces into the room.

"Blake!" she screeches and throws her arms around him. I glance towards Liz, assessing her reaction. She grimaces slightly and takes a deep breath before pasting on a smile just in time to receive her own hug. "Hi, Liz. I'm so glad you guys are here." Amy turns to look at me. "Hi, Sara. How are you?"

"I'm good, Amy. It's good to see you again," I state wanting to shake my head, but hold myself back.

Amy is a pretty girl. She's about the same height as me, but skinnier. She has blonde hair, blue-grey eyes and I swear she loves attention. She has the energy and enthusiasm along with the clothes she wears to get that attention and look fantastic doing it. She seems nice, but I can't always handle her liveliness.

Like Blake, she also grew up with Bree and they are pretty close. They have had their problems, one of them being Christian, but they always work things out in the end. Bree says they've been friends for too long to lose her; it would be like losing family and she already lost her mom and grandma whom she was really close to. Blake moved to their high school during his junior year. Blake and Bree ended up becoming best friends and Amy is part of the package. So, since Blake and Liz began dating, I've seen more of all of them.

"Matt wanted me to let you know he's sorry he couldn't make it," Blake informs Bree referring to another one of their friends from their hometown. "Who else is coming? Anyone we know?" Blake asks Bree and Christian.

Christian responds, "Actually my mom really wanted to do something, so we agreed as long as we could keep it small. We wanted just friends and family, so it's just my

40

roommates, Joe and Dean left." He stops and looks directly at me, "Watch out for Dean. He's a player."

I nod my head in acknowledgement with a light smile. "Thanks."

"Christian's sister can't get out of her intensive therapy program yet and his brother Matt couldn't get a flight from Texas that fast. He just got back there from being here for the holidays and before that he was here because of Theresa's accident," Bree explains.

"And I sure as hell was going to make sure Bree's dad would be here," Christian adds. "So, it was now or never. We have a few snowmobiles, if anyone wants to go this afternoon, but really, we just thought we'd all hang out. Like I said, my parents wanted to do the party for us."

Just then, the doorbell rings. While Christian walks to answer the door, I turn to take in the rest of my surroundings and gasp when I face the back of the house.

The kitchen flows into the living room, which is situated at the back of the house, completely covered in windows overlooking what must be the lake. My eyes are glued to the sparkling white grounds beyond the windows. Where the sun is shining through the trees, the snow looks like a collection of sparkling diamonds. I think I see the outline of their dock from here at the bottom of the hill, so I have an idea where the lake begins. It looks stark, fresh and new, that's one of the things I always liked about winter…clearing everything for a new beginning. We all need that sometimes.

Liz steps up next to me and comments, "Wow, it looks so different, but still so beautiful."

"It's incredible," I admit with wonderment. "It looks so peaceful don't you think?" She nods her head in agreement.

Christian walks into the room with two guys I've never met and we turn towards them. "Guys, this is Joe," he gestures towards a tall guy with blonde hair, before turning

41

towards the one with longish black hair with a pointed look in my direction, "and Dean, my roommates." He turns towards us, "You know everyone except Blake's girlfriend, Liz and her friend, Sara." I give them a polite smile and shake their hands.

"So, Sara," Dean begins as he steps up to me with a sly smile and a quirk of his eyebrow.

I quickly speak up before he can say anything. "So, you must be Dean, the one I'm supposed to stay away from," I declare with a smirk.

"Dude!" Dean glares at Christian and he just shrugs his shoulders in response, and chuckles in amusement.

"Blake, I also wanted to let you know that there's more than enough room for all of us to stay here. You and Liz are welcome to Matt's room, and I guess Sara you and Amy can share my sister's room if that's okay. Joe and Dean get the singles in the spare, unless you want to share, then you can sleep on the pull out in the basement," he jokes getting a punch in the arm by Dean. "We didn't want anyone to have to worry about driving on the icy roads at night, even if it's only the short drive over to Bree's," he adds with a small smile.

I watch Blake swallow hard before answering, "Thanks, man." Christian just gives an answering nod before turning to reach for Bree and giving her a chaste kiss.

Turning away from the exchange, I let my eyes run over the rest of the living room. The first thing that catches my eye is the massive stone fireplace with a large round ivory rug sitting in front of it. The room is covered in old wood, almost like you're looking at wood from an old barn. There is even a faint smell of wood and I inhale deeply, loving it. The large oval coffee table appears to be made out of similar wood and it sits in the middle of a large U-shaped navy and ivory plaid couch.

"No TV?" I can't help but question.

Christian shakes his head. "Nah, the seventy inch is in the basement with the other toys." He smiles big, insinuating it's his favorite room in the house.

"Anyone hungry?" Christian's mom yells from across the room. I hear a few people murmur, "Oh yeah," in response while we all turn back towards the kitchen.

His mom has a whole spread of appetizers spread across the counter from basic cheese and crackers, to meatballs, to hot spinach dip to a hot seafood dip and more. "This looks delicious. Thank you," I tell her.

She smiles at me, "We're just grateful to be able to celebrate with Christian and Bree's friends. We're thrilled all of you could make it. We know travel isn't always easy this time of year."

We all fill up small plates and walk over to sit down at the large oak table. I sit next to Liz and a moment later, Joe walks up, questioning, "Mind if I sit?"

"It's all yours," I proclaim, gesturing towards the chair beside me. "So how long have you known Christian?" I ask.

"Actually, we were put together as roommates our freshman year in the dorms and we've been close ever since." He pauses and glances over towards him and Bree. "I'm glad they finally got all their shit straight." I look at him curiously. "How long have you known them?" he inquires.

"The same as Liz. We all met at a concert last summer," I explain. "But I've heard a little about what they went through."

He nods in acknowledgement, "Yeah." He pauses before changing the subject, "So, where are you from Sara?" he asks giving me a friendly smile.

Just then the back door opens, and I look up to see two good looking older men who must be Bree and Christian's dads, followed by a tall younger guy with dark brown hair and his head down, his broad shoulders shaking as if he's laughing. "Portland," I answer Joe still watching

43

the men curiously as they hang up their coats on the hooks by the door. The younger man stops laughing and slowly lifts his head up, his eyes landing directly on me. My heart stops and I completely forget to breathe. I hear Liz's gasp of shock in my ear, while I stare into Jason's sparkling blue eyes. He's sexy as hell in a tight navy-blue Henley with a faded light blue button down open over top with the sleeves rolled up to his elbows. Dark blue jeans are covering his strong legs and LL Bean work boots are loose on his feet.

I think back to how he introduced himself as Jason Emory. He looks a lot like Christian in so many ways. I don't know why I didn't put it together, but I didn't. I swallow hard trying to catch my breath when someone touches my left arm making me jump and I finally choke in a breath. I look to my left and Joe asks me, "Are you okay?" sounding as if he's underwater.

I just nod my head numbly in response before I'm able to croak, "Excuse me." I quickly push my chair back and it screeches across the floor. "Um, where's the bathroom?" I squeak trying not to panic, but I know it's already too late for that.

"I'll show you where it is," Jason offers from across the room and my heart skips a beat from the low rumble of his voice.

"Sara, that's my brother, Jason," Christian introduces us unknowingly.

"We've met," Jason admits, not taking his eyes off me. I ignore the surprise on Christian's face as I attempt to gulp down the huge lump that has formed in my throat. I take an unsteady step in the direction Jason is pointing. He falls into step right behind me, placing his hand on the small of my back to guide me, sending tingles throughout my body from his touch.

I swear everyone is staring at us as we walk out of the room causing me to struggle just to put one foot in front of the other knowing my face has already turned beat red. As

Jason slowly guides me down the hallway, I know he's waiting until we're out of earshot before he speaks. "Right here, Sara," he states, gesturing to our right. "Sara, I..." he begins.

I cut him off immediately by stepping into the bathroom and blurting, "Thanks, Jason!" before quickly slamming the door in his face. I grip the sink, my knuckles turning white and stare at myself in the mirror. I notice my eyes are wide and my face is flushed and blotchy as I still try to catch my breath and calm my nerves. I can't stop shaking, but I do everything I can do to make it happen anyway. I'm not about to walk back out there looking like I'll pass out at any moment and the truth is, I just might. I can't believe the guy who left me breathless is here, *and* he's Christian's brother.

Chapter 6

Jason

I walk in the back door from helping my dad and talking with Bree's dad. We're still laughing about one of my dad's snowmobile, stories when I finally look up and gasp softly as I freeze. I'm staring into the same hazel eyes I haven't been able to forget about this past week. I've been praying I would see her again and now she's sitting in my house eating dinner with my family.

How the hell did she end up here?

Tearing her eyes away from mine, she looks at Joe, one of Christian's asshole roommates. He's not really an asshole, but I don't want him near her with the way he's looking at her. After the way I haven't been able to put her out of my mind, I need to talk to her first and hope she's on the same page or at least open to getting to know me. I kick off my boots not taking my eyes off her. She quickly shoves her chair back, asking, "Excuse me, Um, where's the bathroom?"

I jump at the chance and volunteer, "I'll show you where it is."

"Sara, that's my brother, Jason," Christian introduces us unknowingly.

"We've met," I admit, not taking my eyes off her. Out of the corner of my eye, I notice the shocked look on Christian's face and I concede his look is truly priceless, but he's not getting shit from me. He can ask all he wants.

I guide her down the hall and gesturing to our right, I state, "Right here, Sara." Pausing, I take a deep breath, quickly gathering my thoughts and begin, "Sara, I…"

She cuts me off immediately by stepping into the bathroom and blurting, "Thanks, Jason!" before quickly slamming the door in my face just as I'm about to attempt to talk to her.

I let out a breath of frustration and fall back against the opposite wall to wait for her. She's not getting away that easy. I let the memory of her lips on mine settle while I wait for her to come out. My head drops against the wall in panic when a horrendous thought crosses my mind. What if Joe is her boyfriend? "Shit," I whisper to myself. She better not have a boyfriend. I can't get this girl out of my head.

After about five agonizing minutes, the door finally opens, and my eyes slowly rise to meet hers. I take her in starting with her slender feet in hot pink socks that don't match anything she's wearing. A grin tugs at my lips at how fucking cute she is. My eyes slowly make their way up her legs, appearing sexy as hell in those tight dark blue jeans, followed by her gorgeous curves in a fitted brown sweater. Her chest rapidly moves up and down at my obvious perusal. I pause at her lips remembering our kiss and the taste of her lips as I lick my own as if in anticipation. When my eyes meet hers, I know she's doing the same. Damn, she looks better than she did the first time I saw her. How is that even possible?

"Jason Emory," she mumbles on an exhale. "I guess I should've known," she concedes shaking her head in disbelief.

Narrowing my eyes, I look at her curiously. "How do you know my brother?"

"Um, Blake's girlfriend, Liz and I grew up together. She's my best friend. And since Blake and Bree are so close…" she shrugs trailing off. "I guess we all spend a lot of time together," she rambles somewhat nervously, attempting to explain.

My lips quirk up as I feel an enormous amount of relief that her connection isn't through my brother's roommates. I don't want her dating Joe, or anyone else for that matter. "I'm glad you got home safe the other night. I would've called or texted to check, but…" I trail off, wincing as I watch her stiffen and look away from me.

"Yeah, but you didn't bother with my number," she spits out with a tight smile making me cringe. "Why would you? I'm just another girl you helped, and made sure I got home safely," she grumbles dismissively. "Just doing your job," she emphasizes, visibly flinching. "It's okay, Jason, it's no big deal. I appreciate the help," she adds with a grimace, looking anything but grateful.

Yeah, she's pissed, but she has every right to be. I'm the idiot who forgot to ask. I don't want her to think I do shit like that all the time. "Sara, I…" I begin.

"You guys going to talk in the hallway all night?" Christian prods, interrupting us. I tighten my fist in frustration and glare at him. He shrugs his shoulders, smirking at me. "I gotta' use the bathroom." He steps between us giving Sara the opportunity to escape, rushing back down the hall towards everyone else causing me to groan in frustration.

"I gotta' fix this," I mumble as I turn back towards the back of the house. At least I have the chance to do just that; something I didn't think I would get.

I step back into the room and immediately tense, noticing Sara already back in conversation with Joe. I'm about to walk over to interrupt when my mom stops me. "Did you boys get everything all taken care of out there?" she inquires. I nod my head in confirmation, still watching Sara. "So, how do you know her?" my mom questions.

My eyes snap down to my mom. "Sara?" I prompt. She nods her head, giving me a sweet smile. She thinks she's being so discreet, but I know my mom better than that. I need to make sure she doesn't assume too much. "She just came in to eat at the pub with her friends last week," I explain, shrugging like it's no big deal.

Just then a tall thin, but strong looking guy with brown hair and brown eyes steps up to me with his arm wrapped around a beautiful girl with dark brown wavy hair and green eyes that seem to be eyeing me skeptically. I don't think I've ever met them before, but I have this strange feeling I've seen them before, but I'm just not sure where. "Jason, it's so nice to meet you. I'm Liz and this is Blake. We saw you at the pub last week when we came in with Sara," she enlightens me.

"Hi, nice to meet you," I mumble with relief, happy to now know why they look familiar. My mom chuckles as she walks away. I shake my head imagining what she's thinking now. "So, you must be the best friend and her boyfriend," I proclaim. Liz laughs at my question, and I quickly realize it's because I referred to them in relation to Sara, not in relation to my brother and future sister-in-law, but I'm okay with that and raise my eyebrows in challenge.

"Just to clarify, Sara's best friend, yes," Liz answers. I nod my head and glance over at Sara again, wincing at the sight of Joe leaning into her to whisper something in her ear. Liz sighs sounding exasperated and I turn back to her. "Look, I know I don't know you and I don't know what happened with you two the other night, but she's my best friend and I have to say something," she declares staring at me with a warning in her eyes. "Sara's a good girl. She deserves someone who will treat her right. I see how Christian is with Bree and if you're anything like your brother..." she pauses shaking her head, "it just seems to me that you both seem interested. If I'm wrong, I'm sorry to overstep. But I think you should go talk to her," she suggests.

I grind my jaw slightly turning back towards Sara, pondering over Liz's words. As her best friend, I don't think she would tell some random guy her friend might be interested if she wasn't. I figure I should give her something in return. "She's pissed I kissed her, then forgot to ask for her phone number and yes, I seriously forgot," I grumble. I shake my head, acknowledging my own idiocy.

Her boyfriend laughs at me and when my eyes pin him, quirking my eyebrow, he quickly clears his throat rasping an apology, "Sorry, man."

Liz laughs and shakes her head like it's no big deal. "Then change that!" she proclaims.

I nod my head towards them as a thank you and turn to walk towards Sara. I sit in the seat Liz vacated and face Sara's back. Her whole body immediately tenses, but she continues to face Joe who's still talking to her. "So, what do you think?" he asks. When she doesn't answer, I grin to myself, knowing her silence might be because I have an effect on her and she's not listening to whatever he's saying. "Sara?" he prods.

"Hmm? What?" She shakes her head and apologizes, "I'm sorry Joe. I guess I'm still tired from the drive or something. I think I need to get up and go do something before we eat or I might fall asleep at the table sooner or later." He eyes her warily and she quickly adds, "It's not you, it's just been a long week."

"Ok, why don't," he begins, but I quickly interrupt, not giving him the chance to weasel his way into any more time with her right now or anything else.

"Sara?" I prompt, touching her back lightly as she stands and rising with her. She flips quickly around as if my hand burned her.

I flinch letting my hand drop to my side. Clenching my jaw, I slowly exhale to calm myself down before I speak, hoping it's just anger I can help her see past. "Can we talk for a minute? Please?" I beg. "I really need to talk to you," I emphasize never taking my eyes off hers. She nods stiffly and I gesture towards the front of the house where there's a smaller living room right to the left of the entryway. She starts walking in that direction and I let my hand fall to the small of her back to lead her into the room. I feel her tense again at my touch, her reaction about fucking killing me, but I feel like I need to keep touching her and hope she'll accept it.

The room has a cranberry-colored velvet like sofa and two chocolate-colored chairs of the same material with mix and match throw pillows. There are two oak side tables on each side of the couch, along with an old family portrait above the couch that Sara's eyes veer towards as soon as we enter the room. The picture was taken about a year before I left for West Point, so although it's an older picture, you can still tell which one is me.

I sit on the couch, my eyes drawn to her and I can't help but stare. Her skin appears to be flawless and so incredibly soft. I want to reach out to touch her, but I don't think I can handle watching her flinch away from me again. I need to fix this first. "I'm so happy you're here, you have no idea," I confess quietly.

She turns to study me with her eyebrows raised in question. "Really?" she asks surprised and unsure. I don't really blame her though.

I nod my head with increasing confidence not taking my eyes off her. "Yeah, really. I completely messed up the other night," I admit. Her eyes narrow, assessing me. "I haven't been able to stop thinking about you, Sara. Yet, I've had no way of getting in touch with you, but then again, I was the idiot who never asked for your phone number."

She grimaces and instantly straightens her shoulders, standing with false confidence. "And now you want it?" she asks, challenging me.

I nod my head in confirmation, trying to plead with her through my eyes. "I wanted it then. I just couldn't take my eyes off you long enough to get my brain to work and ask you for it," I proclaim. I know I'm laying it on thick, but every word is true. This girl has to give me a chance, there's just something about her that takes my breath away.

She smirks at me like I've lost my mind. "Yeah, right. I'm sure that's the reason and not that stuff like that probably happens to you all the time working in a pub. I'm sure you help out girls like me all the time."

My stomach twists, not liking her response. I cock my head to the side and gesture to the space next to me. She finally sits down, but on the opposite end of the couch. When I catch her eyes again, I continue, "Girls like you, no." Her eyes widen and she looks at me like she doesn't believe me, but I go on, needing her to understand. "Stuff like girls hitting on me, yeah, I'll admit that happens a lot. But I don't take them up on anything. I don't bring them into the employee break room, and I definitely don't kiss them," I emphasize. I stare into her eyes, willing her to believe the truth in my words. "You are different for me. I'm not exactly sure why besides the obvious fact that you're gorgeous. I just know there's something special about you," I insist. A strange, almost haunted look quickly passes over her face before it disappears causing my stomach to twist. Clearing my throat I add, "I need to find out what it is."

I cautiously scoot across the couch and closer to her, so our knees are touching. When she doesn't flinch away from me this time, I practically sigh in relief, but hold myself back, not wanting to scare her off. "Wh…what do you want, Jason?" she stammers shakily.

"I want to get to know you, Sara. I want you to go out with me. I want you to give me a chance," I declare never letting my eyes waver from hers. "Say yes," I encourage, "please."

She looks at me nervously and the indecision I see so clearly on her face makes my heart pound faster. "I…I…I don't know," she stutters.

"Do you have a boyfriend?" I prod. I assume Liz wouldn't have encouraged me to talk to her if she did have one, but I have to ask.

"No, no, it's not that," she mumbles hesitantly with a shake of her head. I feel a slight amount of relief with her admission, but not enough as I anxiously wait for her to elaborate her reasons. "It's just that I'm not sure I'm really what you want," she states nervously looking anywhere but at me.

My eyes go wide, and my mouth drops open in shock with her response. Is she fucking joking? I shake my head and pull myself together trying to find the right words before I begin, "Sara, I…"

"Hey guys, we're going to head out on the snowmobiles for a little while. Do you want to come?" Bree asks popping her head into the room causing Sara to jump right up to her feet and head to the door. She doesn't even give me a chance to finish before she's trying to escape.

"Sure, that sounds like fun!" Sara exclaims before her expression turns into slight disappointment. "I've never been, though."

"That's okay," Bree insists. "I never go on my own either. I ride on the back of Christian's snowmobile. One of the guys can take you, his roommates come up here with him to ride all the time," she suggests glancing briefly over to me. "I know they wouldn't mind."

"I'll take you," I quickly offer. "You'll be safe with me." Sara turns bright red, her face looking doubtful and if her mind is anything like mine, she might be right. I smile at her and follow her down the hallway. "There are extra snowmobile suits in the mudroom off the kitchen. You're going to want one to stay warm," I proclaim pointing towards the back of the kitchen. She nods stiffly and heads in that direction, while I struggle to keep the satisfied smile off my face. I'm not about to let her escape from me this time and holding onto me with her front pressed to my back is a definite bonus I can't deny.

Chapter 7

Jason

After we're all dressed in snowmobile suits, we grab ski masks and gloves for everyone. Christian and I lead the way trudging through the snow to make the path out to the garage a little bit easier to maneuver for those behind us. The snow has been falling lightly and it's already covering our tracks from earlier.

We have six snowmobiles lined up in the garage. My dad always wanted to make sure there were enough for all of us to go out together. My mom's and my sister's snowmobiles are mostly red with a little bit of gray. My dad always half joked it was so we could find them easily if anything happened to them. I say half joked because they didn't like when he said that, but I know my dad really was trying to protect them the best he could. My dad's ride is mostly black with white accents, while mine is black with some silver and Christian and Matt both have ones that are a bright blue with a little bit of black.

Christian and I step up to the rack against the back wall and start handing out helmets we think will work for everyone. I grab one for Sara first and step up to her. "Pull your ski mask on," I instruct her. "I don't want you to be cold and I need to make sure this fits right." She narrows her eyes at me, but she doesn't argue. She quickly pulls the ski mask over her head. I pull the helmet on and fasten the straps, playing with them for an extra minute or two as an excuse to be close to her. "Perfect," I whisper looking into her ever-changing hazel eyes. Her eyes are seriously incredible. I don't think I've ever seen anything like them. I can't stop staring.

Eventually, I clear my throat and step back, trying to get my head on straight just from gazing at her. I busy myself by helping Christian make sure everyone else is ready. As soon as we know everyone is all set, Christian turns to Bree and reaches for her hand pulling her swiftly to him. He lifts her effortlessly and sets her down on the back of his snowmobile before climbing on himself. He directs his roommates to take Matt's and Dad's snowmobiles and Amy quickly climbs on with Dean.

Liz looks at Christian and I with confidence and asks permission to go on her own, "I'll take my own if that's okay with you guys. I go with my brother Jax sometimes. He taught me how to ride."

"That's cool. You and Blake can take Theresa's and my mom's," I declare nodding towards the red ones. Christian nods his head in agreement.

"Sara, you can ride with me," Joe offers with a small smile.

"She's riding with me," I declare, leaving no room for argument with my hard tone. Joe narrows his eyes at me, but I turn my back to him, preparing to leave. I grab Sara by her elbow, guiding her towards my snowmobile, not giving her a chance to change her mind. "Stick to the trails. Follow either Christian or myself only. We know where the trails are and how to get back," I call over my shoulder to the rest of the group. "Nobody goes off on their own," I reenforce. I don't mind being the bad guy to Christian and his friends for their own safety. I'm used to it.

I stop next to my snowmobile and look at Sara. I tilt her chin up with two fingers, urging her to look at me. "I'm not going to be able to talk to you while we're riding. It's a little loud and with your ears covered everything is already muffled," I enlighten her. "All you have to do is wrap your arms around me and hold on really tight. Got it?" I prompt. She nods stiffly at me in response.

55

I climb on and pat the seat behind me. She slowly steps closer before finally cautiously climbing on behind me. I can feel her inch up the seat to get closer. She lightly places her hands on my waist. I chuckle and reach for both of her hands. Tugging them around me as tight as I can, I emphasize, "I said tight, Sara." I hear her gasp as she presses her front to my back. I can't help but grin to myself before starting the engine. It's too bad we have all these layers between us because being this close to her is already driving me absolutely insane.

We ride down near the lake to head west towards one of the designated trails. I start out slow, so I don't scare her and soon Christian and all his friends are passing right by me. Being at the back of the group with Sara works for me, until she starts to loosen her hold. I speed up and take a couple turns, causing her to tighten her grip again and press closer to me just like I hope, but in my head she's still not close enough.

I take one of the easier trails so there aren't as many twists, turns or jumps. I'll wait until next time to take her on one of the other ones and only if she wants to. I don't want her thinking I'm a reckless dick when it comes to her. I believe Blake and Liz are the only other ones on the same trail as us. It works for me; nobody is alone, and I don't have any assholes besides myself drooling over the girl wrapped around me.

Eventually Sara's head drops to my back causing me to grin at the trail in front of me. I'm loving every second of this relaxing ride. I can already hear some muffled motors and hollering ahead as we approach the turn-around at a clearing. I stop on the outside of the clearing and pull my mask down under my chin. Dean kicks snow up at Joe and I laugh appreciatively. "You guys should come back on the other trail. It has the best jumps!" Dean exclaims.

Blake and Liz immediately agree. I turn my head to ask Sara, my face only inches from hers. I gulp and question with a grin tugging at my lips, "Want to do more of the same on the ride back? Or do you think you're ready to try a little something more with me?"

She has her mask pulled down as well and presses her lips together in contemplation, but it just makes me want to kiss her sweet lips. I watch her mouth, holding back a groan, before she finally answers a little breathlessly, "We can try the other trail." I look down into her eyes with a grin. "Just please be careful with me," she pleads.

"Always," I answer vehemently, staring into her eyes. I release a harsh breath through my teeth. "Hold on tight, sweetheart," I grit out. I'm going to lose my fucking mind if I don't get to kiss her again soon. I spin around towards the other trail and take off. Sara squeals happily and holds me tightly. As we go over the first jump, Sara shrieks and grips me tighter, almost causing me to lose my breath, but I don't care. The laughter that follows, even muffled is pure fucking heaven. We go over jump after jump and my grin gets wider and wider as her laughter continues while her body remains pressed tightly to mine.

When we reach the end of the trail, I slow down as we head towards the garage. I don't want this to end, but I don't want Sara to freeze her ass off either. She starts to pull back and I let go of one of the handles so I can grip her hands wrapped around me and keep them there for as long as possible. When we stop and I turn the engine off without letting her go, I feel her stiffen. I grind my teeth in frustration before releasing her. She immediately pulls her hands back as everyone else pulls up to the garage.

I remove my helmet and hat and set them on the ground next to me. Sara doesn't get up hastily like I expect, so I try not to let it bother me she pulled away so quickly. I just had her wrapped around me for nearly two hours. I really can't complain.

As everyone else starts to put everything away, I know I need to get up to help. I reluctantly stand and stretch my arms above my head before I turn around to help Sara. She loses her balance when she tries to stand and falls into my chest. I wrap my arm around her to steady her and smile. "Um, S...sorry," she stammers.

I grin even wider. "Don't be, I like having you there. You have to be stiff after being wrapped around me so tightly for so long." It's hard to tell with the cold, but I could swear she blushes. "You, okay?" I prompt.

"Yeah, thank you," she whispers as she nods her head, not looking me in the eye. "That was a lot of fun, Jason, but now I'm freezing!" she admits with an exaggerated shiver. I chuckle at how adorable she looks, and I have to stop myself from reaching for her.

"You can go on in," I offer nodding towards the house. "Christian and I will finish up and be there in a minute." She finally looks up at me and gives me a small appreciative smile making my heart skip a beat before she turns away from me to walk inside. Unfortunately, Joe follows right behind her causing me to grimace before turning to get to work cleaning up.

"I'm hungry," Dean yells spinning towards the house. "I can't wait to eat more of your mom's food!"

"Don't touch anything without me Dean!" Christian yells chiding his friend.

"Well hurry your ass up then!" Dean jokes.

Amy, Blake and Liz follow Dean back to the house, while Christian and I quickly put everything where it belongs. Bree stays behind with us and helps by putting the last of the helmets back on the shelves along the wall. Christian steps over towards Bree and gives her a chaste kiss with an adoring smile before stepping back to line up the snowmobiles.

"That was a fantastic idea, Christian! Good ride," I declare grinning at my brother. He just smirks at me knowingly and pats me on the back as he walks back towards our house hand in hand with Bree.

As soon as we walk through the door, we strip off all the extra clothes we wore to keep us warm on the trails. I turn towards Sara who just finished doing the same and inquire, "So what did you think?"

She smiles genuinely up at me causing my chest to tighten before responding, "That really was a blast! Next time can I drive?"

I laugh, thrilled she's already talking about next time and ignoring the fact that she might not be talking about going with me next time. "I'd be happy to teach you," I offer, hoping it will encourage her to accept and spend more time with me.

Her smile slowly fades making my stomach twist. Before I have a chance to ask her about her reaction, I hear my mom call, "Dinner's ready, everyone."

I sigh as Sara swiftly turns away from me again, watching her as she rushes out of the room like it's on fire. "Thanks for riding with me Sara," I call hoping she hears even though I don't even see her slow down.

I stifle a groan as I step into the dining room. Most everyone is already seated, and I can't do anything but watch as Sara slides in right between Liz and Joe, exactly where she was sitting before. Taking a deep breath, I stride towards her anyway and let my fingers trail across the back of her neck when I reach her. I lean down slightly and mumble into her ear as I maneuver closely around her, "I guess we'll finish talking later." I watch as goose bumps cover the back of her neck and smile to myself in satisfaction. I can't help but hope we'll figure things out by the end of the night knowing the way she just reacted to me. She can't ignore me forever.

I make my way around the rest of the table to where my mom has me seated between her and Christian. I swallow hard and grind my teeth, not at all happy with this set up. I don't know if I'll make it through dinner watching Joe flirt with Sara the whole time directly across the table from me. I grimace, seeing he's already at it! I sure as hell would be too if I had her close to me. Taking another deep breath, I remind myself I can't lose it at my brother's engagement party. He deserves better from me more than anyone. So instead, I focus on my breathing and the meal in front of us as I sit across the table from her and imagine her legs wrapped around me without all the layers.

Chapter 8

Sara

I'm a nervous wreck. I barely ate any dinner and what I did eat, I didn't taste. Joe keeps talking to me, but I have no idea what he's even saying most of the time no matter how much I struggle to concentrate on him. I feel terrible.

He's exactly the kind of guy I've been dating since Brad, and I broke up and the kind of relationship that's easy for me. He's the kind of guy that when I'm dating him, I don't feel pressure or stress. It's the kind of relationship that's fun, but I don't care what happens. Absolutely no worries and it's exactly what I need. He's cute, smart and seems really nice, but...I sense Jason's eyes on me the whole night. I don't know if he's actually looking at me, I just feel like he is and it's driving me absolutely insane. The thought of Jason just being in the same room as me puts pressure on me. It already feels different with him and I sure as hell act different with him.

How do I know what he said before is true?

I don't know if I should take that chance. For some reason Jason makes me so nervous. Whenever I'm near him, my heart begins beating so hard and fast I'm afraid I'm about to have a heart attack. I feel flushed and I have trouble catching my breath, while talking seems to be almost impossible. I've never been like that around a guy before, except for maybe when I first starting dating Brad, before anything happened, which explains my hesitation.

I'll be better off going out with someone like Joe. He's like guys I normally date. I like him, but I can keep my head on straight. I don't have to worry about him hurting me like I would Jason. Is that what it is? Is it because I don't want this guy I don't even know to hurt me? I sigh in frustration because I already think it would break me if Jason would prove Brad right.

Liz looks over at me. "You, okay?" she asks her voice full of concern. "You didn't even eat your cake," she observes, nodding towards my plate. "You always eat your dessert," she adds and gives me a small smile. I nod stiffly with tight lips and her eyes narrow even further. "Did you talk to Jason and figure everything out?" she prods quietly.

I whisper, hoping nobody can overhear me, "Sort of." She raises her eyebrows in question. I know I need to give her a real answer so she'll stop badgering me. "He apologized. Basically, he said he hasn't stopped thinking about me and he asked me to give him a chance," I ramble as quietly as I can.

Her eyes gleam with excitement. "That's great! You said yes, right?" she prompts. "That's why you went snowmobiling with him?"

I shrug my shoulders in response. "I don't know," I mumble since I never really had the chance to answer him and I didn't know what I should even say. I did love having my arms wrapped around him while we were snowmobiling though.

"You're smiling!" she exclaims. I immediately drop the smile from my face. Narrowing her eyes, she insists, "I know you're going to give him a chance, Sara. You have to. I haven't seen you like this about a guy maybe ever. You deserve to be happy. Talk to him!" She pauses, shaking her head in amusement. "Honestly, it's like dealing with children," she jokes.

I grimace and sigh reluctantly. "I don't know," I repeat.

She opens her mouth to say something else just as Blake leans in. "Sorry to interrupt girls, but we're all going to head down to the basement to hang out. You coming?" he prods, placing a kiss near Liz's ear. She smiles big, her whole face lighting up and stands to wrap her arms around her boyfriend. I feel a slight twinge of jealousy, but I quickly tamper it down. I can't have what they have, so I'm not about to let myself dwell on it. At least that's what I tell myself as my mind drifts to being in Jason's arms.

"Okay, let's go, Sara. You can do what I told you to do downstairs," she declares, smirking. I can't do anything but roll my eyes and shake my head at her; arguing with her right now is pointless.

I groan in protest instead as she drags me downstairs. We step into a large room that appears to run the length of the house. It's covered in tan carpeting and pale walls with sports paraphernalia from all over the east coast. Pictures of what I assume is the Emory family involved in different sports throughout the years line the walls as well. There's a massive television on the main wall along with a couple game consoles with a huge U-shaped black leather couch facing it. To the left of the TV sits a pool table along with several cues. To the right of it sits a pinball machine, dartboard and an old Arcade version of Pac Man. Along the opposite wall is a mahogany bar with several cherry wood stools lined up in front of it.

"Do you play pool?" Joe inquires, coming up behind me.

"Not really, I've played a couple times, but I don't have a clue," I admit.

"I can teach you," he suggests with a small smile curving his lips.

I feel my face turning red at the way he's looking at me. "Um, I don't know," I stammer. I don't know why, but for some reason I don't want him to teach me. It doesn't feel right when Jason is here.

Liz grabs my hand and starts tugging me away. "Sorry, Joe, I'm stealing Sara. She has to be my partner for darts," she announces.

He smiles politely and nods his head in acknowledgement as I gratefully let her pull me away. I quickly whisper, "Thank you."

"It was either that or let you throw up on his shoes," she mumbles. My mouth drops open at her statement making her laugh.

"What about me?" Blake questions.

"We're playing you and Jason," she proclaims. She smirks at both of us and runs to the board to grab the darts before either of us can respond. "Right, Jason?" she prompts, arching her eyebrows in challenge.

He sets his iPod down right after "Good Lookin' Girl" by Luke Bryan begins to play through the surround sound speakers. Then, he strides up to me while watching Liz curiously and she starts laughing again. "What? Sara and I against you two?" he questions.

"No, girls against boys," she argues, smiling mischievously.

His smile widens and a wicked glint sparkles in his eyes. "So, do we get something if we win?" he prompts.

"Great idea!" Liz shrieks. I know I'm about to strangle her for whatever idea she has in her head, but I don't know how to stop it. "If we win, you two have to take us out, wherever we want to go."

"I'm all in," Jason proclaims and winks at me. My heart jumps up into my throat as I watch him move.

"I know what I want," Blake claims with a playful grin.

"Um, no," I stammer my face completely flushed now with Blake's insinuation.

Blake looks over at me and smirks. "Keep your mind out of the gutter, Sara. I'll make it doable for you too. I want a kiss right here from my girl telling me I'm the sexiest man in the world." He raises his eyebrows at me in challenge before winking at Liz.

"I'll be gentle," Jason teases with a small smile.

"Shit," I mumble under my breath. "I did it once, I guess I can do it again." I turn towards all of them glaring. "Fine, I'm in," I concur already asking myself why I'm agreeing to this obvious set up. Liz squeals and gives me a quick hug. "Liz goes first," I state and the boys nod in agreement.

Jason steps up right behind me and whispers, "Thank you," in my ear sending shivers down my spine. I take a deep breath to calm my nerves before I admit to myself, I don't know whom I want to win this game. I take a step away from him so I can try to concentrate on the game. He chuckles softly, the low, sexy sound making my stomach flip-flop. It's obvious this is fun for everyone but me.

Jason

Sara is really good at darts. I love watching her eyebrows come together over her perfect little nose when she's trying to concentrate right before she releases the dart at the target. It's almost like she's blocking everything else out, or maybe she's just trying to block me out. I can't help but notice how flustered she becomes when I step close to her as well as the amusement in her friend's eyes. I'm thankful to have Liz as an ally right now or Sara might be over letting Joe teach her to play pool and I don't think I could deal with that shit.

The game is pretty close, and I step up to the line, ready to finish the game, but when I glance over at Sara nervously watching me, I know I have to lose. I'm not about to force her to kiss me again until she's ready, especially not in front of all these people. A guaranteed date with her looks like a start in the right direction. As I release the last dart, the girls shriek and jump up and down excitedly with their win. I shrug my shoulders at Blake, giving him a crooked smile. He raises his eyebrows in question and then shakes his head, laughing.

"Yeah, everything Christian said about you is definitely not true," he emphasizes. "You are a good guy."

I huff a humorless laugh and scan the room to find my brother. "Christian, what the hell have you been telling your friends about me?" I yell across the room. He just shakes his head and waves me off like it's no big deal as he wraps his arms around Bree and plants a kiss on her neck making her squeal. I shake my head and shrug again, causing Blake to laugh even harder. "So," I begin turning towards the girls, "I guess I owe you a date."

"You don't owe me anything," Sara blurts out, but I'm not about to let her get away from me or get out of this date. Especially after giving away my kiss.

"I make good on my bets and you girls won. We can go out when we go back to Portland," I suggest.

"Classes start this week. It's going to be pretty busy with my new schedule," she rushes for another excuse.

I smile and declare, "Well then, next weekend." I'll have to change my work schedule, but she doesn't know that. She looks like she's about to protest again, so I stop her. "Unless you changed your mind and you want to forfeit your win," I challenge. I smirk at her with my arms open wide. She snaps her mouth shut and openly glares at me. My arms drop to my sides and my expression turns soft as I take a step towards her. "A girl's gotta' eat, right?" She sighs heavily like she might be giving in to my request. "It's just dinner and you get to pick the place and anything else we might do," I remind her gently.

She looks up at me with those dazzling hazel eyes and I have to shake myself out of my stupor. "Fine," she grunts sounding exasperated. "I'll go to dinner with you."

I let the smile immediately cover my face. "Don't sound too excited about it, Sara," I tease. She eyes me skeptically, but what she doesn't realize is my only ulterior motive is to get her to go out with me again without a bet holding her to it. I absolutely must have this girl. It's the first

66

time I've actually wanted to hang out with my brother's friends in years. When we were younger, hanging out with Christian and his friends always caused trouble for everyone involved, especially my brother and me.

I watch Christian and Bree approach all of us hand in hand. I have to admit, I've never seen my brother this happy, and I'm thrilled he has that with Bree. "So, by the reaction over here I'm assuming the girls won?" Bree asks innocently.

"Oh Yeah!" Liz smiles and high fives a somewhat disgruntled looking Sara. I have to hold back my laughter at her reaction.

Christian smirks. "If you beat Jason, you either shot perfect or he wanted to lose," he mumbles jokingly. I take a quick glance at Sara and she's eyeing me, probably trying to assess the truth in those words.

I clear my throat. "Nah, we lost fair and square," I insist, trying to brush off his statement. "Your friends kick ass at darts."

He shakes his head at me before smirking at Blake. "Friends?" he challenges. Bree instantly elbows him in the gut stepping away from him while he laughs and Blake laughs right along with him. "I was kidding," he chuckles and accepts a bottle of water from Joe who steps up to join us with Dean and beers in hand. Blake is actually Bree's best friend and Christian has a hard time dealing with it in some ways, but he's also thankful as fuck for Blake. Bree has been through a lot and Blake saved Bree's life twice and helped bring her back to him in more ways than one. Christian and Blake aren't exactly the best of friends, but they respect each other and would have each other's back in most cases. It seems they enjoy giving each other shit to tease Bree, as well.

Christian steps in towards me and places a hand on my shoulder like we're extremely close. We're brothers and we'll always have each other's back, but what most people don't realize is the two of us definitely have our issues. I'll take the blame for those problems, but I can't wait for the day we don't have any issues standing between us. He speaks quietly so only I can hear him, "I don't know what you're doing Jason, but please don't fuck with my friends."

I look him in the eye and take in his silent warning. The truth is, I don't blame him for feeling like he has to warn me. I don't let my eyes waver from his when I insist, "I'm not with this girl. I fucking promise you that." He stares at me for another minute trying to read me before clapping me on the shoulder and walking back over to Bree without another word.

Now, let's see if I can convince the girl of the same thing.

Chapter 9

Jason

As the night continues, I am drawn to Sara's every move. She seems to do everything shy of telling me to 'Fuck off' when I go near her. What I can't figure out is why, unless she's still pissed about me not asking for her phone number. Since I am the one that fucked up already, I'm trying to be patient and make up for it. I do have a date with her next weekend, so if tonight keeps going downhill, at least I know I'll have another chance. Hopefully by then she will have forgiven me.

After tossing my beer, I step towards Sara to try talking to her one more time. She has her back to me and I pause when I notice Joe glance at me nervously before quickly focusing back on her. I step up next to Bree instead, without saying anything and toss my arm around her like she was my intended target. She's standing just a couple steps away from Sara and I'm hoping to hear some of the conversation next to me. "How's my future sister-in-law?" I ask and Bree blushes in response.

My ears perk up when I hear my name behind me. "So, is something going on with you and Christian's brother, Jason?" I listen intently as Joe asks her. I hold my breath waiting for her answer.

"No!" she shrieks. I release my breath forcefully, grinding my jaw with aggravation. She doesn't have to say it with so much vehemence. What the hell? "There's nothing going on with Jason and me," she begins to clarify. "We're just..."

She doesn't finish her statement and I want to turn around and interrupt their conversation to set her straight, but

I have no right. "Listen, you don't need to justify anything to me. I would just really like to ask you out, but I don't want to step on any toes, and I heard you might be going out with Jason. Christian is my best friend," Joe adds as further explanation for his rambling.

I'm about to turn around again when Bree grabs my arm and smirks at me shaking her head. She whispers, "Let her handle it." I relent with a huff and cross my arms in annoyance, waiting for her response. Bree chuckles quietly at my reaction, but I ignore it, straining to hear behind me.

"Um, well, I um have met him before and well, I um do have an um date with him next weekend," she stutters. A slow grin covers my face. Relaxing slightly, I attempt to hold back my chuckle at how fucking adorable she sounds. "But, um, I don't know if well, um..." she stammers trailing off.

"Well, think about it. If it's nothing with him, give me a call," he urges. "I'd really like to take you to dinner or something sometime," Joe declares, stopping her so she doesn't have to continue. I can't help but think he really is a good guy, just not the right guy for Sara. At least that is the story I tell myself and hope it's true.

"Sorry, Joe," I mumble smiling. "I'm going to do what I can so she doesn't take you up on that offer." Bree laughs louder shaking her head at me before releasing my arm. "What?" I ask her, grinning. She really is going to be a great sister-in-law.

She rolls her eyes at me and prompts, "Be good and just go talk to her." I nod and immediately turn around without another word. I take a step towards Sara feeling much more confident. Joe smiles stiffly at me before walking away after quickly mumbling something to Sara, while my focus remains on her.

Sara

I'm about to hyperventilate. The guy I should be going out on a date with just asked me out and I couldn't even explain to him what was going on between Jason and me. Joe's such a good guy that he steps away anyway. Jason stands in front of me looking at me with that sexy smile. I pray he didn't hear any of my conversation with Joe. I not only sounded like an idiot, but I don't want Jason to jump to any conclusions. There's also the fact that I don't want to feel any more foolish around Jason than I already do.

"So," Jason begins his smile fading as his eyebrows scrunch together in concern. He reaches for my arm asking, "Are you okay?" I swallow hard trying to catch my breath and nod at him hesitantly. He obviously doesn't believe me when he starts guiding me towards the couch saying, "Maybe you should sit down." I let Jason guide me to the couch and allow my knees to buckle, flopping down on the cool leather. He sits so close to me our knees are touching. I push myself away just slightly to reduce our contact, hoping it will help ease my nerves. My breathing seems to only become worse with his touch.

I stare at the black TV screen in front of me and concentrate on breathing in and out. Why can't I wear my normal mask around him? Every time he's there, I look like a fumbling idiot. I have never been like this in front of any guy! I can't even imagine what he must think of me. Around anyone else I'm normal or I can fake it, but around him I'm anything but. As I catch my breath from my mini panic attack I blurt out, "Why do you keep helping me?"

I refuse to look at him while I anxiously wait for him to answer. "Are you fucking kidding me right now?" he prods sounding completely exasperated, causing me to look up to see his face. "First of all, any decent person would help you if they could." He shakes his head in disbelief before continuing, "Second, I like you, Sara. I want to get to know you. I haven't been able to take my eyes off you, so if

71

something is wrong with you, I'm bound to notice. And, when I do, it sure as hell is going to be me helping you."

My heart flips erratically in my chest with his words before jumping up into my throat. His blue eyes seem so sincere as he's talking, but it goes against everything I've ever really believed. I take a deep breath and swallow the lump in my throat before I answer with a shaky, "Thank you. I guess I'm just a little tired," I add as the only excuse I can come up with hastily.

"Do you want me to get you some water or something?" he offers obviously not buying my excuse, but thankfully not calling me on it either.

I shake my head and mumble, "No thanks." I give him a small smile of appreciation as I try to put my confident mask back in place. "I'm already feeling a little better."

"Good," he states. He smiles relaxing into the couch next to me. "So, what do you like to do for fun Sara?" he asks looking at me intently.

I shrug my shoulders in response. "I don't know. I guess I like to go skiing this time of year."

He smiles suggesting, "We should go together sometime. I usually snowboard, but I like to go skiing too."

I grin at his offer. "You don't have to sit here and keep me company," I let him know without responding to his suggestion.

"I want to," he declares before cocking his head to the side and narrowing his eyes to study me closely. The butterflies take flight in my stomach again and I give him a shy smile.

Christian drops down on the couch next to Jason. "Is my brother bothering you?" he asks grinning at me.

I laugh as Jason's eyes narrow. "No, he's not as bad as you said he was," I joke.

Jason's eyes assess me before focusing back on Christian with a slight smirk accompanying his glare. "Thanks a lot, bro."

"Anytime, Jason." Christian's smile grows. "Don't let his charm fool you," he laughs. "Seriously though, we were just going to throw a movie in."

"No horror movies Christian," Bree demands as she tries to sit down next to him. He wraps his arms around her waist and pulls her onto his lap instead.

"But those are my favorite kind with you," he teases her. She rolls her eyes at him and focuses on me, dismissing him with a shake of her head.

"Anyway, I'm so glad you're here Sara. Are you having fun?" Bree inquires sweetly.

"I am, thank you for having me," I state, smiling genuinely back at her.

Bree is the kind of girl you can't help but truly like. She is one of the nicest people I have ever met. For a long time, I wasn't sure how I felt about her because Liz was jealous of her relationship with Blake, and I am more loyal to my best friend than anyone in my life. But once you get to know Bree, anyone can see how kind she really is, let alone how deeply in love she is with her fiancée Christian.

A loud scream sounds through the speakers and both Bree and I jump. Jason and Christian burst out laughing. I look around frantically before realizing it came from the TV. I sigh, relaxing into the couch, and giggling myself. "Christian!" Bree shrieks twisting to smack him on the chest and attempting to wiggle out of his arms. "Really?"

"You can bury your head in my chest the whole time if you want," he proposes. "I don't mind at all," he claims, smiling. Receiving another smack in the chest for his playful teasing, he laughs even harder. "Dean put it in, Bree. We can go upstairs if you want," he suggests wiggling his eyebrows. She sighs in defeat burying herself in his chest like he recommended and clings to him like it's a matter of life and death. He chuckles lightly before placing a kiss on her forehead and leaning back into the couch with her in his arms appearing completely content.

"Do you like horror flicks?" Jason asks studying me.

My attention quickly snaps back over to him on my other side. I shrug my shoulders and mumble, "They're okay, I guess."

I watch as Liz sits on the other side of the couch with Blake and Dean sits with another beer in hand next to Amy who quickly scoots a little closer to him. My eyes land on Joe when he sits down on the other side of Christian and I realize he's staring at me. I look away feeling slightly uncomfortable with the attention.

After a few minutes, my anxiety grows. Looking around at the couples and with both Joe and Jason focusing on me, I need to find a way to escape. I glance at the phone in my hand and realize I have three missed calls from my dad. "I'm sorry guys, but I have to return a phone call and then I think I need to get some sleep. I've been so busy lately and I'm really tired," I give my lame excuse as I stand.

Everyone nods their understanding and I practically sigh in relief. Instead, I smile and turn towards the stairs. I feel someone behind me, but I don't turn until I reach the main floor. Jason is standing there with a small smile curving his lips. "I want to make sure you and Amy are all set in your room," he explains, and my mouth snaps shut without responding to him at all.

I stop suddenly remembering my bag is still in the car. "Shit!" I groan.

Jason runs into my back and grabs me by the hips to steady me, although I think he's more off-balance than I am. A gasp escapes my lips and he asks, "Are you alright?"

I sigh. "Yeah, I just remembered we never brought our bags in, so they're still in Blake's jeep. We weren't sure where we were staying," I elaborate.

"I can go grab them for you," he offers. Before I have a chance to argue he's gone. He goes downstairs and comes back up with Blake. The two of them step out the front door and return almost immediately with all three of our bags.

"Thanks Blake," Jason proclaims as he comes down the hall towards me with my bag.

"Thank you," I mumble, smiling politely. We walk down the hallway, and he opens the door to his sister's room, waiting until I step inside to follow me with my bag. He sets it on the floor before looking up at me. I turn away from him to take in the room. Her room is a pale pink with a four-poster canopy bed covered in a pale pink and white quilt with a mountain of pillows. All the furniture has a whitewash to it making it look worn, but beautiful. On one wall she has a huge six-foot pin board covered with pictures and a bookshelf lined with books as well as a few stuffed animals.

"I don't know how well this room really fits Theresa anymore, but my mom had to go pink since she's the only girl in the family," Jason justifies.

I turn towards him with a smile nodding my head. "I understand that. My mom used to do that with me. When she left, I used to dress up Liz whenever I had the chance just like my mom always did with me." I won't mention we just did that together the other night.

"I'm sorry," Jason states looking genuine.

I shake my head and mumble, "It's fine. It was a long time ago." I turn away from him and walk over to look out the window. "She's re-married now. I guess she's very happy with her new family."

"Do you still see her?" he asks hesitantly.

I shake my head refusing to look at him when I answer, "Not really. My mom would do anything to avoid coming to our house to see my father, even if it was just to pick us up. When my brother started driving though, we were able to visit her more often. But by then," I shrug my shoulders as if to say it didn't matter, but we both know I mean by then it was too late. "I guess I feel like an outsider when I'm at her house. I go when I have to," I add with a heavy sigh.

Jason places his hands on my shoulder and rubs gently as I let out a gasp. "I'm sorry," he whispers again in my left ear spreading goose bumps from my neck and down my arms. His touch feels comforting, making me want to fall back against him and soak it all in.

I give myself a mental shake and twist away from him and the window. When his hands drop away from me, I instantly feel cold. I change the subject, surprised at myself for how open I'm being with him. "So, I heard some rumors that you're a better dart player than you let on tonight."

Jason laughs lightly and I turn to face him again with a small smile. "I don't know about that, but I will say I'm not going to pressure you into anything. I really want to kiss you, but I'll kiss you again when you want me to, not because you lost some bet." I smile to myself at his partial admission.

"So does that mean we don't have a date next weekend?" I prod raising my eyebrows in question.

He steps towards me with a smirk. "No way. You're not getting out of that one. I'm willing to put a little pressure on you for a date. I need a fighting chance so I can earn another kiss. He takes one more step towards me and I back up bumping into the wall. He's so close I can feel his breath on my lips. I'm breathing heavy as my eyes drift from his blue eyes to his mouth, back to his eyes. I want to lean forward and take that kiss for myself. He tucks a stray chunk of my blonde hair behind my ear before stepping back stiffly himself.

"Do you need anything else?" he asks after clearing his throat.

"I...I'm...I'm okay," I stutter. I gulp down my nerves. "Th...Thank you, Jason."

"Wait, I need your phone." I pull my phone out and hand it to him without question. He types something in real quick and hands it back as his own phone beeps with a text. "There, now I have your number and you have mine," he declares, smiling in satisfaction. "There's no way in hell I was going to forget that again!" he emphasizes, smirking. He leans close to me again and my heart stops as he places a sweet kiss on the corner of my mouth, taking my breath away. "Goodnight, Sara," he whispers along my cheek.

I unsuccessfully attempt to hold back a whimper as he pulls away from me. I try to keep my voice steady as I reply, "Goodnight, Jason." He gives me one last look filled with hope before he steps back and out of the room, leaving me completely breathless.

Chapter 10

Sara

I drop down on the bed and stare at my phone with dread before I gather up my courage to hit my dad's number and return his call. When he answers I barely whisper, "Hi, Dad."

"Sara! Why didn't you tell me you were going out of town? And you don't even call when you get there? I went to your apartment, but nobody was there. Then you don't even have the decency to call me back. I finally got in touch with your roommate just before you called and she just informed me what you were up to," he rambles sternly, not giving me a chance to explain. He doesn't want answers anyway. He just wants me to do what I'm told. He treats me like I'm always gone getting into some kind of trouble.

"I...I'm sorry, Daddy," I stutter attempting to hold back my tears knowing how much he hates them. "It was a last-minute thing. I was going to call you when we got home tomorrow. It's only for one night. I promise. We just didn't think it was a good idea to drive back at night on the icy roads," I explain hoping he understands and stops yelling.

He sighs into the phone. "I taught you better than that Sara. Call me next time," he insists ignoring my comments. I nod in agreement even though he can't see me. "We will have lunch when you get home. Your brother is here, and I told him Brad and I would take all of you out for lunch tomorrow," he demands. I cringe at the thought of Brad being included in our already dysfunctional family lunch. "It's about time you turn yourself around and start acting like a grown up."

78

"I'm not really sure when we'll be getting home. Liz's boyfriend drove us here," I state trying to make any excuse to get out of this situation. I don't want to go to lunch with my dad and Brad. "I can drive up to see Stephen next weekend at his apartment," I offer.

My dad's voice comes out angry when he responds, "You are not going to drive to your brother's apartment by yourself!" I roll my eyes at the thought of him thinking I'm incapable of so little. He's only a few hours south. "We will eat an early dinner before your brother leaves. You will be there. Call me as soon as you know when you'll be home," he stresses. He hangs up without a sound from me, leaving me no chance to argue.

I sigh in frustration and drop my head against the bed. I wish I could just stay here and never make it to lunch or dinner. I let the tears fall knowing my dad will once again attempt to push me towards Brad. He will also have zero interest in anything actually having to do with me, nor any confidence in my decisions.

I jump up and stride to my bag Jason placed on the floor for me. I grab my pajamas and quickly change into purple and grey striped flannel pajama pants with a matching long sleeved thermal top before brushing my teeth and climbing into bed. I want to be asleep before Amy comes in or if Liz comes to check on me. I don't have the energy to tell Liz my plans for tomorrow just yet. She'll want to talk about it and ask why Brad is going along. I don't blame her, but it's too complicated to explain without telling her the truth, especially when I'm this emotional and I don't think I can handle that right now. If I add the fact that I'm under the same roof as Jason, I'm positive my emotions will overflow, flying off the charts. As for him, I seem to want to open up around him more than anyone and that's even more terrifying.

I focus on my breathing as I settle against the pillow, attempting to concentrate on happy thoughts like my date next weekend. Instead, I'm soon consumed with haunting memories and wrapping my arms around myself in comfort, although it seems futile. As my eyes finally drift close, my dreams are anything but happy thoughts...

5 ½ years ago...

I'm wearing a pale blue tank top with a dark blue and white flannel shirt over top, tied in front. I paired it with one of my short jean skirts and brown cowgirl boots etched with blue stitching that Liz had given to me for my sixteenth birthday. Our birthdays are only a few days apart and we are headed to a party at a friend's farm with a bunch of our classmates to celebrate. My brother's friend, Brad, who's also my boyfriend will be there too, and I want to look good for him.

I skip towards the kitchen and cringe at the sound of my dad's voice calling my name from his office. Stopping dead in my tracks, I turn slowly and trudge back towards him. Pausing in his doorway, I begin fidgeting nervously with the hem of my skirt.

"Yes, Daddy?" I prompt sweetly knowing he won't like how I'm dressed. He never does.

"What the hell do you think you're wearing little girl?" he challenges, looking at me with a disgust I've gotten to know all too well.

"Liz gave me the boots for my birthday," I whisper my response, even though I know that's not the part of my outfit he's talking about.

"I'm not talking about the damn boots. Those are the only normal looking things you're wearing. You look like a slut in that skirt. Is that the only way you can keep that decent boyfriend of yours? Fucking him?" he accuses. I shake my head as the tears I was barely holding in spill over onto my cheeks. I try to brush them quickly away before he says any more, but it doesn't do me any good.

80

He laughs bitterly at my reaction and stomps up to me. "I'm friends with his parents, Sara! His dad is my business partner. Your brother is his best friend. You can't mess with that! You'll ruin everything!" he screams in my face, whiskey rolling off his breath as I tremble under his demeaning gaze. "You're a whore just like your mother! You take whatever the hell you want and don't worry about anyone but yourself. You're just a useless slut that destroys everything she touches, just like your mother," he grumbles. "Get out of my face!" he screams bitterly and spins away from me.

I run to my bathroom and lock myself in sobbing. Eventually I'm able to get myself under control and wash my face to rid my cheeks of the tears. I swallow the lump in my throat refusing to let him get to me again. I reapply my make-up and take a deep breath before looking at myself in the mirror. "Don't let him get to you," I command my reflection one more time before I head outside to wait for Liz.

Liz's brother Jax is driving us to the party since he's going too. He's a year older than us, but the guy who's having it is a junior like Jax and he invited a bunch of people. My brother will probably be there too, but he never even came home from school today. I jump into the back of his old Buick as soon as he pulls up. "Hi, Jax. Thanks for driving us." He smiles and nods his head in acknowledgment, while looking at me through the rearview mirror. "Hi Liz," I murmur with a smile looking over at my friend.

"You look so cute! I love the boots on you. They're perfect!" she exclaims.

"Thank you," I reply. I force myself to widen my smile, trying to get some of my confidence back, even if I'm faking it.

When we arrive at the party, Jax pulls into the grass near a bunch of other cars and trucks parked next to a large field. Music, I think might be The Dave Matthews Band

81

blares out of the barn, but it's hard to tell with the base pumping so high. A bunch of our classmates are scattered around the barn and the open fields behind it making the party appear endless. "Come on, let's go!" Liz squeals tugging at my arm. "Text me when we're leaving Jax," she calls over her shoulder.

"Be Careful!" he warns us. "Call or text me if you need me. I'll find you."

Liz links her arm through mine as we walk. "I'm going to go get a soda, do you want one?" Liz asks innocently. She's always so good. She never breaks the rules, no matter what other people might say.

I smile at her knowing she won't judge me for what I do either. "No, thanks. I think I'm going to grab a beer and go look for Brad." She raises her eyebrows at me and hesitates. I can see the doubts rolling through her mind. "I'll come find you in a little bit," I insist and turn away from her before she has a chance to try to stop me.

I get to a small keg, finding Tony, one of my classmates helping to fill the red solo cups. "Can I have one of those?" I ask with a flirty grin.

He leers at my legs, then my chest, before he finally meets my eyes with a low whistle. "For those legs, anytime," he declares handing me a cup. I take it and roll my eyes as I spin away. He slaps me in the ass making me jump and spill a little of the beer on my shirt. I grit my teeth and keep walking away to look for Brad.

"Slut," a girl I don't know mumbles glaring at me while she puts her arms around Tony.

I ignore her and keep looking for my boyfriend. After wandering through the crowd for about fifteen minutes, I finally spot him in back of the barn talking with a group of guys and girls. I begin walking towards him when I realize Kenni is one of the girls.

I hate that girl.

She's the same age as my brother and Brad and always doing everything she can to make me look bad. She makes me nervous. I slow my steps towards them as she starts dancing with one of her friends shaking her ass in Brad's face. He doesn't seem to be discouraging her either making my stomach turn. In fact, he's laughing with his friends when she backs up into him and grinds into him a little before stepping away, proclaiming, "Let me know when you're ready for a real woman." She laughs stepping away from him and he shakes his head with a smirk.

"Maybe it's time you take her up on her offer," his friend Jeff suggests nodding in Kenni's direction. "It's not like you're getting any from your girlfriend," he emphasizes and they all laugh at my expense.

I flinch and look down at my feet, fighting off the lump trying to lodge itself in my throat. I stare at the golden liquid in my red solo cup with an overwhelming feeling that my dad might be right about me. I blink back the threat of tears, chug down the beer in my hand without taking a breath, then pull my tank top down a little further to show off a little bit more of my cleavage. I push my shoulders back and walk confidently up to Brad placing my hands on his chest.

"Hey, babe," I murmur right before I smash my lips to his, savoring his look of surprise.

He pulls me closer to him, letting his hand slide to my ass and giving it a squeeze. I pretend it's what I want, wiggling myself against him. Brad pulls away with a devilish grin when his friends start whistling. He grabs a blanket out of the back of the truck bed and pulls me along behind him yelling over his shoulder, "See you guys later." I smile with satisfaction as Kenni glares at me before again fighting down my nerves.

Brad stops at an area on the outskirts of the fields, covered in grass and mildly surrounded by trees. With a quick glance in my direction, he shakes out the blanket and *spreads it out on the ground. "I've been waiting for you to get here. You look fucking hot." I smile and willingly lay in his arms on the blanket. He starts to kiss me again, while one hand pushes my tank top up shoving my breasts out of my bra. "I've been dreaming of these," he mumbles kissing my breasts. My heartbeat picks up, but not from excitement, from fear.*

This is not what I want.

Brad pushes my short jean skirt up and slides his hand up between my legs. I tense even more when he reaches my underwear, trapping his hand between my legs. He huffs in frustration at my reaction, "Don't be a fucking tease again. If you're not going to let me have you, I'll find someone who will," he warns. "I need you though, Sara, I want it to be you."

I can't do anything but nod stiffly at him. I don't want this, but I can't lose him. I need him to love me. I force myself to relax as he takes off my underwear and rubs me before pushing his fingers inside of me. I whimper with distress but close my eyes trying to force myself to relax. Brad looks at me and kisses me hard. "It's okay Sara," he urges, whispering against my lips. I try so damn hard to believe him.

He slides his pants down and grabs something out of his back pocket. I realize it's a condom when he brings the small black plastic square up to his mouth and rips it open with his teeth. My breathing picks up as he rolls it on then looks at me. "Are you ready for me?" he prompts. I nod stiffly trying not to hyperventilate. I just want to get this over with.

He pushes into me without any more pretense, and I let out an involuntary gasp of pain as he takes away my innocence. "Are you okay?" he questions. I nod my head before looking away to cry silently and pray for it to be over, while he pushes into me over and over again. He finally makes one last grunt and collapses on top of me. I silently push the tears away while he pulls himself together. "That was awesome, Sara. Remember, you're mine now." The way he says that gives me the chills from head to toe but not in the way I expect, not in a good way.

He grabs the blanket and walks ahead of me back to the party. I try to straighten myself up the best I can and hold back any more tears from what I just did. When we get back, his friends all seem to be sneering at me. Kenni glares at me. Turning towards her friends, she grumbles loud enough for all of us to hear, "What a slut!" Gasping, her words cause me to blush a deep shade of red.

Brad leans towards me and I hold my breath, waiting for his words of comfort, but they never come. Instead, he whispers in my ear, "Cover up a little more next time before you come to a party. My girl doesn't need to look like a ho in front of my friends, that's just for me." He smirks and I suddenly feel nauseas as an overwhelming feeling of shame washes over me. I tune out as his friends all pat him on the back with a knowing grin. He reaches for me, and I don't know what else to do, but go willingly. I may have kept him for now, but all I've really done is proven my father right.

I hate myself.

Present Day...

"Sara! Sara, wake up," Liz whispers in my ear while gently shaking me. I groggily lift my head and push away the very real tears from my cheeks. I look around the pink frilly bedroom trying to remember where I am and finally realizing I'm in the Emory's house, Christian and Jason's parents. "Are you okay?" Liz prods.

I take a deep breath and shake my head attempting to clear out the fog. I clear my throat and answer automatically, "I'm okay." I slowly lift my head and glance warily at my friend. "Just a bad dream, I guess."

"Do you want to talk about it?" she offers, her voice full of concern.

I shake my head gently again looking back down at my hands crushing the pink and white comforter in my lap. "My dad had called earlier, and I guess I worried him. It must have set off some old memories of when I did the same," I state, giving her an explanation as close to the truth as possible. Liz doesn't know the truth about my dad or Brad. My embarrassment with the way my dad treats me has always felt too horrible to share with anyone, even your best friend. As for not telling her about Brad, I didn't want Liz to think any less of me. She's the only one besides my brother I have always felt really loves me unconditionally. I can't take a chance that the truth might change how she feels. Besides, I like feeling normal around her. "I'm just going to try to go back to sleep," I mumble quietly not looking her in the eyes.

Liz wraps her arms around me and squeezes me tight. "Thank you," I rasp, hugging her back.

She smiles sweetly at me while she stands up. "I'm glad I came to check on you." She steps toward the door before turning back to me. "I'm going to get ready for bed, but please let me know if you need me. Blake and I are right next door to you," she adds pointing at the wall opposite my bed. I nod reflexively knowing I won't be bothering her tonight before looking down at my pillow.

I slowly lie back down as Liz pulls the door closed behind her. I curl myself into a tight ball, attempting to hold myself together. Taking a few deep breaths, I pinch my eyes together as a few tears escape. I don't want to feel like this anymore. I hate that my dad always brings my nightmares back. Shaking my head, I try to rid my mind of my horrendous thoughts. I hope and pray I don't have any more dreams of my past. I don't think I can handle it tonight, or any other night for that matter, but for now I want to get through one night at a time.

Chapter 11

Sara

I wake up the next morning feeling completely exhausted. I have no idea what time it is, but Amy is already gone, if she even slept in here last night. I can't really tell from looking around the room and I definitely never heard her come in. Shaking my head, I roll out of bed, it's not like it's any of my business anyway. I pull on a sweatshirt and stumble to the bathroom to brush my teeth and throw my hair into a ponytail.

I wander downstairs to the kitchen only to find it completely empty. Inhaling deeply, I follow my nose to the fresh coffee and pastries on the counter in the corner, the only evidence someone else is awake. I grab a small raspberry filled Danish and set it on a plate before I load a heaping spoonful of fruit salad onto the side of my plate. Grabbing a coffee cup, I fill it up. I close my eyes taking in the heavenly scent before I open them to add sugar and cream. I pick up my plate and cup and stroll over to the table carefully, so I don't spill. Taking a deep breath, I set everything down at one of the chairs facing out the large windows. I think I could look out these windows all day, I ponder as I curl my legs up under me.

I love staring out at the endless sea of white. It has a calming effect on me in a way. I think it's because it makes me feel safe. Maybe it's because the ceaseless view of nothingness gives me the feeling of being alone. I like the thought of a world where I don't have to worry about my dad or Brad or what a horrible person I am. A tear slowly escapes with the thought. I close my eyes and take a deep breath trying to pull myself together.

"Good morning," Jason grumbles softly into my ear. Gasping, my eyes snap open and goose bumps instantly cover my flesh. I turn to look at him and my stomach flips at the sight of him. His short dark brown hair is surprisingly beautifully messed from sleep, and his blue eyes are sparkling bright. The corners of his lips that are turned up, immediately curve down when he sees my face. His eyebrows immediately scrunch together with concern. "Are you okay?" he prompts, gently reaching for me.

I reflexively flinch slightly away but force myself to stop as he visibly cringes at my reaction. I steel myself, hating my body's instincts. Thankfully, he tries again. Reaching towards me cautiously, he wipes away my forgotten tear with the pad of his thumb. I attempt to swallow the large lump in my throat. I open my mouth to answer him, "I'm okay. I just have a lot on my mind," I whisper hoarsely.

He sets a cup of coffee down I didn't even realize he was holding and sits down next to me. "Do you want to talk about it?" he questions.

I grimace and shake my head. "No, that's okay." I shrug like it's not a big deal.

He doesn't say anything for a few minutes. He continues to watch me like he's looking for answers before he finally releases a heavy sigh. "Okay, then how about I grab my breakfast and I can stare out the window with you," he suggests, the corner of his lips twitching like he's fighting a smile. I nod my head in agreement and release a breath I didn't know I was holding, finally able to give him a small genuine smile. He beams at me, appearing relieved. He stands up squeezing my shoulder on the way, giving me a shock of warmth.

He's back within seconds carrying a large plate filled with fruit and a few different pastries. "Hungry?" I prod with a smirk.

"Not really," he remarks with a shrug as he shovels a mouthful of fruit and pastry into his mouth making me laugh.

He watches me for a minute his blue eyes sparkling before he proclaims, "You have a beautiful laugh." My stomach flips as I feel myself blush slightly, but not responding. "I wish I could get you to smile more. I think that's my new goal," he proposes.

I grin shyly at him. "I…" I start but then instantly snap my mouth shut as I turn my head to look back out the window. I'm rarely at a loss for words, but there is just something about this guy that seems to keep making that happen over and over again. I'm honestly shocked to hear him say he wishes I would smile more. I smile all the time. In fact, so many people comment on how I'm always smiling, always so happy. Nobody ever knows I'm just putting on a show. Does he mean real smiles? Does he actually see the real me? The me I don't let anyone in to see? I attempt to swallow down my growing anxiety with that thought.

We eat in comfortable silence, but I can feel his eyes on me most of the time. I fight with myself not to look back at him and to keep my breathing steady.

"Did you see that?" he asks excitedly.

"What?" I prompt, finally glancing over to him. I can't tell him all my focus was concentrated on him sitting next to me.

"A bald eagle just flew into that tree," he declares pointing outside.

I stand up and walk towards the windows, grateful for the distraction. "Where?" I inquire searching through the trees and seeing nothing but white.

He saunters over to me, stepping up right behind me. I feel his body heat closing in on me and I have to remind myself to concentrate on controlling my heart rate as well as breathing in and out. He places his left hand gently on my shoulder, eliciting an unexpected soft gasp from my lips. He bends down towards me and leans in really close to my right ear before pointing with the same hand. "You have to look up," he whispers into my ear, his breath sending shivers down my spine. "He's in the tallest tree, right down near the lake. You can see the nest all the way at the top, just barely over the other trees." I hardly register what he's saying with the irresistible feel of heat from his breath on my cheek and his hard body pressed up against mine.

I gulp and my eyes slowly follow the line of sight from his hand out towards the trees. Lifting my gaze, right near the lake, I finally see the dirty white head of a bald eagle sticking up out of his nest. "I see it!" I whisper excitedly.

The bird gracefully flies out of the tree, swoops down over the frozen lake and back up into the sky and away from us. I watch until I can no longer see it. For some reason the freedom of the bird itself, not just the symbol of the bald eagle, completely overwhelms me.

"Beautiful," I murmur under my breath.

"Yes, you are," Jason mumbles. I blush, as my chest tightens, feeling the sincerity in his words. I turn my head slightly to peer at him, almost expecting his eyes to tell a different story than his words, but a lump forms in my throat from the intensity of his look instead. Our faces are only inches apart. He looks like he may want to kiss me as much as I want to kiss him in this moment. He slowly moves his hand to my cheek and leans towards me. He's so close, I can feel his breath on my lips. I know I'm going to give in to him. I want to. "Sara," he rasps my name.

"Good morning, big brother!" Christian hollers as he ambles into the room with Bree. I swiftly jump back from Jason. "Morning, Sara," he adds with a low chuckle. I smile nervously back at both of them without saying a word, trying to catch my breath. I hear Jason quietly sigh in resignation behind me and I move shakily back to my seat.

"Did you sleep okay, Sara?" Bree asks grinning at me.

I reach for my coffee cup and take a sip so I can catch my breath before I answer. "I did, thank you," I lie attempting to be polite.

"Are you guys going to hang around for a while today?" she inquires as everyone else tiredly trails into the kitchen for breakfast.

I look over at Liz and Blake since I haven't had a chance to talk to them about what time we're driving back today. After my dad's phone call though, I know I can't be too late in returning. "I'm not sure," I pause looking over at Liz to make sure she hears me, "that's why my dad called last night Liz. He planned something with my brother and needs me to be there." I glance over at Blake and apologize, "I'm sorry, I would have said something sooner, but he didn't tell me about it until last night when he called."

"It's okay. It's no big deal, Sara." Blake states, shrugging it off. "What time do you have to be back?" he questions.

"I don't know exactly. He originally wanted me for lunch, but he said an early dinner would work if we weren't going to be back in time. Whatever you and Liz want to do is fine, Blake," I answer.

"I could give you a ride," Jason offers. "I'm heading back to Portland anyway because I have to work tonight. I'll get you there whenever you need."

I feel a slight panic at the thought of riding back with him, but Liz doesn't give me a chance to argue. She lights up at his offer, "That's a great idea! Thank you, Jason. Blake and I were going to stick around until lunch and then grab an early dinner on the way home." My eyes widen knowing I'll make everyone feel bad if I argue, so I pinch my mouth closed and breathe slowly through my nose.

"Excellent! Then, let me know when you want to leave and I'll have my truck all warmed up for you," Jason proclaims. He glances at me, grinning wide, causing the butterflies to stir in my stomach.

"Thanks," I mumble.

Liz steps over to me and leans over my chair before asking me quietly, "Are you sure this is okay with you?"

I nod and smile reassuringly at my best friend, "Yeah, it's fine Liz. I promise." I know she means well and I'm sure she'll enjoy spending time with her boyfriend without me tagging along. She definitely deserves it. I don't need to make her feel bad because of my issues.

"Did you sleep any better after I left your room last night?" Liz whispers. "I was really worried about you."

I nod my head not wanting to answer too loudly, fearing someone could overhear. "I'm okay," I insist ending that part of the conversation. I don't need anyone else to know I was up half the night with bad dreams, especially Jason.

"Good," she declares, grinning.

"I'm going to go shower and get ready. I'm not in a hurry, but I don't want to keep my dad waiting for too long today," I announce so Jason knows we'll have to leave soon.

I stride over to the sink to clean up my dishes as Christian steps up next to me. "I can do that," he offers. I give him a small smile as a thank you and he takes the dishes from my hands. He hesitantly adds quietly with a quirk of his brow, "Be careful, okay?"

I look at him trying to decipher his meaning when Bree steps up placing her hand on Christian's arm. "Thanks for coming, Sara. And don't worry, Jason will get you home safe." She leans in and gives me a big hug. Lifting my arms around her, I give her a squeeze, gently hugging her back.

"Thank you for having me," I state, glancing from one to the other. "And congratulations again. I'm really happy for you two," I add smiling genuinely at the two of them. You can tell how crazy they are about each other.

"Thanks," Bree murmurs. She smiles at me, still holding onto Christian. She glances up at him with such obvious love and he leans in to give her a quick kiss like he can't help himself. I love that they have that together. The kind of love they have seems rare.

As I step away, I glance back to Christian giving him one last puzzled look, attempting to decipher his comment before turning to go upstairs. I really wish I knew what he was trying to say. Exhaling harshly, I shake my head and try not to think about it. I need to take a quick shower and get ready before I get my things together, especially if I'm going to be in a car with Jason for an hour.

I send a quick text to my dad to let him know that we're heading back soon, and I'll be able to make it for lunch. I don't want to go, but I know the sooner I get this over with the better. Plus, my dad will be happy that I didn't cause him to have to change his plans. I groan to myself already dreading the day ahead.

Chapter 12

Sara

The ride back to Portland starts out relatively quiet. Jason turns on ninety-two Moose and lets it play softly on his stereo while driving. I keep staring out the window at the endless white contemplating what Christian was trying to tell me as the new boy band song plays in the background. Was he trying to warn me about Jason? If he were warning me, why would he do that? I don't know why I'm stressing about it because it doesn't really matter anyway. It's not like a girl like me could actually have a relationship with a guy like Jason.

I sigh in frustration and Jason glances over at me with his eyebrows raised in question. "Are you alright?" he asks his voice full of apprehension.

"You ask me that a lot," I respond. He glances over at me, arching his eyebrows, urging me to answer before focusing back on the road. I heave a sigh and reply with a nod of my head. "I'm alright," I mumble without confidence. I turn to look out the window again. He reaches over and gives my knee a light squeeze. I gasp, a bolt of heat electrifying me from his gentle touch and my eyes flash over to him.

"You sure about that?" he prods glancing towards me every chance he can get. Momentarily holding my breath, I shrug my shoulders in response. "Does it have anything to do with this lunch you have to get back to Portland for?" he probes. My throat instantly goes dry as he comes closer to part of the truth. "Or maybe something to do with your brother or your dad?" he pushes. My body instantly heats with embarrassment. I'm not about to tell him the truth, but for some reason there's no way in hell I can lie to him either, so I maintain my silence, not saying anything at all.

He reaches for my hand and intertwines my fingers with his sending warmth throughout my whole body. He squeezes softly and I'm a little shocked as I feel instant relief consume me with his comfort. "I'm here if you want to talk," he prods gently.

I smile over at him, my heart pounding with the thought of really having someone to confide in. I'm not ready, but...I want that so much it hurts. I rub my chest with my free hand, hoping to rub away the dull ache. "Thank you, Jason. I really appreciate that," I whisper.

He gives my hand another squeeze and thankfully changes the subject. "So, where are we going on our date next week?" he inquires with a wry smile.

"I'm not sure yet. Liz and I will have to talk and figure it out. I promise it will be something good though," I claim, grinning.

"I know it will," he concurs smiling wider.

"Yeah, I'm sure you're on pins and needles waiting to find out what we'll be doing," I grumble sarcastically.

He laughs and shakes his head slightly. "You have no idea!"

I smile to myself and swiftly change the subject. "So, I heard you went to West Point," I state. He nods his head in confirmation. "That's pretty impressive."

He shrugs like it's no big deal. "Thanks. My dad had gone there too, and I guess you could say being the oldest, I was strongly encouraged to go in that direction as well," he states dryly. I want to ask more, but he quickly turns the tables on me. "What are you going to school for?"

"I don't know, business, I guess. I'm really good at math," I add without a lot of enthusiasm or confidence.

He chuckles, repeating, "You guess, huh?" He glances over at me with a smirk. I just shrug my shoulders like it's really not a big deal, but the truth is, I'm doing what

I'm supposed to be doing according to my father and my ex, not according to me. I don't know what I want. Anything to do with the future scares the crap out of me.

"I don't really know what I want to do with it, it's just something I'm good at," I reiterate. "Plus, my dad strongly encouraged me to go into business," I add in a deep voice, attempting to mimic Jason. He bursts out laughing, giving me my desired effect.

"Oh, I love this song!" I screech as Honey, I'm Good by Andy Grammer booms over the radio. I pull my hand from his to turn it up and start singing and dancing in my seat to the song. Jason laughs taking in as much of me as he can while driving and I enjoy every second of it.

For the rest of the ride, I attempt to entertain Jason to the best of my ability, singing and dancing to the music even when I don't know the words. We're still laughing as he pulls up to my apartment, my stomach starting to hurt from laughing so hard. Glancing out the windshield, the smile instantly drops from my face as I notice Brad's truck in the parking lot. My chest tightens and I feel myself starting to panic, not wanting Brad to see me in Jason's truck. I don't need that right now.

"Are you okay?" Jason prompts, his eyebrows drawn down in concern. "You look really pale all of a sudden."

Of course, he seems to notice everything about me. Why does he have to be so perceptive and kind? "Yeah, I'm just…uh…" I stammer, not knowing how to answer him. I begin scrambling to reach for my bag, but Jason reaches behind the seat before I do and scoops it up for me.

"I've got it," he states. Reaching out my hands, I try to protest, but he looks at me sternly and insists again, "I've got it, Sara." I nod stiffly and hold my breath as he steps out of the car. I reluctantly do the same, so he's at my door by the time I'm closing it. He places his hand on my back to guide me towards my apartment. "Which one is it?" he questions. I point to my door numbly, without opening my mouth and forcing myself to take a breath. We step up to my door and he stops and looks at me. "You're shaking," he observes. "What's wrong, Sara?" he repeats, this time sounding slightly desperate.

"N…Nothing…I'm f…fine," I stutter. "Th…thank you for the ride, Jason."

He grinds his teeth and looks up at the sky as if begging for answers before excruciatingly slowly bringing his gaze back down to me. I reach for my bag and his hand grips me around the back of my neck, so he can tilt my head up towards his. I'm in a state of panic wanting this with him and knowing Brad is in the parking lot, terrified of what he's going to say or what he might see.

"I don't know what's going on Sara, but I really wish you would talk to me. You were fine before we pulled into your parking lot. What set you off?" he prods staring intently into my eyes, willing me to answer him with just a look. I pinch my lips shut tight as I eye him warily, trying to calm my nerves with him so close. "Can I come in and make sure everything is okay inside?" he prompts.

I shake my head vehemently. "That's okay. You don't need to do that. Everything's fine," I insist.

He clenches his jaw and grumbles, "I understand you're not ready to talk to me yet. We haven't known each other for very long, but I hope you will be ready soon enough. I'd like to help you, but I have no fucking idea where your head is at," he emphasizes. Sighing in exasperation, he reluctantly lets go of my neck and wraps his arms around me, hugging me tightly. "I'll let it be for now cause that's obviously what you want, but please let me know if you need anything."

I keep my hands between us, lightly lying on his chest and curl myself into him, giving into the warmth of his body and the strength of his arms, without saying anything. I inhale deeply, wanting to breathe him in while he'll let me. Eventually, he loosens his hold on me and places a kiss on the top of my head before unlocking my front door for me. He pushes it open and finally hands me my bag and my keys while asking, "Are you going to be okay, Sara?"

I nod stiffly and mumble, "Thank you Jason." I step into the apartment and before I shut the door I wave and say a quick, "Bye."

He gives me that heart-melting smile, making my heart skip a beat. I barely hear his, "Goodbye," leave his beautiful full lips before I shut the door in his face, but I have to. I know I have to deal with Brad right now. The thought alone makes me cringe.

I rush to my room and toss my overnight bag in my closet when I hear the expected pounding on my door, but I flinch anyway. I sigh harshly and paste on my fake smile as I trudge back to the door. "Brad, what a surprise," I mumble stiffly.

He shoves inside past me, grumbling, "Sure, it is." I shut the door quietly and wait for it. I feel him seething, his energy sucking all the air out of the room. "I had to wait in my truck because it's too fucking cold outside and I didn't want to deal with interrupting you with that asshole. What the fuck were you doing with him, Sara?" he challenges.

I close my eyes trying to keep calm. I don't owe him anything, but it will be easier if I give him something. "Liz and I were at our friends Bree and Christian's engagement party. Liz and her boyfriend Blake weren't leaving yet, and I wanted to make sure I made it home in time for the family lunch. Jason is Christian's brother and offered to drive me home."

"It's morning," he states the obvious vehemently. I keep my mouth closed tightly and he continues glaring at me, "What the fuck was that assholes hands doing all over you?"

"They weren't Brad, but I don't owe you any explanation anyway. You aren't my boyfriend!" I glare back at him.

"It's time to change that again. I'm graduating soon, which means it's time for you to grow up. You obviously can't handle this shit," he declares.

"Brad, I'm not doing this with you," I complain, trying to hold back my frustration. "We have to go meet my dad and my brother."

"Not wearing that you're not!" he fumes, looking at me with disgust.

I wasn't planning on it, but I can't help but feel slightly defeated with his obvious insult anyway. "Just please let me go change and we can go. Okay?" I prod. I glance at him cautiously for confirmation and he finally nods rigidly in response.

I quickly change into a nice pair of ivory pants and a red blouse buttoned up high, with short black high-heeled leather boots. I definitely don't feel like myself in these clothes, but I can't deal with any further criticism from Brad or my father today. I'll do what I can to appease them for now. I run a brush through my hair and touch up my make-up before stepping out of my bedroom and right into Brad.

"Excuse me," I mumble, trying to step around him.

He stops me, wrapping his arms around me. "Now you look like the woman that should be by my side," he declares brushing his lips against my neck.

I grimace and try to shove him away. "Brad, don't." I push again, urging, "We have to go Brad." He doesn't budge, tightening his arms as his kisses begin trailing down my neck. "You don't have to come with me, but I won't be late for my father," I insist trying to keep my voice steady. "I can drive myself anyway. There is no reason you even need to be here. Why don't you just leave?" I suggest bitterly.

He finally responds to that, "There is definitely a reason I'm here and you know it. Your father loves me. He's the one who invited me to lunch with your family today. He's the one who told me to come pick you up and bring you with me," he grins proudly causing my stomach to turn and instantly making me feel sick. I really don't want to go. I love my brother, but I don't want to have anything to do with my dad or Brad. I wish they didn't coincide.

I take a deep breath trying to ignore my panic. "Then let's go, so he doesn't have a reason to hate you." I don't understand why my father always pushes me towards Brad. He respects him more than he respects me, but I guess I keep proving my father right when it comes to Brad, so why shouldn't he feel that way?

He groans into my neck and reluctantly grumbles, "Fine." He gives me one more kiss before stepping away. "After you," he smirks. I numbly grab my purse and try not to flinch as he smacks my ass as he follows me out the door. "You will be mine again, Sara. It doesn't matter how much you keep fighting it. You always come back to me in the end. It's what everyone wants," he claims, chuckling.

"Not everyone," I grumble inaudibly.

Chapter 13

Sara

I try to push aside thoughts of Brad and my father so I can focus on my brother as we walk into the restaurant. My father has picked an upscale steakhouse for lunch. I guess it's Sunday, so it can work, but it still feels like a little much to me for a Sunday afternoon. My shoulders stiffen as my father and brother stand to greet Brad and me as we approach. Stephen eyes us suspiciously looking back and forth between Brad and I while straightening his tie. Stephen doesn't know what really happened with Brad and me because I don't want him to look at me any differently and I don't want to be the one to blame for him fighting with his best friend.

"Hi, Dad," I state. I approach my father first and push up on my tiptoes, giving him a kiss on the cheek. I turn away quickly at his disapproving look trying not to let it bother me. I walk over to Stephen and throw my arms around him, momentarily ignoring everything else. "Hi, Stephen!"

He laughs in my ear. "Hey, Sis!" He gives me an adoring squeeze. "Did you come with Brad?" he whispers in my ear before I pull away without answering him. I need to explain but I can't do that right now, so I'm better off saying nothing at all. Instead, I turn to find a seat, which Brad is already holding out for me. I smile tightly at him before sitting down.

My father clears his throat demanding all our attention, "Thank you for making sure she got here on time."

Brad, for all I've grown to hate about him, at least he still has some decency and nods uncomfortably while my brother pleads with my father, "Dad, please stop."

101

His lips purse like he's trying to decide what he wants to do. Fortunately, we don't have to find out when the waitress arrives to take our drink order. We quickly order drinks, coke for Brad, Stephen and me and a Bloody Mary for my father. We all quietly reach for our menus. I quickly glance down to the salads and find one I can tolerate while eating with my father. I'm starving, but I know I'm not really going to eat in front of him for more than one reason.

My dad clears his throat again and sets his menu on the table in front of him, staring directly at me, waiting for my full attention. I cautiously set down my menu and take a sip of the table water before looking back at him. "So, Sara, how was your little party?" he asks his voice full of sarcasm.

I swallow hard, gathering my courage to speak to him. "Friends of mine had an engagement party for just close family and friends. I didn't want to miss it. I went with Elizabeth and her boyfriend."

He purses his lips and nods his head in acknowledgement. If he doesn't know someone or if they aren't friends of his, he doesn't care or doesn't think it's important. "Engagement party?" he repeats. I nod my head stiffly. "And these friends are the same age as you?"

"Yes, I go to college with them," I explain. "Christian will graduate in the spring like Stephen and Bree is a junior with me."

He nods his head and I eye him quizzically, trying to decipher what he's thinking. He never gives away too much when my brother is with us because Stephen always stands up for me. Instead of giving me any insight, he turns to my brother and changes the subject, "I'm so proud of you, Stephen! I can't believe this will be your last semester and then you can join the business and take on some projects of your own." My brother smiles at him modestly and I can't help but grin with pride at Stephen as well. He deserves the praise. He works hard and he's a good guy, unlike my father.

"Thanks, Dad. I'm ready to get this year done," he admits. Although my brother sticks up for me with my father, he has an okay relationship with him. My dad respects him and I'm glad he has that respect. He deserves it. Sometimes I wonder if my dad doesn't look at me that way because I'm a girl or maybe it's because I look so much like *her*.

My dad looks to Brad. "Your father and I have been talking and with both you boys graduating this year, we have some ideas to merge our businesses together some more. I guess you could say a new project for the two of you to spearhead." Both my brother's and Brad's faces light up. My dad asks, "What would you think of that, boys?"

"That would be great!" Stephen exclaims.

"Awesome!" Brad adds with obvious excitement.

"Of course, your father and I have quite a few details to work through yet, but we'll get to that as the two of you get closer to graduation. In the meantime, our families need to be attending certain functions together to do some networking. I'll make sure to let all of you know where and when you need to be somewhere as will your father, Brad." Brad just nods his head in agreement and my brother grins in acceptance.

Then my father looks to me for confirmation as well. "Okay Sara?" he prods firmly.

I jump, slightly surprised. "Oh, I'm sorry, I didn't realize you needed me to be at some of these things too," I state somewhat stupidly. I should've known better than to put it that way.

My father looks like he has steam coming out of his ears when he responds through gritted teeth, "You are a part of this family young lady whether you like it or not! I expect you to be where I tell you to be when I tell you to be there, wearing what I tell you to wear and with whom I tell you to be with. Do you understand me?" he challenges.

I nod, wide-eyed, swallowing down my fear. "Yes, Dad," I answer obediently, not really knowing what I'm

103

agreeing to. I just need to do what's necessary to get away from him.

My brother reaches under the table and gives my hand a slight squeeze in support. I don't know if he's trying to comfort me or encourage me, but either way it's not really working. The rest of lunch I make it through, responding mostly with yes or no, while picking at my salad. I'm not really hungry, but I think it has more to do with having to eat lunch with both my dad and Brad, along with listening to my father's criticism.

After my father pays the bill, I'm thankful when he immediately looks at his watch announcing he has to go. Although, I thought our schedule was about Stephen. At this point, I don't really care, just get him away from me! I'm so done.

My father stands and the three of us follow his lead. He turns and shakes Brad's hand first. "Thank you for coming and thank you for bringing my daughter, Brad. Good luck with the end of school."

"Thank you, Sir," Brad replies, shaking his hand before stepping out of the way as my father focuses on me.

"Sara," he states my name as a command and I step into his arms dutifully, placing a kiss on his cheek. "Call me this week," he instructs. I nod my head in agreement and step away.

I watch almost bitterly as my father embraces Stephen beaming with so much pride. I love my brother, but why the hell am I not good enough for my father? Why doesn't he ever look like that when he's talking to me? I swallow hard and turn away trying to shake the jealousy off. He deserves it. I don't want Stephen to worry about me when he has to leave in a few minutes.

After my father finishes speaking with Stephen, he turns and strides out of the restaurant without a second look in my direction. Stephen steps up next to me and prods, "So, do you have time for a beer before your big brother has to go?"

I smile over at him with obvious relief. "That would be great," I proclaim.

"That okay with you, Brad? I'll bring my sister home before I head back to school," he offers looking towards Brad. I feel an even greater reprieve at his offer, my body relaxing.

Brad gives Stephen a head nod and a fist bump. "Of course," he agrees. "I'll catch you later." Then, he steps up to me and I stiffen reflexively as he places a kiss on my cheek. "I'll see you soon, Sara."

I squeak out, "Bye," with my brother's eyes narrowed on me as Brad walks away. I turn to Stephen and roll my eyes at him, teasing, "I can't believe you guys still fist bump. Who even does that anymore?"

Stephen chuckles and swings his arm around my neck pulling me close to him as we walk out and next door to a pub without saying another word. For the first time all day I feel completely relaxed. Stephen doesn't let go of me until we reach the bar and plop down on the stools laughing.

"Jerk," I grin over at him.

He smirks and orders us two beers. After the bartender places them in front of us he turns to me and asks, "So, what the hell is going on with you and Brad?"

"Ugh," I groan. "Nothing!" He raises his eyebrows in challenge like he doesn't believe me. "Dad sent him to pick me up. When I pulled in this morning, his truck was already sitting in the parking lot at my apartment building. I guess dad was afraid I wouldn't show up on time," I grimace, proclaiming bitterly.

He shakes his head at me in exasperation. "Don't do that, Sara. Don't let dad get to you. It's not worth it."

I huff. "How the hell can I not, Stephen? He gets you a dream job and he tries to get me a boyfriend that he deems fit for someone with his name. He could give two shits about me!" I argue.

"If you don't want me to take the job, I won't. I'll find a decent job somewhere. I may have dragged school out a bit, but I've done well. I'll be fine. I don't have to work for dad, Sara," he offers seriously.

I shake my head like he's lost his mind. "That's insane! Take the job, Stephen. It's what you want to do. Plus, you know you'll start off with a fantastic salary, benefits and vacation time that you won't get anywhere else. Let alone you won't be starting at the bottom like you will in most companies. If you don't take the job, dad won't be the only pissed off one you'd have to deal with!" I rant. I'm not letting him ruin his future for me.

"Okay, okay," he relents, putting his hands up to stop me. "You're right, but I see what you go through with him and I know my standing up for you only goes so far." He looks at me sympathetically and I take two large gulps of my beer. He shrugs helplessly. "I just wish I could do more for you. It makes me feel like a shitty brother sometimes you know."

I shake my head and roll my eyes at him. "Knock it off! You do enough for me, I promise. I couldn't handle it if you didn't do this because of me." He nods his head slightly and takes a drink of his beer. "You know I love you, Stephen," I whisper and watch the cocky grin slowly spread across his face, "but if you tell anyone I'll kick your ass!" I joke. Smirking at him, I quickly look around as if I'm afraid someone might be listening.

He chugs the rest of his beer and stands to sloppily wrap his arms around me in exaggeration. "I love you too, Sis."

"Get off me!" I joke, laughing.

He chuckles and messes up my hair as he steps away. "Come on, let's get you home. I have to get back to school."

I follow him out to his car knowing I'm going to miss him like I always do. My brother and Liz are truly the only ones who really know both sides of me. The side my father wants me to be and the extremely positive side I show everyone when he's not around. Every once in a while, I have the opportunity to sneak a little of myself in there without the masks making me feel free, like I feel with Jason, someone I barely know. That's the me I wish I could be every day. I don't want to be the one who must be constantly proper or the me with fake cheeriness that explodes from every part of my soul. I want to be the me I am without all the disguises whomever that might be. Maybe someday I'll be able to share more of me with my friends and family, but will they even want that part of me?

Chapter 14

Sara

Later that night I plug my phone in and crawl into bed feeling completely exhausted. I drained the battery on my phone playing a mindless puzzle game this afternoon after my brother dropped me off. I didn't have the energy to do much of anything and honestly, I was too lazy to get up to plug it in afterwards. I didn't really want to talk to anyone anyway. I needed the quiet after dealing with my dad and Brad today, but I guess I should know if someone wanted to get in touch with me today.

I curl up on my side and wait until my phone powers up to look over my messages. I notice first that I have a couple missed texts from Brad I guess he sent earlier tonight. I close my eyes and take a deep breath to muster up the courage to read what he has to say. I know he won't be happy I haven't answered him yet with whatever he wants. I release my breath slowly and open my eyes before tapping his name.

"I've missed you. It's time we talk." His first text comes through simple, and it might even sound sweet if you didn't know him, but I do. Without a response from me, he becomes more irritated and demanding. "I guess we're doing this by text for now. With my graduation coming up and our families working together, it's time for you and me to grow up. It's time we get back together." I swallow hard and shake my head at the words. I definitely can't do that. "You need to be grateful, Sara. I at least deserve to hear from you." I cringe at his last text knowing he's pissed.

I notice I have a voice mail from my brother and I quickly hit the button to listen to his message. "I just heard from Brad and he says he's been texting you all night and he hasn't heard from you. I know I normally don't get in the middle, but he said he was worried. So, now I'm worried. Tell anyone and I'll kill you!" he jokes. "But seriously, Sara, call or text me just to let me know you're okay. Love you," he adds quickly before hanging up.

I hit my brother's contact information and send a quick text.

> *I'm sorry. My battery died, but I'm at my apartment and I'm fine. Love you too.*

> *Ah, likely story. Glad you're ok.*

Stephen texts back. While I'm debating what to say to Brad, another text comes through from my brother.

> *Please send a quick text to Brad to let him know you're ok.*

I acknowledge Stephen knowing I need to answer Brad. I finally tap his name to text him.

> *Sorry, my battery died. I promise, I wasn't ignoring you, but I don't think it's a good idea for us to talk right now.*

I start shaking as soon as I press send and wait to hear back from him. His response comes through almost immediately.

Sooner or later, we will talk.
We will be back together
soon.

Tears finally spill over onto my cheeks after reading his last message. I try to shake away the sadness before it consumes me. I keep my thoughts occupied by checking my other messages and emails. I'm just about to set my phone down when Jason's name pops up in bold and my heart skips a beat.

How was lunch?

Fine.

I answer lamely. After a few minutes my phone finally beeps with another text from him.

That's it? Fine?

I can almost hear him huffing in frustration through the text making me giggle.

Ok...

What are you doing?

I'm still working. Not as
much fun without you here.

His claim makes my stomach flip. I almost forgot he's at the bar right now.

You?

Nothing, I'm in bed.

I answer honestly.

F*@!

I read making me laugh, but I don't respond. What do I even say to that? Then only a few minutes later my phone beeps again,

> *Did you really have to tell*
> *me that when I'm at work?*

> *Sorry.*

I respond grinning at his reaction. He's such a guy.

> *Don't be. You've given me a*
> *great image in my head to*
> *get through my shift tonight.*

Warmth floods my body, but then my smile dims slightly, thinking he has to be too good to be true. Maybe he does only want one thing from me. The only thing I'm good for. Before I start to feel too down, another text comes through from him.

> *Get some sleep. Can't wait*
> *for our date!*

I take a deep breath hoping that's true.

> *Goodnight.*

I answer, not wanting to hope.

> *Sweet dreams.*

He responds making me cringe even though he means well. If only he knew my dreams are anything but sweet. I set my phone down and curl up on my side, closing my eyes. I take a deep breath hoping my dreams don't wake me tonight. I would love to be able to dream about Jason every night, but I know I'm not good enough for him. I'm never good enough. Unfortunately, I finally drift off to sleep thinking of my past.

4 ½ Years Ago...

I look at my father across the table from Brad and me, while I struggle to hold back my tears. If Stephen were here, my dad wouldn't be talking to me this way, but I can't always depend on my brother to be here. He doesn't even know our dad is like this when he's not around. If it wasn't for my mother having to call him in the middle of our dinner though, tonight might be tolerable. Instead, she turned his mood from bad to worse. I grip Brad's hand in support as my father continues, "Have you been living on junk food?" he probes looking at me with disgust.

"No," I answer weakly gesturing towards the salad in front of me. "I eat pretty healthy and I'm the same size I've always been."

My dad raises his eyebrows with doubt before glaring over at Brad with clear disappointment. "Well, maybe Brad needs to do a better job of looking out for you. I already told you once Bradley, if you want to be with my daughter, you take care of her like I expect you to. Sara has way too much of her mother in her. She needs a lot of guidance." My mouth drops open in shock. I can't believe that he would put this on Brad and talk about me as if I'm nothing, as if I'm not even here.

I don't know what to say to him. I have no idea what Brad should say to him either. I glance nervously at Brad just as he pales and sets down his fork, finishing the bite in his mouth. He swallows his food and slowly takes a drink of his soda before he finally nods his head in agreement.

He clears his throat and responds, "Yes, Sir. I promise I'll do a better job taking care of Sara."

I gasp in surprise. I quickly try to pull my hand away from Brad, but he just holds on to me tighter. I don't know what I expected him to say, but how could he agree to something like this? How could he do this to me? I want to get as far away from both of them as possible, especially my father, but I don't know how.

My dad shakes his head with disappointment. He looks back at me and I know he's about to say more things I don't want to hear before he even speaks. I hold my breath panicking at what's about to come out of his mouth. "Between that horrendous dress you wore to our company Christmas party last week and this," he gestures to me with distaste, "I don't know what I'm going to do with you, Sara, but something has to change."

"Mom gave me that dress," I whisper defensively, even though I knew it was the wrong thing to say. I rarely get anything from my mother anymore, so I appreciate when she does give me something, especially when it's just because she thought of me. She gave me the dress because she said she thought it would look good on me and it wasn't even a birthday or Christmas present.

"Your mother is a whore who abandoned you!" he declares with revulsion, barely controlling his rage. "You already look like her, don't act like her too."

For the rest of the dinner, I do everything I can to stay hidden from my father's scrutiny, but it doesn't work too well when you're sitting across the table from him. Brad drives me home afterwards since my father is meeting someone and isn't coming right home. The ride to my house is quiet and as soon as he pulls up to my house I jump out of

*the car and run inside. Unfortunately, Brad follows me,
walking right in like it's his house.*

*"How could you do that to me?" I ask accusingly,
shakily turning on him.*

*"What was I supposed to say, Sara?" he prods in
exasperation. "He basically says your fat and dressed like a
whore. Then he insists it's entirely my fault and if I don't do
a better job, I won't be able to see you anymore. I'm going to
tell him I'll do a better job taking care of you. He's your
father," he states like that's the reason to do everything he
commands.*

*A couple tears roll down my cheeks and I quickly
wipe them away. Does he have to say that so bluntly? Am I
really that bad? "I'm sorry," I whisper. It's not Brad's fault
I tell myself feeling defeated. I just wish he would stick up for
me once in a while like my brother does. Then again, if I
can't say anything to my own father, I don't know how I can
expect him to. Brad yelling at my dad probably wouldn't go
over very well with either of our parents.*

*"Come here," he urges, opening his arms up for me. I
step into them stiffly. "You know I love you and I'm not going
anywhere. Someday we'll even be getting married, and you
won't have to listen to him anymore." I nod into his chest
wishing that I didn't have to listen to him now. He pinches
me in the side, stating, "So, if I have to help you lose a few of
your extra pounds in the meantime, that's what I'll do."*

*His words only make me feel worse and I choke down
my sob. Both my dad and my boyfriend think I'm fat. I look
down at my body as Brad starts trailing kisses down my neck.
I can't help but think they're right. "Relax, Sara, everything
will be fine," he urges, attempting to comfort me. I can't
relax at all though. The only thing I can do is pretend this
isn't my life. "It's okay, no one is here but us," he
emphasizes. He probably thinks I'm emotional and stiff
because I'm upset with my dad and afraid to get caught. I am*

upset with my dad again, but really, I just don't like myself very much right now.

He backs me up to the couch and I fall backwards. Brad starts to kiss me, and I let him. No one else will want me. I stare at the ceiling and try to imagine I'm somewhere else, while I let Brad do what he wants to me. I don't know when he went from my prince charming to my only way out, but he did. I nearly choke on my hatred for myself as I kiss him back.

Present Day...

I startle awake and look around wide-eyed into my dark room. I'm covered in sweat and wipe away the very real tears that cover my face. I glance over at my clock reading 4:58 a.m. and groan in defeat. There's no way I'm ever going to be able to go back to sleep after another dream like that. I stare at my ceiling trying to shake away my bad dreams and the sick feeling in my stomach.

Feeling defeated, eventually I give up on going back to sleep with a heavy sigh. I throw my covers off and trudge towards my bathroom to take a shower. I hope the hot water will help wash everything away.

Chapter 15

Sara

I've been doing everything I can to avoid Jason this week, texting I'm busy with classes or homework when he calls. I just couldn't see him after how I acted the other day when he dropped me off. I don't know what it is about him, but I can't seem to put on a fake smile for him and act like everything is fine. Between the drama with my family and Brad, school starting back up, my dreams keeping me up at night and just the thought of Jason, I'm a complete wreck.

I finally texted him back last night telling him when to be here for our double date. So now I'm digging through my closet in disgust trying to find something to wear when I hear a knock at the door. "What?" I whine in frustration. Liz walks in the door and bursts out laughing the second her eyes land on me. I turn my glare on her only making her laugh harder, causing me to groan in annoyance.

"What the hell are you wearing?" she questions trying to contain her laughter.

I look down at myself and attempt to explain my process knowing she's not being critical. "I tried to pick something cute and threw the sundress on. Then I realized it's winter and freezing out and there's no way in hell I can wear that, so I threw on some leggings and some boots. I thought the sweater might dress it up a bit, but then I looked in the mirror and discovered I've actually become mismatched Mary." I groan, "You're right, what the hell is wrong with me?" This time when Liz bursts out laughing, I join in and I have to admit it feels good, even if this time I'm the one who needs help. "Help me," I beg Liz with an exaggerated pout.

Liz squeals excitedly. "You're actually going to let me help you?" she emphasizes, exaggerating. I nod my head and she jumps up and down before she begins rummaging through my closet. "This boy obviously has you all kinds of messed up inside because you are always dressing up everyone else. Did you even look at what you were grabbing before you put it on?" she challenges. She plants her hands on her hips and smirks at me making me chuckle, swiftly stripping off my clothes to start from scratch.

She pulls out simple thick black leggings and a long ivory sweater with a V-neck that fits snug, so he'll still be able to see all my curves. Then, she grabs short black boots with a one-inch heal and a clasp on the side joining at a V. I quickly pull everything on before putting my gold heart necklace on that Liz gave me and wrap three gold bangles on my left wrist. I don't want to dress up too much, but I want to look good. Liz smirks at me again and I smile in gratitude. "Thank you."

"You're welcome. Next time I want to dress you up when you're going out dancing or something though. I could have fun with that!" I roll my eyes and laugh. "You have to bring your snow boots though," she adds, "so you don't fall on your ass."

"I already threw all that stuff in the tote bag with yours. Did you tell Blake where we're going?" I ask and she shakes her head in response.

A knock at the door makes me jump and Liz squeals before racing for the door announcing cheerfully, "I'll get it!" I follow slowly behind her and grin, my heart skipping a beat when Jason steps inside with Blake right behind him.

Jason walks right over to me and looks at me timidly. He pulls out a single white rose from behind his back. I smile shyly up at him and murmur, "Thank you, that's sweet."

The corners of his mouth turn up just slightly, causing my stomach to flip-flop. "Well, I have to do a lot more than sweet if I want to get that second date. I'll work on that," he

117

adds playfully. I grin even wider and watch him full of curiosity.

"Well, I'm definitely not going to stop you from working for it," I tease. His smile grows and just as he's about to say something else, we're interrupted.

"Are you guys ready?" Blake questions with raised eyebrows and his arm slung around a grinning Liz.

I blush slightly and proclaim, "Yup, let's go!" I grab my coat and purse and follow everyone out the door.

"What's with the bag?" Blake asks Liz.

"Sleepover?" Liz states as more of a question, smirking.

Blake grins and concurs, "Works for me." I can't help but laugh and Liz joins me giggling.

We all walk up to Blake's jeep, and I climb in the back with Jason, while Liz tries to take the keys out of Blake's hand. "I'm not telling you yet!" she insists. He finally relents and hands the keys over to her in exchange for a kiss. Their kiss makes me want to lean into Jason and do the same thing to him.

When they finally climb in the Jeep, my whole body heats when I look at Jason. He's grinning at me, his blue eyes sparkling. I just pray he can't read my mind, but the way he's looking at me right now, I'm afraid that's exactly what he's doing. I breathe a sigh of relief when he lets me off the hook asking, "So it's obviously a little early for a dinner date, so where are we headed?"

I beam at him, liking the thought of surprising him with something. Liz and I like to goof around. Maybe it's my time to forget about everything else. If this ends up being the only date Jason and I have, I want to make sure it's fun and memorable. Hopefully he doesn't mind relaxing and acting like a kid. "Patience," I tease. "You have to wait until we get there like everyone else."

His grin grows and my heart pounds so hard I think it might pound right out of my chest. "All in," he mumbles under his breath causing my heartbeat to burst into my ears. I shake away any thoughts of a happy future and attempt to focus on having fun today.

Within minutes we pull into Reny's making Blake laugh. "What are we doing here?" he prods.

"We have to pick up a few things first," Liz claims, smirking. I jump out of the jeep laughing and rush quickly into the store. Reny's is one of those stores that has a little bit of everything at pretty good prices.

Instead of following Liz I turn in the opposite direction and Jason follows. "We'll meet you at the register in ten minutes," I call out to Liz and Blake. She waves in acknowledgement as she's walking away.

I walk into the clothing section mostly geared towards tourists. Almost everything in this section has the words Maine on it or something to do with Portland, the state of Maine or even the general New England area. Shirts, hats and even underwear have moose, lobsters or even puffins pictured in different poses. Moving on, we find pajama pants with the Portland head lighthouse, as well as tights overflowing with blueberries. Some are funny and some are meant to be beautiful. Either way it feels like a playground to me. I do love dressing people up and although I don't expect Jason to try on any shirts, the hats can be just as much fun.

I figure I'll be able to see if he's playful like me by starting out easy. I grab a green hat that states, "Wicked Good times." It's definitely a New England phrase and I reach up to pull it onto his head. His grin melts my heart and I smile back at him. He glances over at the small mirror next to him and chuckles. He turns back to me with a mischievous glint in his eyes.

"Yes, I am," he declares. I laugh at his innuendo, only blushing slightly.

"How about this one?" I prompt, reaching for one that looks like a moose with antlers and a protruding nose and using it to replace the hat on his head. "I think that's the one," I claim. I grin holding my breath so I don't laugh.

He just continues to smile, unfazed, but reaches for a hat of his own and places it on my head. "Adorable," he states. I look in the mirror next to him and laugh. On my head is a lobster hat with red claws and antennae sticking out.

"I'm the one who's supposed to dress you up," I whine halfheartedly.

He chuckles, challenging, "Who made those rules? You?" I shrug my shoulders making him laugh again. "Well then, I need picture proof that you're not the only one who gets to play dress up," he jokes pulling out his phone and snapping a quick selfie of us with our hats on. He turns to me as he puts his phone back in his pocket. He smirks crookedly. "You good with that?" he prods. I can't do anything but nod my head and try to control my breathing with him in my space. I love how he just proved to me he doesn't mind embarrassing himself.

I swallow down the lump in my throat and turn away from him. "Come on," I urge, "We have to go meet Blake and Liz at the register." Before I can get very far, he reaches for my hand, entwining our fingers together. I don't pull away, I don't turn to look at him, I almost don't acknowledge it at all. Instead, I let myself enjoy it. I nearly plow back through the store until we reach the registers and we join Blake and Liz who we find just putting our sleds on the counter.

"We're going sledding?" Jason prompts. I turn towards him giving him a slight nod of my head. "Awesome!" he proclaims. He grins and steps up with his wallet to help Blake pay. Just as I'm about to argue, I remember that they owe us this date for losing the game of darts. Even if they lost the game on purpose, I'd make a scene trying to argue at this point.

Blake turns around and laughs, "Nice hats, guys."

120

Jason just grins and tosses his hat down next to the register before reaching for mine and doing the same. He pays for the hats before I realize what his intentions are. "I don't want you to forget today," he mumbles as explanation. He shrugs like it's no big deal, but my blush says otherwise.

"You always do like to play dress up," Liz teases making all of us burst out laughing as we make our way back to the jeep.

We barely fit all the sleds in the jeep along with the four of us, but we manage to shove them in the back along the side with the seats on the right side of the car folded down. I sit in the middle right next to Jason and with how big he is it feels like I'm practically sitting on his lap. He stretches and puts his arm around me as we pull out, eliciting a giggle from my lips.

"What?" he asks innocently. "I'm too big to shove in a corner like this," he claims. "My arms have to go somewhere."

I shake my head in amusement, still giggling. "It just feels like a complete middle school move."

"What kind of guys did you date in middle school?" he jokes as he plays with my hair on the short drive over to Payson Park. It's not the biggest sledding area, but it's a pretty large park and not as busy as the Eastern Promenade can be that overlooks East End Beach. The Bay is visible from the park, which is another reason I love it here.

Honestly, it's incredibly beautiful, even in the grays and whites of winter. Besides sledding, the park is open for snowboarding and ice-skating in the winter months, so it's definitely one of my favorite places in the winter. I hope Jason likes it too I think as my heart flips again as I glance over at him. I take another calming breath, reminding myself I can't get my hopes up for anything beyond today, but I'm going to be sure to enjoy every minute I do have with him.

Blake parks the car near the sledding hill. While Liz and I change into our winter boots, Jason and Blake quickly jump out to grab all the sleds from the car and begin hauling them up the hill. As soon as we're bundled up with hats, gloves and boots, we trail behind them arm in arm. "I'm so excited! I haven't been sledding in years," Liz announces, giggling.

Blake turns and smiles at her reaching his hand out to her. She immediately drops my arm and steps up to him wrapping her arm around his and cuddling into him. "I took my sisters over Christmas break when you were with your family. We had so much fun, but it will be better with you," he insists.

Liz grins at his comment while I roll my eyes. "Is that the kind of lines you fed her to convince her to date you?" I challenge, smirking. "Aw, come on Liz, I thought you had better taste than that!" I tease and they both chuckle in response before she tilts her head up to give him a chaste kiss.

Jason slows down to walk side by side with me, dragging our sleds up with his left hand. "So, if you don't like pick-up lines, how'd I get you to go out with me?" he asks, smirking.

I laugh and claim, "I'm pretty sure I was conned into today."

He grins and shrugs admitting it with a question, "Can you blame me?" I just shake my head, actually giggling at the adorable way he cocks his head at me. When we reach the top of the hill, Jason holds a straight foam sled and a tube. "Which one do you want to try first?" he inquires.

I reach for the tube smiling. "You can give me a push first."

His smile is so big as I flop ass first into the tube, his dimple is digging deeper than I've ever seen it. I'm tempted to lean in and lick it, but I don't need him to think I'm crazy, yet. His arms go on either side of me and I feel his heat on my back even through our layers. He brings his head down near mine, his mouth at my ear as he whispers, "My pleasure," sending shivers down my spine. I take a deep breath just as he shoves me down the hill filling my lungs with cold air. I shriek with the sudden jolt and drop my head back on the tube laughing.

When I reach the bottom, I turn to watch for Jason. I quickly jump out of the way as he yells for me to watch out and flies by me on his stomach. He's soon followed by Liz and Blake spinning to a stop. The guys continue to haul all the sleds up the hill as we all take turns racing or just flying down the hill, while trying to stay clear of all the little kids.

After about the twentieth time down the hill, Jason goes airborne on one of the long foam boards as he flies over a small jump a bunch of 10-year-old boys built halfway down the hill. When he crashes back to the ground the sled breaks in half causing him to skid across the snow before he rolls hard and smashes into a snowbank. My eyes widen and I rush over to him and kneel down next to him. "Are you alright, Jason?" I prod, urgently. All he gives me is an answering groan. I flop down on my ass to get closer to him and ask somewhat desperately while lightly shaking him, "Jason, are you okay?"

He groans again before looking up at me with a glint in his eye before asking, "Who?" I smack him in the chest and start laughing, my chest releasing all the nervous tension. He grunts again, "Ow! What's with hitting a man while he's down?" he challenges, but I see the smirk tugging up the corners of his lips and finish breathing a sigh of relief.

I move to stand up, my butt going almost completely numb. When I'm up, I dust off my hands the best I can with my gloved hands. "I think it's time to go with you breaking the sled and my numb ass," I joke.

I glance down at Jason, still lying on the ground unmoving, staring at my ass. I feel my face heat, blushing. What the hell is that about? I never blush anymore, except around him apparently! He clears his throat and lightly shakes his head before dragging his gaze up to my eyes. I

123

stand there with my arms crossed and my eyebrows raised to let him know I caught him ogling me. He has the nerve to give me his full watt smile, catching whatever I was about to say in my throat. Jason finally pushes himself off the ground and stands right in front of me, placing his hands on my hips. "How about we go down one more time before we go?" he asks sweetly.

I look at him in disbelief. "How can you want to go down again after that?"

He chuckles at my exasperation. "That was nothing. Come on, go with me."

I search for another excuse, not ready to move one way or the other. Embarrassingly enough, my voice comes out sounding like a whine, "But I'm absolutely freezing."

"Come on," he continues to beg, "we'll go together in the tube. You can sit on my lap. I'll keep you warm," he proclaims wiggling his eyebrows at me. I chuckle and give him a playful shove in the chest. He laughs, "You're so rough with me." I smirk and consent with a curt nod before I follow him up the hill.

Right now, I think I'd jump at any reason to have his arms wrapped around me. I'm really in so much trouble with this man!

We reach the top of the hill and he sits in the tube holding it still with one hand, while reaching for me with the other. I step a little closer and just as our fingertips touch, he reaches a little higher and grabs me by the wrist pulling me into his lap. I squeal in surprise and immediately quiet as he wraps one muscled arm protectively around my waist and I feel his face in my neck. My heart begins to pound from adrenaline, but not from sledding. I can't feel anything but him in this moment.

After what feels like an eternity and at the same time just a moment, his left hand comes up to brush my cheek and turn my face towards him, our noses touching. His chest is rising and falling fast just like mine as he leans in and presses his lips lightly to mine. I whimper softly, wanting more when the side of our sled is kicked hard, reminding me where we are and about all the kids around us. "Hey guys, why don't we get out of here?" Liz asks as her and Blake smirk down on us. I nod my head and clumsily scramble out of Jason's lap. He jumps up with ease right after me. It seems he does everything smoothly.

Blake and Liz walk in front of us back towards his Jeep as Jason tosses the broken sled in the garbage. He grabs the remaining tube in one hand and reaches for my hand with the other entwining our fingers together sending chills down my spine, even without the skin-to-skin contact. He tosses the other tube in near a waiting Blake and steps around to the other side guiding me along in front of him, never letting go of my hand. I might be starting to like the feel of having him close a little too much. The thought of him not being around brings a gnawing pain to my chest. I don't want to think about what I will do when the time comes and he's gone.

Chapter 16

Sara

Since we're trying to surprise the guys as much as we can today, Liz drives us to a nearby specialty chocolate store along the waterfront as I strip off some of the extra layers of clothes now damp from the snow and toss them all back into the tote bag in the way back. Liz parks right in front of the door and all of us pile back out of the jeep. I shiver from the whipping wind, my chill feeling bone deep at this point. "I think we need to get you something warm," Jason suggests releasing my hand to put his arm around my shoulders and pull me in close.

"That's the plan," I announce with obvious pleasure as we quickly stride through the front door of the shop.

The store looks just like an old-fashioned candy store and soda fountain. The walls are painted with thick blue and white stripes. The front half of the store is all candy with hundreds of glass canisters filled with nearly every candy known to man lining the walls. Then towards the back of the shop on the left-hand side is a long glass-enclosed counter filled with various specialty chocolates. Then on the right-hand side is a white Formica counter with silver gooseneck spouts on one side and red leather stools seated in front of it.

We walk towards the back to sit on the red stools and look at the wall behind the counter covered with an enormous mirror and lined with glass shelves. Instead of the shelves being filled with alcohol bottles like in a bar, it's filled with old-fashioned sundae glasses, soda bottles and drinking glasses. Underneath is a work counter covered with containers filled with colorful candy toppings, nuts, and fruit. "I've never been in here. This place is pretty cool," Jason comments. "But I thought you wanted something to warm you up, not cool you down?" he probes with a bit of confusion.

I attempt to stifle my giggle at his adorable expression. "I do," I agree. "This place has the best homemade hot chocolate known to man," I giddily enlighten him like I created it myself.

"Nice," he mumbles grinning as he lets his hand fall to my knee, sending yet another chill through me. "Well then we better get you some before you freeze to death," he states smirking. I don't respond, as the waiter behind the counter with light blue pants and a pinstriped white, blue and pink shirt takes our order.

"So, if you could choose one candy, and only one candy," Jason emphasizes, "out of this whole store, what would it be?" he asks. He eyes me as if the world might end if he doesn't find out causing my stomach to do another summersault.

I shake my head to rid myself of the ever-present nerves when Jason is around. I don't know what it is about him. "Umm, that's a tough question. This is a candy store and anything with chocolate is bound to be good," I murmur, smiling. He waits patiently for me to give him a real answer. "I guess if I had to, I would pick the turtles." He nods his head with a small smile like my response was the answer he expected. I add to my explanation, "I just love the combination of caramel, nuts and chocolate."

The waiter, or soda jerk as some people call them, places our hot chocolates down in front of us piled high with whipped cream. I slide the cup towards me and lightly blow on the hot chocolate before I take a small sip. I close my eyes and let out an involuntary groan savoring the warm, thick chocolate taste on my tongue. When I open my eyes, I find Jason staring at me with his eyes flaring and his mouth hanging slightly open.

My eyebrows draw down as I look at him quizzically and prompt, "What?"

He ignores my question and leans in close to me lightly pressing his lips to mine, like he's tasting me, making me fight to hold onto my self-control. He pulls back slightly with a satisfied grin. "You're right," he concurs. "That's the best hot chocolate I've ever tasted." I feel my heart lodge itself in my throat as my face flames red. "You had a little something here," he softly brushes my top lip with his fingers. "I thought I should help you out," he claims.

I take two more deep breaths and exhale slowly before I tear myself away from his gaze and focus on the drink in front of me. I cup my hands around the cup to warm them and sip slowly attempting to rid my insides of the chill. When I'm feeling a little calmer, I ask, "So what about you?" Jason's eyebrows draw down in confusion, looking at me like he doesn't know what I'm asking. "What would be the one candy you'd pick?" I repeat his question without looking over at him.

"Oh, I'd take them all," he jokes. My head snaps over towards him with my eyes narrowed. His sexy smirk makes me realize he just wanted my full attention. "I guess you could say I like the hard candies like the candy sticks. They're full of flavor and I can suck on them for hours," he emphasizes.

I shake my head, feeling unsure about his innuendo and my defenses instantly come up. "You did not just say that," I warn, scrunching up my nose in displeasure.

"I meant nothing by it, Sara, I swear. Get your mind out of the gutter," he teases. I don't know if he means it or if he just didn't like my reaction to his comment, but I nod my head accepting his excuse this time anyway.

"Hey," Liz interrupts my errant thoughts. I keep forgetting they're here with us. When I'm with Jason, he seems to demand all my focus. "Blake and I were wondering if you would mind if we backed out of the rest of the evening?" she inquires looking extremely apologetic. "I just got a call from Katie asking me to cover for her tomorrow morning because she's sick and I really owe her. She's helped me out so much and I'm really tired. We'd like to just go back home and rent a movie and maybe order pizza for dinner."

"That's fine," I begin, feeling like a lead weight has been dropped into my stomach. I'm honestly not sure if it's from disappointment or relief.

"We can bring you back to Jason's truck and you two can still have your date," Blake suggests.

"That's a great idea," Jason adds, the corners of his lips curving upwards. "I'll take care of the check," he offers. "You guys head out and I'll be right there," he continues gently guiding me towards the door like he's afraid I'm about to argue with him.

Liz links her arm through mine and tugs me along through the door before saying, "Thanks Jason," over her shoulder.

"No one wants to hear what I think?" I question Liz as soon as we're out the door.

She shakes her head mumbling, "Not really. You just had that look on your face like today was a mistake. I don't want you to go there," she admits. "You promised you would give today a chance. I want to see you truly happy again and for some reason when you're around Jason, you seem relaxed, and I can even feel your happiness."

I roll my eyes, challenging, "What do you mean? I'm always happy."

She takes a deep breath and turns to Blake, requesting, "Give us a second in the Jeep?" He nods his head in agreement, and tips his head down, giving her a chaste kiss before opening the passenger side door for her, while I walk to the driver's side and slide in the back. I fist my hands together, anxiously waiting for her explanation. "I feel like the worst friend in the world," she starts.

"Liz, no," I begin with my eyes wide, but she ignores my interruption.

"You're right, you always act like you are the happiest person in the world. You're always smiling, constantly doing everything you can to make other people happy and other people laugh. You've definitely done that for me my whole life and I honestly couldn't ask for a better best friend. Anyone who doesn't know you believes you are always happy," she states. Then, she glances down at her lap before looking back up at me and concedes with defeat, "But I'm your best friend and looking back at all those times, I'm almost positive you were only pretending, while I sat by and did nothing. I convinced myself it was only my imagination."

"Liz," I mumble her name again, trying to get her to stop. I don't know if I'm ready to hear this right now.

She shakes her head and forges on, "Today proved to me what a horrible friend I've been and I'm so sorry," she apologizes needlessly. "Your eyes light up when you're with Jason. I see your happiness on the inside, not just on the outside." I wipe away a single tear from my cheek, overwhelmed with emotion. "I don't know what put the sadness back in your eyes, or what put it there at all for that matter and that kills me."

Liz pinches her lips tightly together before continuing. "I don't know if Jason is the answer, but I didn't realize how long it's been since I saw you full of what I can only describe as pure joy until today and I think you have to take that chance. Please don't let something stand in the way," she whispers desperately looking at me with wide eyes full of regret.

I swallow the lump in my throat, knowing if I don't, I'll be sobbing in seconds, and I can't lose it in front of Liz. I lean toward her in the front seat and hug her as tightly as I can, albeit awkwardly over the car's armrest. "You are my best friend, and I would never want anyone else to hold that position," I whisper hoarsely.

"I hope one day you'll tell me why you're holding on to so much sadness," she whispers in my ear. I don't know if I'll ever tell her, but I'm thankful for her offer anyway.

I open my mouth to tell her just that when both the front and back doors of the jeep open. "Is it safe to get in?" Blake questions.

"Yeah," Liz answers. I swiftly turn my head, looking at the sleds jammed next to me so I can quickly wipe away the rest of the stray tears that have fallen. I never cry in front of anyone, and I can't start now. I don't want to let Jason see me like this. I'm not even sure if I could explain it to him.

I feel Jason's leg press up against mine and I can't help but enjoy the simple warmth of it. The door slams shut pushing him even closer when I feel him reach across to buckle my seat belt followed by the click of his own. I guess I can't even remember to do the little things right now because I'm struggling to even force out a thank you. Jason must sense my anxiety because he keeps his mouth closed and I'm grateful for it. I concentrate on his controlled breathing to calm me down.

Eventually, he taps me lightly with his leg and gives my knee a gentle squeeze. I turn towards him with a pasted-on smile and his mouth instantly curves down into a frown, already seeing right through my facade. "Are you alright?" he prods, his eyes full of concern.

I nod my head and whisper, "I'm okay." He snaps his mouth shut, his jaw twitching slightly as he wipes away a tear I'd missed. I sigh looking down at my hands twisting in my lap. He reaches for me and wiggles his fingers in between my two hands and squeezes before letting them drop back into my lap with his hand firmly planted in between.

The drive back to Liz's and my apartment remains quiet and I'm thankful for the time to pull myself together. Although, I'm nervous about what Jason will say when we get there. I don't want him to ask questions I'm not sure I'm ready to answer.

I also can't help but wonder if Liz is right. Should I take a real chance on Jason? I'm terrified of what will happen if I do. I don't want to find out he's just like my father or Brad. I like the image I have of him. I need it to be real. But I'm also scared of what will happen if I don't even try. I like how I am with him. I like how I feel when I'm with him. Honestly, I like him like crazy already and I truly like myself when I'm with him. I honestly don't remember the last time I could say I really liked myself. How the hell did that even happen?

Chapter 17

Jason

Blake and Liz go into the apartment, and I gently drag a still quiet Sara back to my truck. "How about we do the same as them?" I ask and she looks up at me with a question in her eyes. We can go back to my place and rent a movie and order dinner. Whatever you want," I offer, "pizza, Chinese…" I trail off hoping she'll say yes.

Eventually she twists her face into a smirk. "Are you trying to get off easy, Jason?" I raise my eyebrows and she continues with a challenge in her voice, "You know trying to make tonight into a cheap date?"

I laugh hard and reach for her hand again hoping I can tug her over and coax her into my truck to come with me. "I promise, I'll still owe you another date with a real dinner. I just thought it would be nice to spend the rest of the night in after a fun, cold day out." I stop in front of the passenger door and lean into her slightly until she falls back against my truck. I start to breathe heavy being in her space and I watch as our chests begin to rise and fall in unison. I search her beautiful face for answers, hating how lost she looks right now. I want her to feel good about me. I don't want her to think I'm pushing her for sex, but I can see in her eyes she has her doubts, so I push away.

I hold her hand lightly while I wait patiently for her answer. Eventually she sighs, and nods her head, nearly imperceptibly. "Okay," she agrees. I don't try to hide my smile when I open the door for her and help her into my truck quickly before she changes her mind. I jog around the back of my truck and jump in behind the wheel. Starting the truck, I back out without saying a word. The last thing I want to do right now is give her any reason to change her mind and go back into her apartment instead.

I glance over at her, noticing her twisting her hands nervously making me wonder if I made the right decision pushing her to come with me back to my place. "Are you okay?" I ask cautiously.

After an agonizing moment of silence, she looks over to me with her fake smile making me cringe. "I'm good," she murmurs all too sweetly. I sigh and shake my head slightly disappointed. "What?" she prompts now sounding irritated.

I glance over at her before looking back at the road in front of me. I pull into the parking lot behind my building and turn off the car before turning to look over at her, giving her my full attention. She's eyeing me warily, her body angled away like she's ready to bolt and I fucking hate it. I want her to trust me. For some reason I think saying that will scare her away, so instead I tell her another truth. "I wish you wouldn't do that, hide behind your smile." Her eyes go wide like I'm already seeing too much, and I scramble to ease her mind, if only a little bit. "It's just you have such a beautiful smile when you're really happy," I admit, the corners of my mouth quirking up.

She swallows hard but relaxes slightly into the seat reaching for the door handle. "Thank you," she whispers.

I grin back and cock my head towards my building "Come on, I'll show you around." I step out of my truck and find her already climbing down when I come around to her side. I reach for her to help her the rest of the way out. I grasp her hand tightly as we walk towards my building, trying to let her know I'm not about to let go.

I pull her in the back entrance and up the stairs. We walk in the door, and I help her with her coat, hanging both hers and mine over the back of the stools at the counter. I watch as she inhales deeply and smiles, appearing content. "It smells incredible in here!" she declares in awe. She takes another deep breath then looks at me slightly puzzled. "How

134

in the world does it smell like you were just baking in here when we've been gone all day?" she challenges. "Do you have a roommate?"

I chuckle and take a step towards her. "I live above the bakery," I answer simply.

She nods in understanding, mumbling, "That's trouble."

I grin and concede, "It can be, but it can also be heaven." I shake my head slightly forcing myself to stop staring at her before I spread my arms wide and announce, "Well, this is pretty much it. The bathroom is the door on the left and my room is the one on the right."

She smiles and looks around. "I like it, but I think with that smell, anything would look good to me." She giggles and I can't help but revel in the sound.

"So is that a hint to tell me to order you some food," I tease, smirking. "Are you hungry?"

She shrugs like it's no big deal and admits, "I could eat."

"So, what would you like for dinner?" I prompt.

"Pepperoni pizza," she answers before I can even make any suggestions.

I grab my phone and quickly order pizza and chicken wings before I say anything else. "Sooooo," I mumble, dragging out the word while trying to decide how to ask her what was wrong before. I don't want her to keep shrugging it off. She looks at me curiously and I nod towards the entertainment center. "Do you want to pick an old movie or something off Netflix or Demand?" I ask instead.

She turns and walks towards the cabinets under the TV in response. "Why don't you show me what you've got, Jason," she suggests.

With those words and her ass swinging, I take a deep breath and exhale through my teeth to control myself. "Don't tease, Sara," I grumble. She just laughs in response without even glancing my way. Seriously, this girl is going to be the death of me.

She quickly thumbs through my movies and pulls out, Gone in 60 Seconds, with a grin. "Really?" I ask surprised.

"It's a great movie," she proclaims, shrugging her shoulders.

"That it is," I concur and drop myself down onto the couch.

"Do you want me to put it in?" she asks innocently. I close my eyes and bite the inside of my cheek, internally begging for a subject change. My body doesn't want to seem to let go of dragging this girl to my room, but it's pretty obvious I need to treat her with care. I slowly open my eyes back up and shake my head, pinching my lips shut tight. She's standing in front of me, the movie already beginning to play in the background.

"Are you tired?" she asks. "We can do this another time," she offers, oblivious to where my mind just wandered.

"No, no," I insist. "I was just thinking about something," I tell her vaguely. "I'm not tired at all.

"What?" she asks innocently.

I'm not about to tell her where my dirty mind was headed, but instead ask her what I wanted to earlier. "What was wrong before? You seem better, but…what happened?" I probe, honestly wanting to know.

She sighs heavily and sits down next to me, leaving over two feet of space between us on the couch. "Liz just brought up some things from the past she wanted to apologize for, but there was no need. She's always been a good friend, my best friend." She pauses and looks up at me hesitantly from under her eyelashes like she's deciding if she should continue. I remain silent, waiting for her to do just that. She opens her mouth and admits, "She was also encouraging me to give you a chance. She said she thinks we'll be good together." She watches me carefully for my reaction.

I can tell how hard that was for her to admit and I struggle to fight the grin wanting to take over my face. "Well, I think Liz is a pretty smart girl," I respond simply, trying to keep things light and Sara comfortable.

She smirks, giggling, "You do, huh?"

"So do you think she's right?" I prod. She shrugs her shoulders again amusing me and frustrating me at the same time.

"I guess we'll see. You already manipulated your way into a second date," she comments, but I can tell she's fighting a grin, which helps me relax.

"You seemed really tired and cold after all that sledding," I proclaim, smirking mischievously. "I thought I was just being helpful, considerate even. The fact that it guarantees a second date with you is just a bonus," I add.

She groans, grumbling, "Stop with the lines!"

"Is that a line?" I ask, arching my eyebrows in challenge. "I'm just being honest," I declare, shrugging my shoulders like she's done so many times already.

She opens her mouth to respond when the buzzer of my doorbell rings. "Be right back." I quickly jog down the stairs to grab the food and bring it right back up. I set the pizza and wings on the counter and grab two paper plates and napkins, handing one of each to Sara. She grabs a slice of pizza and two wings, while I grab three slices and half a dozen wings before bringing my plate to the coffee table. She follows me staring at my plate with her mouth hanging half open adorably. I grin, shrugging at her again. "Oh wait, what can I get you to drink?" I inquire, leaving my plate as I walk back towards the kitchen. I open the refrigerator and mumble, "I have coke, water and beer. There's also milk but," I scrunch my face up in disgust at the thought of milk and pizza, glancing back at her.

"What kind of beer?" she prompts.

"I have Maine Beer Company Lunch or Heineken," I inform her.

"I'll have a Lunch," she states making me chuckle. I don't know why it makes me laugh every time, but it does. I pop the tops and offer her the beer before sitting down on the couch right next to her, evaporating the two feet she had between us before. She raises her eyebrows at me and takes a sip of her beer but doesn't say a word.

"So, I know I kind of took over the rest of our date, so do I get to plan the next one or is it still your turn?" I question trying to keep the conversation light for now.

"Well, I guess you could convince me to let you have a turn," she says shrugging her shoulders again.

"You guess?" I prompt, bumping her leg with mine.

"Sure. How about you play a game with me?" she prods. I nod my head in agreement, loving how playful she's being with me. I wonder if she's always like this. "Well, I was thinking we could play a form of twenty questions," she proposes and immediately continues to explain what she means. "So, we ask each other questions, but whatever question you ask me, you also have to answer." I raise my eyebrows in surprise. She smiles shyly at me before proclaiming, "I'll start and I promise I'll go easy on you. What's your favorite color?"

"Black, like my truck," I answer simply.

Her grin grows before she teases, "Typical. Mine is blue like the sky. I like the idea of something being endless like possibilities." She looks down in her lap like she might be embarrassed before shrugging her shoulders and looking me directly in the eyes. "Your turn."

"Alright, what's your favorite time of year?" I prod. Watching her, I devour my slice of pizza while I listen to her answer.

"Spring because it's like a fresh start," she responds.

I have trouble tearing my eyes away from hers with her answer leaving me wanting more of an explanation, but it never comes. "I'd probably say summer because there's so much to do in the summer, although I can find things to do any time of year," I declare, smirking.

She just outright laughs at me in response causing my stomach to flip-flop. I love the sound and relax further into the couch as we continue eating our pizza, drinking our beers and talking about our favorite foods, movies, TV, music, bands, places, activities, and any other general information we can come up with. I'm thoroughly enjoying every single second of learning about her.

"I have to say, you're not like I thought you would be," she admits with a sheepish grin. I quirk my eyebrow up at her in question and wait for her to elaborate. "Well, going to West Point and all, I didn't know you'd be so much fun," she teases. I narrow my eyes and poke her in her side in warning, while my lips curl up, defying me. She laughs, the melodic sound warming my insides. I could listen to that sound all day.

On my last question I ask, "What's your perfect date?" I can only hope her answer will help me prepare for next time, but it's worth a shot.

She takes a deep breath and pinches her lips together thoughtfully. "Umm, that's a tough one," she admits. "I guess the guy would come to my door bearing gifts," she begins, the corners of her lips twitching up in amusement.

I interrupt, questioning, "Gifts as in plural?" She nods her head, giggling. "Any particular type of gifts?" I prod, my eyebrows raised in question.

She smirks and insists, "Oh he would know what to bring me if it was the perfect date. He doesn't even have to spend any money to do it," she proclaims confusing me slightly. "Then we would do something fun together. No stuffy restaurants or business parties," she demands almost bitterly. I know she has an explanation for that answer, but for now I don't ask, not wanting to push. I wonder if it's an ex or maybe even her father. I cringe at the thought. "He would definitely make me laugh. He would treat me with respect. He would pay if anything needed to be paid for," she insists making us both laugh. She turns thoughtful and shakes her head slightly mumbling, "I don't know, just..." she trails off sighing, biting her lower lip as she goes completely silent.

"Well, I think today with you has been pretty damn perfect as far as dates go," I confess, directing the attention away from her answer and giving her a reprieve. "There's just one thing that's missing," I tell her honestly. I reach for her and tuck a loose strand of her golden blonde hair behind her ear. I let my finger trace down the soft skin of her jaw to her chin and tilt it towards me as I slowly move towards her and lightly brush my lips across hers. "A kiss," I whisper before pressing my lips against hers again. I let my hand drop from her chin and tangle in her silky hair at the nape of her neck to pull her into me and deepen the kiss. I groan at how good she tastes and how she just melts into me, kissing me back, igniting me from head to toe. Our tongues collide at the same time, both of us tasting, exploring and searching for more.

She slowly starts to lower herself onto the couch and I follow her, not letting my mouth tear away from hers. I hold myself above her, so I don't crush her as her hands begin to move up and down my sides, over my back and down my abs. Her feathery touch feels incredible, burning a path on my skin. Moving my hand down, I slide it just underneath the hem of her shirt skimming my fingers over the velvety soft skin of her belly. I instinctively roll my hips towards her and she gasps in my ear response, right before I feel her stiffen and freeze. She stops moving, she stops kissing me, she stops breathing at all. My heart pounds with dread realizing I pushed her too far.

"Sara," I plead her name as my apology, guilt overwhelming me.

She pushes me away and stiffly stands up without looking at me or saying a word. She immediately pulls off her shirt and drops it to the floor leaving me speechless. She

140

then moves to her pants and quickly shimmies out of them and stands before me in just her lacy pale blue bra and underwear causing my throat to go completely dry. That's not at all what I was expecting. Taking a deep breath, I swallow the lump in my throat and reach out for her. Wrapping my arm around her waist, I pull her towards me. I lightly kiss her belly as I let my eyes drift over her body, "You're so fucking beautiful," I gasp with awe.

I look up to see her beautiful face, but I'm instantly completely taken aback by what I see reflected in her. I swear my heart stops the moment I see her nearly blank, almost vacant expression. My chest tightens and my stomach turns, suddenly feeling like a pit of lava. My eyes focus in on hers, looking straight ahead over the couch but nowhere near me. It's almost like I'm not even here. I think her eyes hold...resignation, disappointment, and emptiness? What...the...fuck? My breath finally catches and I quickly gulp in air as I move swiftly, gently but firmly pushing her away. I quickly reach for her clothes and hand them to her before I look away. "Get dressed," I advise, feeling sick to my stomach. Shit! I need her to get dressed now. What the fuck did I just do?

Chapter 18

Sara

Jason shoves my clothes at me, refusing to look at me. "Get dressed," he demands. I feel the tears trying to surface and breakthrough, not just through my eyes, but it feels like every surface of my body. I really want to cry. I'm so embarrassed. I'm overwhelmed with his rejection. My chest becomes tighter and tighter with anxiety, making it difficult to breathe. I clumsily pull my pants back on, followed by my shirt, before my tears finally spill over and start to fall.

"Isn't that what you wanted?" I prompt, cringing at the strain in my voice.

"Yes...No...Ugh!" he grunts. He drops his head into his hands and pulls at his short hair in frustration still facing away from me.

"I'm dressed. You can turn around now," I spit out and drop myself into the furthest corner of the couch. I pull my knees up to my chest and tightly wrap my arms around my legs holding them close to me, seeking both comfort and protection. I put my head on top of my knees and look in the opposite direction of where Jason is sitting. I want to go home, but I promised I'd give Liz and Blake some privacy for a while tonight. What am I going to do?

"What just happened?" he asks almost desperately. How the hell am I supposed to answer that? I threw myself at you, but you didn't want me? Instead, I remain quiet staring across the room at the brick wall behind the entertainment center, not able to stop the tears streaming down my cheeks. "Sara," he stresses his voice sounding closer, "please tell me what the fuck just happened," he pleads. I still don't answer him. I can't. My whole body aches as if there's tiny bugs crawling just underneath my skin, trying to get out. I'm afraid I'll completely fall apart if I answer him right now. He eventually opens his mouth again, practically begging me for an answer, but at the same time sounding hesitant, probably not wanting the truth. He asks, "Has…has anyone ever…" he huffs trailing off. I can feel the tension rolling off him in waves. He finally blurts out, "Sara, has anyone ever hurt you?"

"No!" I yell defensively before I sigh in defeat. I can't let him think that about me, I need to tell him. "No, no, that's just…that's all I'm ever good for or all anyone ever wants from me," I blurt out, letting my pain bleed into my words, right before I bury my face in my knees. I can't believe I just said that to him. I've never admitted that to anyone before. I'm so embarrassed.

"What?" Jason questions sounding horrified. I feel him move in behind me and both of his hands come down onto my shoulders with obvious caution. I take a deep breath trying to breathe in his warmth. "Sara, you're so much more than that! The reason I want something more with you is because I think you are fucking incredible," he whispers sounding tortured. "I know I haven't known you that long, but every minute I spend with you has me wanting more. And just to be clear, when I say I want more, what I mean is more time, more dates, more laughing, more talking, and yeah more kissing and touching because that's fantastic with you, but I sure as fuck don't want to do anything with you until you want me as much as I want you," he rambles with extreme vehemence.

His words make my heart break a little more. Does he really mean that? It sure sounded like it. "Jason," I barely breathe his name on a choked sob. He twists my body towards him, wrapping me in his arms and I let him, falling into his chest. He rubs my back with one hand, while the other pushes my hair out of my face before smoothing it down my back. After a while I'm finally able to catch my breath, but my embarrassment feels overwhelming and I'm still terrified to lift my head to look at him, afraid of what I might see.

He places a few soft kisses on the top of my head and I can feel him attempting to look at me. Eventually, he sighs softly and asks sounding strained, "Sara, I have to ask why in the hell would you think that's all I want from you?"

I shrug my shoulders, not wanting to answer him, but he remains silent, waiting. I can't handle the quiet from him, knowing he wants answers and it pushes me to speak honestly. "My brother is the only guy I know who respects me and loves me for who I am. Any ex-boyfriends never wanted anything else from me," I generalize not wanting to mention Brad. So many more issues come up when Brad comes into the discussion. I take a deep breath for courage before I continue. "Even my father has always told me that's all I'm good for. He always says I'm just like my mother," I murmur, my voice cracking as I confess.

I feel Jason shaking with tension, but he doesn't say anything right away. Eventually, he whispers with barely controlled rage, "I'm sorry, Sara. I'm so fucking sorry." He pauses and I hear him take a deep breath before he speaks again. "You have to know that's not true and I'm going to do everything I can to be the one to prove it to you," he declares, his voice full of emotion. "Where's your mom?" he prompts.

"Gone," I tell him simply. "She left my dad years ago and lives with her other family. My dad and I have never really gotten along since she left," I explain.

"Do you see her at all?" he questions.

I shrug my shoulders and mutter, "Barely."

"Doesn't your brother..." he starts.

I immediately interrupt him, knowing where this train of thought is headed, "My brother knows my dad and I don't get along. He stands up for me when he's around for it, but my dad is careful. He never says anything over the top

144

around anyone but me and I can't tell anyone. He's good to my brother. He's about to help him launch his career. I'm not about to ruin that for Stephen because if Stephen knew everything, he would walk away from our father and his future. I can't be the one to take that from him."

I'm thankful when I feel him nod his head and hold me tighter because that's all I'm able to tell him right now. I've already told him so much more than I've ever told anyone. He's giving me just what I need being in his arms, although I still don't want to look at him. I feel like an idiot for throwing myself at him. I feel horrible for breaking down on him and I'm embarrassed about my family and my past. "I'm so sorry I ruined the rest of the night," I mumble into his chest.

He tries to lean back to look at me, but I'm not ready to let him see me. I feel like he's already opened me up more than I'm prepared for and if I let him look into my eyes right now, he'll see every horrible secret I'm trying to hide inside of me. I can't be any more vulnerable with him right now than I already am. Eventually he stops trying to see my face. He sighs heavily, insisting, "You didn't ruin anything Sara. I'm thankful I've had this time to get to know you and I'm already looking forward to our next date."

He pauses continuing to rub my back. "Do you want to watch another movie? It's not like we really watched any of this one, so if you want to start this over, that's fine. Or if you want to pick out some girlie movie on demand or something, that's good too. Whatever you want," he offers quietly.

"Okay," I whisper my agreement into his chest. He switches the TV on and flips through the on-demand movies until he comes to Wedding Crashers. I grab his hand, urging him stop. Even though it's an old movie, Vince Vaughn and Owen Wilson always make me laugh and I need a good laugh right about now.

After he presses play, Jason moves us down on the couch so I'm lying face down comfortably on his chest with his arms wrapped gently around me. He brushes my hair back out of my face with his fingers, relaxing me even more into him. I have my face pressed to his chest and with one ear I'm listening to Jason's heartbeat and with the other I'm half listening to the movie, feeling completely content.

I think this is just what I need and I'm grateful he's giving this to me.

Jason

She laughs at something else on the TV and I reflexively do the same. I've seen this movie a bunch of times, but I haven't been paying any attention to the television at all. My focus has been solely on Sara. I want her relaxed and happy. As long as she's laughing, I'm following in her footsteps because the sound lightens me after what she just shared with me.

I'm completely blown away by what she said about her father. We all have issues with our parents, but our dad would never tell us we were worth so little. The thought of anyone saying something like that to my sister makes me want to kick their ass and I know my brothers would do the same! My dad would probably want to kill anyone if they treated Theresa that way, although he's not that kind of man. I can't imagine having a father who would treat you like that, let alone someone like Sara who clearly doesn't deserve it.

Then again, no one fucking does. It kills me that she's being treated that way. No wonder she was so on edge when I dropped her off last week. She must have been stressed about going to lunch with her dad.

I really can't believe she would think I only want her to fuck her. She's so much better than a one-night stand. Yes, I'll admit I've had one-night stands before, but that was with girls who were looking for the same thing at the time. But then again, she said ex-boyfriends; does she think that's all she's good for in a relationship? I've never seen anyone check out like she did with me. Her eyes looked so vacant and haunted it makes me sick. I want her with me one hundred percent when we're together, not just her body. Is that what it has been like for her with her ex-boyfriends? How many people have treated her like that? How many men? I feel my breathing pick up along with my anger. I swallow hard and take a deep breath, exhaling slowly, attempting to calm myself down. I don't want to get her worked up again when I finally have her calm and smiling. Well, the movie has her smiling anyway; hopefully I had a little something to do with it.

I run my fingers through her blonde hair to try keeping my mind on the here and now. I have to get out of my head before she senses how pissed I am at what she just confessed. The way she was talking, she would probably take my anger as me being mad at her, but it's not her fucking fault. I let her silky hair fall through my fingers over and over again, enjoying every time she smiles. "Your hair is so soft," I whisper mindlessly.

"Hmm?" she prods without moving.

"Nothing. I just love your hair," I confess.

"Thanks," she murmurs quietly. "I should probably go home." She sighs curling into me. I chuckle, loving her movements telling me the opposite, but don't dare say a word. "Would you mind taking me home?" she prompts.

I look up and notice that the movie is over and heave a sigh. I give her one more squeeze and take in a deep breath, trying to inhale every bit of her I can before I reluctantly release my breath and her along with it. We both slowly untangle ourselves from each other. I stand and pull her up into my arms and wait until she's looking in my eyes. "Thank you for spending today with me. I had so much fun just being with you today," I emphasize, needing her to know the truth in my words.

She visibly blushes and tries to look away, but I won't let her. I cradle her face in my hands and gaze into her eyes as I gently press my lips to hers, moving with the softness of her mouth, just needing to feel her, taste her. I pull away without deepening the kiss and can't help but smile in satisfaction when she whimpers. "I could kiss you like that all night," I whisper. I need her to know I want her for more than sex. I need her to know she's worth it.

"Jason," she whispers breathily.

I let my hands trail from her face down her neck, to her shoulders and down her arms until I reach her hands, interlacing our fingers and clasping them tightly together. I hold her there for a minute and just take her in. I don't like what the men in her life have done to her. I need to do everything I can to be a good man for her. She more than deserves it and I want to be the one to give it to her.

"So, I have to work at the bar tomorrow, but I could take you to breakfast in the morning if you're up for it?" I ask her.

"Really?" she questions sounding surprised.

I chuckle lightly. "Yeah, I don't want to wait until next weekend to see you for our next date." She smiles at my comment and I feel my heart pick up speed in response. "The diner has everything, what do you think?"

"Okay," she nods shyly at me in agreement. I grin not holding back. I love making her happy. This girl can light up the whole room with just her smile. "What?" she prompts as I unabashedly stare at her.

I lift my right hand up still holding hers and run my thumb across her lower lip in awe. "Your mouth...your smile is fucking contagious. You are absolutely gorgeous." She blushes a beautiful shade of red and shakes her head trying to look away, but I pull her back towards me with our joined hands. "You are, just accept it and say thank you," I insist, grinning.

She purses her lips, but I see the humor dancing in her eyes. "Fine, thank you," she mumbles sarcastically.

Chuckling, I joke, "Good enough, I guess. I'll let it slide this time." I lean down and lightly press my lips to hers one more time but pull away knowing I can't push her anymore tonight. I want her to trust me and believe me, not give in to me. She has to want me just as much as I want her, and I do. I want her more than anything.

I sigh and reluctantly take a step back giving us some needed space. I let her left hand go so I can grab my keys and my wallet, slipping my wallet into my pocket before helping her with her coat. "Come on, I'll take you home," I offer regretfully. I hold her hand tightly as I lead her out to my truck, wishing I didn't have to let go.

Chapter 19

Sara

I'm looking through my closet, trying to piece the last of my outfit together for my date with Jason. He's taking me to dinner tonight for Valentine's Day. He says it's the other half of the date we never finished from the dart game he owes me, but I don't know whom he's kidding, I've seen him nearly every day!

The last couple weeks have been amazing. Jason has been absolutely wonderful. I swear he's too good to be true, especially for me. When he's working on the weekends, he takes me out earlier in the day even if we just go to the diner for breakfast or lunch. Whenever he has a day off, we do something. If I have classes or I have to study, he works around my schedule. We've gone skiing a couple times and he took me ice-skating. We have gone out to dinner or just curled up together to watch a movie. He even comes over to help me with my homework, although it's hard to get much done with him around. My eyes always end up wandering to his abs or his dimple or…who am I kidding…all of him! The man is hot and sexy as hell.

I can't help but wonder if this is how relationships are meant to be. We talk, laugh and have so much fun together. We cuddle and kiss all the time. Lots of kissing and holy shit I didn't know kissing could be so hot, but with Jason it's definitely scorching! He hasn't pushed me any farther than kissing though, deep kissing, but just kissing. I had always been taught that guys only want one thing from me from both my father and Brad. They convinced me, no one would ever want me for more. Without really telling him my whole history, Jason seems to be doing everything in his power to prove them wrong.

I slowly take a deep breath, exhaling slowly. My chest tightens every single time I even think about him, which is basically all the time. I don't think I've ever been this happy in all my life. I told Stephen about him. He says he wants to meet him and he encouraged me to bring him to our next family thing. I don't know about that though. I'm not sure if I can introduce Jason to my father. I kind of feel like that might be a little bit cruel to do to Jason.

I pull on a fitted gray cable knit V-neck sweater with a pair of dark blue jeans and tall black boots. I'm just finishing up my hair when my phone rings and I reach for it only to freeze when I see my father's name. My heartbeat speeds up with nerves instantly. I try to take a deep breath, but I'm only able to inhale and exhale shakily.

I gulp and hesitantly answer, "Hi, Daddy."

"Sara. We have an event we have to attend on Saturday night. Come with Brad," he states, his attempt to try telling me what to do like always. Sometimes I feel more like his employee than his daughter.

I grip the phone so tightly I think it might break and pinch my eyes closed praying for courage. "Dad, I'm sorry, but I can't go with Brad," I stop him before he continues sounding stronger than I feel. I can't believe I said that to him, but there's no way I'm doing that to Jason, no matter what my dad does to me.

He sighs in frustration. "Is this about that boyfriend of yours?" he probes sounding inconvenienced more than anything. "Stephen told me about him," he adds.

"Stephen told you about him?" I repeat, surprised. I didn't tell him not to, but I guess since I don't tell my dad anything, I sort of assume Stephen doesn't tell him anything either. Then again, when it comes to me, my dad doesn't care most of the time, but with Stephen…I let the thought trail off with another suppressed sigh.

"Well, you're never honest with me, so someone needs to be," he declares firmly as if I'm constantly lying to him. I grit my teeth and wait to see what he has to say, feeling like I'm going to throw up. "You can bring your boyfriend if you think he will portray my business appropriately."

My heart nearly stops and I almost want to roll my eyes at his comment. Is he serious? He always seems to think no one is good enough unless he's hand-picked whomever himself. But he actually agreed to let Jason come with me. Does that mean he actually trusts my judgment for once? He continues, interrupting my thoughts, "Otherwise, I expect you to be there with Brad. You do not show up alone. Understood?"

"Yes sir," I whisper in acknowledgement.

"Fine. I'll email you the details and I expect you to let me know who you will be attending with by tomorrow morning for the RSVP," he informs. "I'll see you on Saturday."

"Okay, I'll text you in the morning, I promise." He hangs up without saying another word and I drop my phone onto my dresser. I don't know if I'm grateful or terrified he's letting me bring Jason. I heave a sigh, no longer looking forward to my date with Jason. I don't want to tell him about Saturday. I don't want him to meet my father or Brad but going with Brad is not an option.

The doorbell rings and I groan into my hands before I step back and trudge to the door knowing I'm the only one home. I peek through the peephole and as expected see Jason standing on the other side. My heart skips a beat at the sight of him. I put on a smile take a deep breath, opening the door to a grinning Jason holding a huge bouquet of colorful wildflowers.

He takes one look at me and his smile quickly fades while his eyes fill with concern. "What's wrong?" he prods stepping towards me.

How the hell does he do that? "Nothing, I'm fine," I answer automatically. He quirks his eyebrow at me in that sexy way that makes me tell him anything he wants to know. I release my breath and shake my head. "I just hung up with my dad. I'll be fine," I whisper almost trying to convince myself.

His lips pinch together in annoyance. Although with everything he's done the last couple weeks, I think he's finally convinced me that when things like this happen his irritation is with my father, not me. I remind myself of this again and take another deep breath. "I just need to grab my coat and my purse and then we can go." He nods stiffly still looking like he's trying to calm himself down.

I quickly put my coat on and grab my purse. When I get back to the door, I find Jason finishing up with putting my flowers in a glass. He turns and wraps me up in his arms. He presses his head into my hair and holds me tight. I can barely breathe, but at the same time I've never felt more protected causing me to grin with relief into his chest. He loosens his hold on me and kisses me on the forehead. I enjoy the sweet moment as his lips linger before placing both his hands on my cheeks and tilting my face up towards his. The look he gives me takes my breath away. I gasp for a breath just has his lips lightly brush against mine in the sweetest, softest kiss, like he's cherishing me. My eyes close as my heart begins beating out of control. I can't help but whimper as he slowly pulls away from me with a soft groan.

My eyes flutter open and my breath catches with the look he gives me. I swear I see more in his eyes than I could ever hope to see in my lifetime looking back at me, causing butterflies to take flight in my stomach. He releases my face and one hand slides down to find mine, entwining our fingers together and holding on tight. With a squeeze of my hand, I start breathing again, but I don't want this moment to end. My heart is beating so hard right now I hear the rapid thumping in my ears. I really think it might pop out of my chest at any second. It will be a miracle if I make it to his truck without passing out, but in only a few moments, I do. I give a squeak of surprise as he moves his hands to my hips and effortlessly lifts me up into the cab of his truck. He leans towards me giving me another chaste kiss before slamming the door and bringing me back to the present.

By the time he jogs around to the driver's side and hops in, I've reined myself back in. I take a deep breath, buckle my seat belt and relax back into the leather seat. He buckles his seat belt and starts his truck before glancing over at me with a grin. "You look gorgeous as always, Sara," he proclaims, my cheeks heating instantly. "Happy Valentine's Day, by the way."

I giggle having completely forgotten about Valentine's Day already. I look at him with an even larger grin on his face showing his dimple I love so much. He puts his left hand on the steering wheel and leaves his right hand on my knee. When we're together he always has to be touching me somewhere. I love that he has to have some type of connection with me. I smile over at him and proclaim, "Happy Valentine's Day." He gives my knee a squeeze as he backs out of the parking lot at my apartment. "And I'm sorry, I forgot to say thank you for the flowers. They're beautiful. I'm sorry I didn't get you anything," I add scrunching up my nose, feeling slightly embarrassed. I can't believe I didn't even think about it, but I guess I've never been much of a Valentine's Day person.

"Yeah, you did," he tells me sincerely. I know I look confused when he glances over at me and he adds hoarsely, "You gave me a chance. That's all I need."

Goosebumps instantly cover my body and I blush looking away. After a few minutes of quiet I finally get my voice back. Clearing my throat, I relax next to him and question, "Where are we going anyway?" Pausing, I lick my lips and continue, "I know you said you still owe me for that dart game at your brother's party, which is ridiculous for so many reasons, but anyway..." I trail off. Grinning, I shrug like it's no big deal. "I hope it's not somewhere fancy I'm not really dressed for that."

He laughs. "Well, I guess now's a good time to ask right?" he teases. "I was actually just thinking somewhere with some good food. I had Street and Company in mind if that's alright with you?" He glances at me for my reaction. I consent, nodding my head with a smile. "Definitely not fancy, but really good food and I'm bringing the great company along with me. There's nothing better than that," he adds under his breath.

I smirk and shake my head in exasperation. "Another line, Jason? What am I gonna' do with you?"

He grins, his blue eyes sparkling. "Why keep me of course, but it's not a line." I laugh and think about how he's always able to make me relax so quickly. It's overwhelming how he can truly get me to be myself, unlike anyone else, not even Liz. Let alone, I'm a truly happy version of me when I'm with him. Could this be real? Could he really be my future? Could he be my happily ever after? I never thought I deserved one or even had a chance to have it.

Before my thoughts become too depressing, we're walking hand in hand into the restaurant. The whole place is covered in mostly wood with predominantly brick walls. It's my kind of relaxed atmosphere. After we're seated and we order our drinks, Jason turns to me and inquires, "I'm curious, do you have something against fancy restaurants? Not that I'm complaining," he adds with a playful grin.

The way he talks to me completely eases my mind and body. He makes it so easy for me to answer anything he wants honestly. I shake my head and reply, "Nah, I think it's just because my dad is always very particular. I believe he always picks the restaurants he likes to go to based on how fancy or pretentious they are or who he knows there or even what it will look like to other people if he's seen there. If everyone doesn't have to dress up in at least business attire, it

155

isn't good enough for him. I guess you could say he doesn't want to be caught off-guard running into someone he believes is important." I grimace thinking about what my father thinks is important.

Jason reaches across the table and grabs my hand. He stays quiet until I look up at him. "If you're ever uncomfortable, or if there's ever anything you don't want to do, I need you to tell me." I nod my head in acknowledgement. "I mean it," he emphasizes. "I don't ever want you to be somewhere you don't want to be or do something you don't want to do," he clarifies.

"Okay," I agree, "but sometimes we all have to do things we don't want to do," I remind him thinking of Saturday. Maybe telling him sooner rather than later is a good idea.

"Yeah, but I'll still do what I can to make it better for you if I can," he insists causing my heart to jump into my throat with his confession.

"Thank you," I whisper appreciatively. My chest tightens and my stomach turns as I'm suddenly overwhelmed with emotion.

The waitress steps up to our table interrupting us. We both order the lobster. It's messy, but delicious. As she walks away, Jason turns his attention back to me. "So, what did your father want?" Jason asks with a grimace.

I knew this was coming, but I'd rather avoid it for as long as possible. I sigh heavily, feeling my stomach churn with nerves. I take a deep breath and push my shoulders back for confidence, but I still can't look up at him when I speak. "I was actually just about to tell you about that. My dad has an event on Saturday that he wants me to be at. It's like a networking party. My dad and brother will both be there and my ex," I mumble the last part.

"What was that? Did you say your ex was going to be there?" he probes, his eyebrows raised in question. He waits for me to respond but I cringe away from him. I've been dreading this conversation and honestly doing everything I can to avoid it. "Why will your ex be there Sara?" he prods, sounding slightly hurt.

I look down at my lap while I answer, a lump in my throat as I force out the words, "Brad's dad and my dad are business partners in a lot of projects. Brad and my brother Stephen are also best friends. Then, when they graduate in the spring, they were both offered jobs by my father. They will be working together on some spin off for both of our families' companies. I don't really know any of the details," I ramble as quickly as possible.

Barely breathing, I dare a glance up at Jason only to see his jaw twitching with anger. I fight to keep the tears out of my eyes. I already feel my heart breaking, needles pricking at all of my insides with dread. I know he's going to leave me. "So let me get this straight," he begins, taking a deep breath, he continues, "Your dad wants you to go to this event on Saturday where your ex will be." I nod my head in confirmation and look back down at the table. "I'm going with you," he decides without even asking.

My head snaps up in shock. That is not the reaction I expected from him. "But don't you have to work?" I prompt.

"I'll get out of it," he answers, leaving no room for argument.

"Jason," I plead, not even knowing what I want to say.

"I don't care if I have to quit. It's just a job. I will be there for you," he states as a command. My body nearly gives out with overwhelming relief. I'm thankful I'm sitting down, or I would've embarrassed myself. I thought he would be mad at me. He has every right to be. The corners of his mouth quirk up as he asks, "Am I invited?"

I burst out laughing, hard. I would climb over the table into his lap right now if it were at all appropriate. "Yes, you're invited," I reply, grinning. I'm not about to tell him it's either I go with him, or my father would make Brad escort me. I don't even want to think about how he would react to me going anywhere with Brad, but I don't blame him. "Thank you," I whisper with tears in my eyes.

"You don't have to thank me. I'm not about to let you be around your father and your ex without me there if I can help it." He squeezes my hand in support. "I am looking forward to meeting your brother though," he admits with a smile.

I grin from ear to ear loving the subject change as my body begins to relax. "You're going to love Stephen!" I exclaim feeling so much better.

Just then the waitress returns to our table and sets our bright red, steaming lobsters down in front of us, along with a side of corn, mashed potatoes, cole slaw and a roll. "Wow, are you going to be able to eat all that?" Jason prods, eyes wide.

"I'm sure you can help me if I can't," I mumble with a shrug.

Chapter 20

Sara

When we pull up to my apartment after dinner, I'm feeling so much better than I did before. I shake my head at Jason smiling. "What?" he questions, giving me his sexy grin.

Instead of answering him, I jump out of his truck and slam the door shut. As he comes around to my side to find me, I'm already gone. "Sara?" he inquires playfully. I toss a snowball at his back and take off around his truck laughing. "Hey," he laughs. He quickly rolls his own snowball, tossing it at me, getting me in the shoulder.

Throwing another one, I'm able to get him one more time with a snowball right in the center of his chest as he's jogging directly towards me. I squeal as he tackles me to the ground in a soft snowbank next to the parking lot. "What do you think you're doing?" he challenges, teasing me.

"Jason," I shriek as I laugh hysterically, his body pressing me into the snow. I can't stop laughing.

He grabs a handful of snow and brings it close to my face, taunting me. "I could just rub this in your face and you couldn't do anything about it. Or, I could put it down your shirt. I bet that would be pretty cold."

I'm squealing and laughing so hard as his hand gets closer and closer. Wiggling against him, I attempt to get away, at the same time relishing in his proximity. Suddenly, he throws the snow on the ground instead. He mumbles, "Fuck it," the moment before his lips come crashing down on mine. My laughter is immediately suppressed and I moan into his mouth as he pushes into me. His tongue dives into my mouth and tangles with mine. He tastes of lobster and

159

beer and something I can't describe, but it's uniquely him and I love it, wanting more.

I wrap my leg around the back of his to try pulling him closer. He pushes into me in response, causing warmth to spread throughout my whole body. I want him closer. The movement pushes our heads back into the snow and part of the snowdrift falls onto our heads. We both freeze, stunned. Jason starts chuckling against my lips and I follow. He shakes his head just slightly causing snow to go everywhere. He assesses me with a wide grin. He lightly brushes a few clumps of snow off my face, kissing each spot as he goes. He gives me one more kiss on my swollen lips. Then his smile grows as he murmurs, "You look good in white."

I gasp in surprise. I think my heart stops beating at his insinuation. I can't even try to open my mouth to respond to him. He jumps up with one leg on each side of me and reaches down for my hands. He swiftly pulls me up and into his arms. Giving me a kiss on the nose before gently dusting off my hair, he grins. "Sorry, I couldn't help myself," he claims. With his beautiful smile, he turns towards my apartment with me in tow. All I can do is follow him, overwhelmed in this unfamiliar territory.

I unlock the door and turn back to him standing there looking down at me, expecting nothing but a goodnight. I love that about him. "Would you like to come in?" I ask shyly.

"Are you sure?" he prods only making me more confident in my decision. I want him here.

"Positive," I confirm, nodding my head.

"Is your roommate home?" he prompts.

"No, she's over at Blake's tonight," I admit quietly. He looks hesitant before he takes a step through the door, but I don't feel anything but relief the moment he does. I want him here I reiterate to myself.

I set my purse down on the kitchen table and take off my coat and boots while Jason does the same. When he's done, he stands and takes a step towards me. He places his hands on my hips and pulls me into him. He takes a deep breath like he's breathing me in and I smile up at him, enjoying the moment. He places his hands behind my neck and brushes his lips lightly over mine. He pulls back right away, but I don't want him to. "Would you like to watch a movie or something?" he suggests, his hands sliding slightly from my neck so he can stroke my cheek with his thumb.

"No," I whisper my response, looking him in straight in the eyes, my chest rising quickly up and down with anticipation.

"What do you want, Sara?" he asks his voice sounding gravely and his eyes never leaving mine. "I need you to spell it out for me."

"Just you, Jason," I admit with confidence I didn't know I had.

I watch his Adam's apple bob up and down as he swallows hard with my comment. He leans down towards me and presses his lips to mine, devouring my mouth. I wrap my arms around his neck and hold on tight as he kisses me with so much passion, I think I might burst from the inside out. He lifts me up and holds on to my ass to bring me closer. I wrap my legs tightly around his back and hold on for dear life. I don't want him to ever let me go.

Eventually, he starts walking towards my room, careful with me, and even though no one is here, he shuts and locks the door behind us. When his legs hit my bed he drops me down on it, our lips breaking apart as I bounce. Leaning down, he holds himself over me and takes a deep breath looking me over from head to toe as he caresses my cheek. "You are so gorgeous. Do you have any idea how fucking beautiful you are, Sara?"

He takes my breath away with his words. I try to tell him how much his words mean to me, how much he means to me, how much the sincerity in his eyes when he says those beautiful things means to me. "Jason, I've never felt…" I gasp feeling so overwhelmed. I can't talk. I can't explain it. I just need him as close to me as possible. I pull him in to kiss me. He complies but pulls away again.

Jason slides me the rest of the way onto the bed and spreads himself out next to me. He lays his hand over my hip and lets it gently glide up my side and turn near my breast to follow the lower curve across to the other one then back down to the other thigh. He pauses and looks up at me, but I'm holding my breath waiting to see what he'll do next. "I want to show you how beautiful I think you are. Tell me if you want me to stop at any time, okay?" he emphasizes. I nod my head in confirmation, biting my lower lip in anticipation.

He groans and kisses me pulling my lower lip away from my teeth until it's between his as he lightly sucks it into his mouth. His lips leave mine and gently brush along my neck giving me chills. He gently tugs at the bottom of my sweater. "Can I please take this off, Sara?" he requests hoarsely with a barely controlled plea. I nod my head again in affirmation, my chest rising and falling as I struggle to take each breath.

He quickly pulls it over my head and tosses it on the floor. His hands immediately grip my sides as he places a few feather-light kisses on my belly before coming back to my mouth. Pushing his tongue inside, he begins exploring every inch of my mouth he can find, his tongue tangling with mine.

He pulls back with a light chuckle, asking, "Do you want this off?" I look down at my hands. I have most of his shirt bunched up in my hands nearly pulled up to his armpits. I just nod my head, still tugging. He reaches behind him with one hand and pulls it the rest of the way off, tossing it on the floor with my sweater. I stare at him in awe, tracing the planes of his stomach muscles with my fingertips and smile when I hear his sharp intake of breath at my touch. I love that I have that effect on him.

He leans in threading one hand into my hair and holding me to his mouth while his other hand skims lightly across my skin. His hand follows along the underside of my breast, and I arch into him, wanting him to touch me. He cups my breast as his thumb runs over my nipple making me gasp into his mouth causing him to groan. My breathing picks up and his thumb rubs my nipple over and over again before he finally reaches back behind me and flicks the strap of my bra taking it all the way off. He rips his mouth roughly away from mine, immediately covering the nipple he was playing with. He begins to suck and lick at it with his tongue while his hand goes to my other breast. I gasp in pleasure, arching into him as I grip his shoulders tightly not knowing what to do.

"Jason," I pant with desperation.

He lets go of my nipple with a light pop and looks down at me his eyes now a darker shade of blue and full of lust. "Can I take off your jeans, Sara? I want to make you come," he requests, his voice deep and gravelly. I swallow hard and nod my head. He stands up and grips the bottom of my pants, pulling them off in one quick tug before climbing back on the bed. "Fuck," he grumbles.

"What?" I ask breathlessly but self-consciously. I am lying on my bed with Jason in nothing but jeans and me in nothing but my black lace underwear.

"You're just so damn sexy. I have no idea how I got so lucky," he claims reverently causing my heart to flip flop again.

"Jason," I whimper, not able to get out anything more than his name before his lips crash back down to mine.

I love the feel of his chest pressing against mine. I love the feel of his skin brushing against my skin. I love the feel of everything about him and I want more. He pulls his lips away, kissing and licking me down my neck. He palms both breasts and lightly lets his fingers caress over my nipple as he leans back to admire my body. He groans and leans in to take the other nipple into his mouth and swirl his tongue around it.

"Jason," I gasp yet again, "I need more." He pinches one nipple, lightly twisting it, while he sucks on the other. I beg him, arching into him, desperate for more, "Please!"

He slides his hand down my stomach and lets his fingers push my underwear to the side, his fingers skimming over my folds. "Holy shit," he groans as he easily slides two fingers inside with how hot and wet, I am for him. He rubs his palm against my clit as he pushes two fingers in and out.

It feels like only seconds later when my breathing becomes completely out of control. Feeling like I'm on fire, my whole body alive and desperate, I groan his name, "Jason," as I feel my insides clutch his fingers over and over again. I've never come so hard and so fast in my life. He slowly pulls his fingers out as he crashes his mouth over mine.

"So, fucking beautiful," he whispers in awe against my lips. He immediately presses his lips to mine again, breathing heavily. He moves his mouth over mine with such care, licking my lips, then kissing me with a barely controlled groan.

My hand goes to his muscled chest and starts to slide down. He quickly grabs onto it with the one not holding me. "What?" I ask innocently.

He sighs and looks at me with pure lust and determination. "I need tonight to be about you. It's about me showing you how beautiful you are, how incredible you are and that you're worth everything. I don't want anything in return."

I open my mouth to respond. "I…" I barely choke out before a tear rolls down my cheek. My chest feels heavy, like my insides are overflowing, or growing too big for my body. I feel completely overwhelmed by his words and his actions. I'm not even sure how to react.

"Hey, none of that. What's wrong beautiful girl?" he probes wiping the tear away. He tilts my chin up, so I look him in the eyes.

I shake my head and take a deep breath trying to get the courage to tell him what I want to say. "Nobody has ever done that for me before." I pause trying to swallow down my nerves. "Nothing is ever about me," I admit embarrassed. My body heats and I quickly try to look away from him.

He holds me tight, his jaw twitching like it does when he's angry, but I know it's not at me. "I'm going to do everything I can to change that because you deserve for it to be about you, Sara." He takes a calming breath through his nose before he prompts, "Why don't you throw a shirt on, then come back here and curl up in my arms? I just need to hold you for a while."

I don't answer him. Instead, I just get up and do exactly as he requests. I throw a plain pink t-shirt on and climb back on the bed, quickly making my way back into his arms. He pulls me tightly to him and places a kiss on my forehead before whispering almost inaudibly, "I think I'm falling in love with you, Sara." My heart skips a beat, before it restarts beating erratically. I close my eyes as I let his words wash over me and pray that this is a dream I never wake up from.

Chapter 21

Sara

I look in the mirror assessing my simple black dress. It's sleeveless with the collar lying loose around my neck, then gathered slightly to the right with a circular rhinestone pendant. The dress is fitted along my chest, waist and hips with the skirt flaring out slightly at the bottom. I have on black strappy one-inch heels to match with a rhinestone buckle on the side. I hate wearing these shoes, especially this time of year, but my dad would be furious if I showed up in my high black boots.

I put on more make-up than normal with some red lipstick to add color. I have my blonde hair loosely pinned at the back of my head with a few curls hanging down on each side. I added a couple rhinestone bobby pins to match my dress as well, hopefully contributing to the elegance I'm aiming for.

"Wow, you look great!" I jump at the sound of Liz's voice coming from the doorway. I turn to look at her and she laughs making me raise my eyebrows in question. "You don't look like you're very happy about your outfit," she observes.

I shrug knowing I have a sour look on my face. "I guess it's just not really what I want to be wearing right now. I'd rather be getting pizza and watching a movie on the couch with you guys and Jason."

Liz sighs in empathy and gives me a sympathetic smile. I hate those smiles, but coming from Liz, it's not so bad. "I know you hate going to these things. Are you sure you have to go this time?" she asks innocently.

I nod my head with a grimace. Liz may know I hate going to these things, but she doesn't know most of my reasons have to do with not wanting to be anywhere near my father or Brad or anything that has to do with them. "It's just going to be kinda' weird with both Brad and Jason there," I tell her giving her a partial truth like I usually do.

"I understand that," she mumbles, nodding her head in acknowledgement, "but it will be good for Brad to see you have a boyfriend now and it really is over for you guys." I freeze, blushing at the word boyfriend. "What?" Liz prods, her lips twitching up at the corners of her mouth when she sees the funny look on my face.

"I...I have a boyfriend?" Liz laughs as I stand there in shock, letting reality sink in. I never thought I'd be here with anyone besides Brad. I never thought I'd have a chance at actually being happy. A smile slowly spreads over my face that I feel all the way to my soul, warming me from the inside, out. "I have a very hot boyfriend," I declare proudly.

Liz laughs even harder, concurring, "Yes, you do."

"Hey, I heard that," Blake yells from the other room causing both Liz and I to completely lose our composure. We laugh so hard tears begin forming in the corners of my eyes. "And your hot boyfriend just ordered us some pizza and he's also getting really cold out here on the couch without you," Blake adds playfully.

We both eventually catch our breath as our laughter dies down. Liz steps up to me, grinning. "My stomach hurts from laughing," she grumbles as she releases a slow breath looking content. "Don't let anyone bother you tonight. Just do what you have to do and have fun with your man."

I nod in agreement, hoping I can do just that. "You're right." I give her a quick hug, grateful for her support. "Now go back to your hot and lonely boyfriend before he really starts complaining," I order, giggling.

I take one last look at myself in the mirror and grab my black wrap, along with my clutch and long black wool dress coat when I hear the doorbell chime. "I'll get it," Liz calls.

"Hi Liz," I hear Jason's voice and my heart starts pounding against my ribcage. I step out of my room watching the floor with each step I take when I hear a low whistle.

"Now, you look hot, Sara," Blake proclaims easing my tension. I relax and look up with a smile. Jason's glare at Blake is almost comical. Blake chuckles and informs Jason, "Well, my girlfriend just called you hot, so I thought I'd even it out a little bit." I giggle as Liz's blush tells Jason it's the truth.

My eyes turn to Jason and my breath instantly catches in my throat. He's wearing a black suit with a white button down and a solid dark red tie. His shoulders look huge in his suit. His dark brown hair is perfectly styled and when my eyes finally drift to his face, I see a sparkle in his eyes and the dimple I adore. "You look absolutely stunning, Sara," he murmurs in admiration and wonder. He steps towards me and bends down to gently place a kiss on my lips.

I feel myself blush at his compliment. "Thank you," I whisper. "You look pretty incredible yourself," I add lightly smiling up at him.

"This is for you," he states. He grins holding up a small bouquet of red and white roses. The surprise on my face must be evident when in the next moment he shrugs and adds, "I figured we've never dressed up like this for a date before and I wanted to give you something special."

I attempt to gulp down my nerves that seem to be going first date crazy tonight and murmur another, "Thank you, Jason." I reach out and take them, his hand brushing mine sending chills down my spine with the contact. I put the flowers to my nose and inhale deeply. I love the sweet smell, but really it's my excuse to take a deep calming breath.

I know we've been dating for a few weeks now, but tonight feels different. Tonight, I have to bring Jason to meet my nightmares and hope he doesn't see it all for what it is. I hope he doesn't see me for what I am. Jason will meet my family and although I'm excited for him to meet Stephen, I'm terrified for him to meet my father. What will my father say? What will he do? What will he think? And how will Jason react to him? Then of course Brad has to be there as well. I think I might dread them meeting even more. I'm nervous wondering how Brad will take Jason's presence more than the other way around. I just hope after tonight, Jason still wants to stick around.

"Here, I'll put those in some water for you," Liz offers as she steps up grabbing the flowers from me. "They're really beautiful."

I release my breath and turn towards Liz, mumbling, "Thank you."

"Don't worry about it. You two have fun," she insists, giving me a pointed look. "Go!" she urges nearly shoving us towards the door.

"Are you sure you aren't just trying to get rid of us?" I tease while Jason helps me slip on my coat. His fingers trail along my arms as he pulls it up, again sending chills throughout my body. I shake away my shudder when I hear his quiet groan.

"I am," Blake calls over the back of the couch causing Jason and I to laugh. Liz glares over her shoulder at him, while she fills up a large glass with water and sets the new flowers next to my wildflowers from Valentine's Day. "Well, you're making me look bad," he teases gesturing to my bouquets.

We all laugh. "I'm not going to apologize for that," Jason prods.

"Now you sound like your brother, Christian," Blake grumbles, the corners of his lips twitching up in amusement. Jason shrugs his shoulders in response, smirking.

I button the top two buttons on my coat before turning to grab my wrap and clutch from the table. "Bye guys, be good," I tease as we walk out the door.

169

Just before the door slams, I hear both Liz and Blake reply, yelling, "Bye!"

Jason's hand settles on the small of my back, guiding me towards his truck. He opens the passenger door and before I can move his hands settle on my waist. He steps into me and looks down at me, tilting my head up towards his with his fingertips on my chin. He looks into my eyes a faint smile on his face. "You really do look absolutely stunning tonight," he informs me his eyes drifting all over my face. His words along with the look he gives me, sends chills throughout my body again. He lightly brushes his lips against mine and rubs my arms up and down before placing his hands on my hips and easily lifting me into his truck. "It's freezing. Let's get you warmed up." He slams my door shut and quickly jogs around to the other side. I'm not about to tell him he's the reason I'm shivering.

After he climbs in and begins to back out, he asks, "So, is there anything I need to know about tonight?"

I heave a sigh and lean back into the seat. "I don't think so, not really. My dad will have certain people I have to say hi to and some others he may want to introduce me to, but he'll be mostly concerned with Stephen and Brad," I admit with a grimace.

I turn towards Jason and notice a slight tick in his jaw before it quickly disappears. "So that just means I'll be able to keep you mostly to myself?" he prompts, hopeful.

"I hope so. I've never been to one of these business things with anyone except my brother or Brad," I confess stupidly and his jaw instantly resumes its twitching. "I'm sorry. I've known him my whole life," I inform him, attempting to explain why he's the only one I've ever attended these parties with. "You have to believe me when I tell you that it has been over with Brad and me for more than a couple years. I just never had anyone I wanted to bring with me and since my dad doesn't want me to ever come alone, I always came with Brad even though we aren't together

170

anymore," I ramble on trying to explain myself, but even I know the only thing I'm doing is making it worse.

Jason's body looks suddenly filled with tension when he questions, "What were you going to do if I had to work tonight, Sara?"

I shake my head, already frustrated and not wanting to respond. "I…I hadn't thought about it. I wanted you to come with me," I stammer.

His eyes narrow at the road and his breathing becomes heavier. "Would you have gone with him?" he asks in an eerily quiet voice.

"No!" I retort instantly even though I don't know if it's really the truth. "I would have gone with my brother or something." My response relieves a little bit of the obvious tension in his body and I watch as he slowly exhales.

He reaches over towards me searching for my hand. He entwines our fingers together and gives my hand a light squeeze. When he speaks, I finally release the breath I didn't know I was holding. "No more going with Brad to any of these things. Ever," he emphasizes. "If I can't go with you and you have to attend, go alone. If you can't do that, go with your brother and if he can't go or has his own date, you can go with one of my brothers," he states leaving no room for argument. "My girlfriend does not go anywhere with her ex," he adds, his jaw tight.

I hold in my gasp at his words, loving every single one. I'm overwhelmed with how he's fighting for me. He glances over to me and his eyebrows draw together before he looks back out at the road. "You okay with that?" he prods wanting clarification.

I try to swallow down the emotions taking over my whole body before I speak. "Very okay with that," I'm finally able to whisper as I nod vehemently. I quickly dab the tears away, hoping they don't ruin my make-up.

Jason smiles, appearing relieved. Then, he squeezes my hand, mumbling, "Good." He pauses as he pulls into the parking lot and parks his truck. Glancing over at me again, he requests, "So tonight, with you looking like that, I need you to stay close to me." I grin in response. Taking a deep breath, he adds with a shake of his head, "Please."

I giggle in response. I tilt my head up and kiss him, but he pulls immediately away and buries his face in my neck with a groan, giving me a different kind of chill. I take a deep breath and exhale slowly to calm myself down. He finally pulls away and prods, "Come on. Let's get this over with."

Chapter 22

Jason

I walk into the grand ballroom at a hotel I've never stepped foot in before with Sara looking absolutely stunning. She's walking a bit stiffly and gripping my arm tightly, her anxiety rearing its ugly head and all I want to do is help her. I try to gently loosen her fingers, so I don't have permanent marks on my arm as I look around in awe. The whole place has accents of gold from the elegantly carved moldings to the extravagant gold and crystal chandeliers.

As I try to take everything in, I turn to Sara to see what I can do to help her relax. I open my mouth, but we're immediately interrupted and I don't have a chance to speak. We're greeted by several elegantly dressed couples who are probably around the same age as my parents as soon as we cross the threshold. They all obviously know Sara. She introduces me as, "her friend," Jason Emory. Although I don't like it, I remind myself it doesn't matter how she introduces me to strangers as I shake their hands.

It already feels like hours when we ultimately make our way past the doorway, but in reality, has been less than one. "Would you like a drink?" I ask her, running my hand lightly down her back. She nods her head in confirmation without saying a word or even glancing in my direction. "Sara?" I prompt, just hoping to get her eyes. When I don't say anything else, she finally directs her attention towards me. I know she notices my concerned expression when she sighs and relaxes slightly, it seems only in attempt to appease me.

"I'm sorry, Jason. I'm just looking around to see who's here," she explains hesitantly. I know exactly who she's looking for with that much tension surrounding her, but she doesn't need me to acknowledge it. Instead, I nod once and give her a small smile in support. I place my hand on her lower back to guide her towards the bar for a drink.

"Sara!" I hear from behind us when suddenly she's tugged away from me and in the arms of a tall, blonde-haired guy I don't know. I feel my jaw twitch with tension wanting to rip her right back to me, but I don't want to cause a scene. I look to her and watch her reaction instead as he picks her up in a hug. She surprises me when she grins up at him, giving him her loving, happy smile causing my heart to skip a beat as she hugs him back.

Who the fuck is this guy?

"Stephen," she screeches. I exhale slowly, feeling my whole body relax at the sound of her brother's name. "Put me down!" she urges.

He obliges and sets her on her feet, spinning her back towards me, before looking at me with a genuine smile. "You must be Jason," he proclaims, holding his hand out to me. I place one hand back on the small of Sara's back as I reach the other out to shake his. "It's nice to meet you," he declares sincerely.

"You too, Stephen. Sara talks about you all the time," I admit returning his smile. Her brother chuckles as she rolls her eyes towards the ceiling in fake annoyance.

"All good, I'm sure," he jokes grinning. He looks towards his sister and asks, "Did you see Dad, yet?" Sara just shakes her head in response, not bothering to hide her grimace. "Don't worry, he seems to be in a good mood tonight," he informs her, his obvious attempt at trying to help her relax.

"We'll see," I hear her mumble under her breath before adding louder, "He's always in a good mood for you."

Stephen obviously didn't hear her first remark. He laughs shaking his head, attempting to dismiss her comment. He adds, "You should try to find him. He said if I saw you, I should let you know he was looking for you." He glances over to me with a smile that says good luck and admits, "He wants to meet your new boyfriend."

My fingers twitch near Sara's back at hearing her brother call me her boyfriend and at the same time, I have to hold back my anger towards Sara's father, the man I'm about to meet and already have absolutely no respect for. This should be interesting. I clear my throat to get rid of the edginess, stating, "Thanks, Stephen."

He pats my shoulder with a knowing grin. "You'll be fine," he insists mistaking my demeanor for normal nerves when you're about to meet your girlfriend's father. I just nod rigidly and watch as he gives his sister another quick hug. "You look beautiful, Sis."

"Thank you," she whispers. I hate how her face cringes slightly with her brother's compliment. She loves him for saying it, but she doesn't believe him and I fucking hate that for her! She should know how amazing she is and believe it.

"I'll catch up with you guys in a bit. I need to do a little more networking. That is why we're here after all," he grumbles. Giving us a quick wave, he steps away and disappears into the small crowd.

I tug Sara slightly toward me and again try to guide her to the bar for a drink. "I like your brother. I see why you two are so close," I proclaim.

"Yeah," she murmurs, smiling. "He's a good guy."

I want to ask her why she never told him anything about her dad or her ex after meeting him, but I figure now is not the time to try to have that conversation again. I can already tell he's the kind of guy who would've had her back, even if the war were against their own father.

Just as we're approaching the bar, I again feel Sara stiffen under my hand and I quickly survey the people in front of me. I immediately notice a man standing at the bar with a dark brown colored drink in his hand laughing with two other men. He looks like an older version of Stephen, leaving no doubt as to whom he is. I lean down towards Sara's ear. "You're father?" I prompt for clarification. She gulps and nods her head. I rub a slow circle on her back hoping to comfort her even slightly. I've never known anyone so nervous to see her own father.

"Sara, dear," he calls when he spots us. "I was just talking about you and wondering when you would arrive."

"Hi, Dad," Sara rigidly goes to his side and places a kiss on his cheek. "We've been here for quite a while. In fact, I already spoke with the Johnsons and Kings and I was just speaking with Stephen," she answers almost formally.

He assesses her before speaking. "Well, I'm glad you're here. You remember Mr. McIntyre and Mr. Svelte," he states nodding his head towards the gentleman at his sides. "My daughter, Sara. She's a student at the University here." I watch as both men kiss her hand in greeting and she smiles her empty smile at all of them, making it difficult to breathe.

I want to rescue her from this, but how do I do that?

Her dad eventually turns his attention to me, his eyes slightly narrowed, assessing and I'm assuming judgmental. "You must be Jason? A friend of my Sara's?" he emphasizes.

I don't miss the inflection and my eyes can't help but narrow as well. "Yes, Sir," I mutter politely. I give him a nod and reach out to shake his hand.

He takes it and drops it almost instantly when he asks, "So, I heard you graduated from West Point?" I again nod my head in confirmation as the other two men grunt their approval. "And now, what do you do?" he prods with the corners of his mouth twitching up. After everything Sara told me about him, I should have known. He only wants to make me look bad.

I stand tall and push my shoulders back, contemplating what kind of answer I want to give him. I catch Sara's eyes and I see a touch of fear in them causing my heart to stutter and my breath to catch. I clear my throat before answering with all the confidence I can muster, "My family needed me, so I came to help out. While I'm doing that, I have been doing some bartending at a local restaurant and pub. I'm working on my long-term options now that I know I'll be staying in the area."

Her father continues to contemplate me with his lips slightly pursed before taking a sip of his drink. Then, his focus returns to Sara. "Bradley was looking for you, too. Make sure you find him," he demands. "Don't forget to say hello to his parents too. They will want to see you, since you haven't been around since Christmas."

He turns around putting his back to Sara. Her eyes roam to the ground as she robotically murmurs, "Yes, father."

My heart breaks for her in this moment. She's fighting for the attention of a father that seems to want to use her as a trophy he can set aside when he's done showing off to his friends. I step towards her and wrap my arm gently around her. It's the only thing I can do to try to protect her without embarrassing her and that's the last thing I want. She doesn't deserve this.

I pull her out into the hallway and turn her to face me, cradling her face in my hands. I scan her face like I'm checking for wounds, but there aren't any, at least not any that are visible. Her eyes still look empty prompting me to quietly beg for her attention, "Sara, look at me." Her eyes finally drift to mine and I keep talking, hoping she'll listen. "We don't need to be here. We can go. You're a smart, beautiful, caring woman and everyone who's in your presence knows it. You don't need to take his shit anymore."

Her eyes soften for me slightly before her features again turn to defeat. She shakes her head in refusal. "But I do, Jason," she insists. "He pays for me to go to school, including all my expenses so I don't have to work. I have a year and a half left of dealing with him if I want to graduate."

"We can find another way, Sara. I don't want to see you hurting like this," I confess.

"Jason, this is so new between us still and..." she sighs trailing off. It may be new, but I've never felt so strongly that I need to protect something or someone besides my family. I'm going to figure out a way to do exactly that.

"Sara," an older woman interrupts. I flinch as she jumps away from me like she's on fire. The woman eyes me warily as she steps up to Sara and embraces her in a gentle hug. "It's so good to see you, dear. We were hoping you would be joining us tonight. Bradley was quite disappointed he wasn't escorting you here. You two always go to these things together," she confesses, obviously wanting me to know.

Ah, so Brad's parents. Wonderful!

I feel my jaw start to twitch as Sara blushes with embarrassment. "Um, hi Mr. and Mrs. Moore. It's good to see you." She glances nervously over at me, "This is my friend, Jason Emory."

Again, with the friend thing and to these fucking people? Seriously?

I grind my jaw and slowly release my breath before shaking both of theirs. "Nice to meet you," I mumble as politely as possible. I can at least prove my parents made sure I have manners, I think. I have no idea what they say to me, but I take a step back and let them finish their conversation while I try to control my seething. When they finally walk away, I smile as best I can and nod my head to say goodbye.

Sara steps in front of me looking nervous. "Jason, I'm sorry. I know this is awkward, but please don't be mad at me. I don't know how to handle this," she confesses.

Well at least she's admitting it. I release another breath trying to get rid of the tension. "Sara, do you want to be here with me?" I prod, needing to hear her say it.

"Yes, of course I do," she insists.

178

I relax further and give her a genuine smile. "Then, we'll figure the rest out," I claim.

She nods her head and wraps her arms around me continuing to nod into my chest. "Okay," she whispers. I envelop her in my arms, reveling in her warmth. I lean down towards her, pushing my nose into her hair. I love the soft fruity smell of her. She leans back to look up at me. "We should go back in there," she advises. "There're a few more people I have to see before we can escape."

Yeah, a few more like your ex I think, but don't say it, she doesn't need even more added stress from me. I'm supposed to be helping her tonight, not making her feel worse. I nod my head and gently press my lips to hers before I pull away. I stand to my full height and let my hand settle on her lower back as we turn to walk back into the ballroom.

At the first step inside the ballroom, another man's hands settle on the hips of my girl, and I know I'm glaring at the man of the hour, her ex-boyfriend. "Whoa," he mutters, holding her firm as she nearly runs him over.

She freezes and whispers harshly, "Brad." Her face turns bright red, but his hands don't move as he sneers down at her.

Just as I'm about to physically remove his hands off of her permanently, his hands slip away as he places a kiss on the corner of her mouth. "Hi, Sara. You look very nice," he states with a smirk on his face. I fist my hands at my sides, so I don't punch the asshole in the face. I'm sure none of these people would fail to call the police on me.

Sara steps so close to me, I'm sure she can feel the anger vibrating through me. "Um, Brad, this is my boyfriend, Jason."

He finally puts his focus on me and looks me over sardonically. He shakes his head slightly and asks with his eyebrows raised, "The handsy asshole with the truck? You said he was just a friend, Sara," he accuses.

I don't know what he's referring to, but I don't know if I want to. I keep my mouth pinched shut so I don't do anything to make Sara's situation worse. I have to keep reminding myself this is about her. "Brad," she says his name in warning. She sighs heavily and tries to make our escape. "We have to go talk to some people."

Brad mumbles, "I will get you back."

At his words I stop. I have to. She turns to look at me and I encourage her to keep going with a nod of my head. "It's fine, Sara. I'll be right behind you." She eyes us both warily, but she eventually turns reluctantly and walks further into the room towards her brother. I'm sure desperate to get away from him. But I'm not moving without saying something to this asshole and she doesn't need to hear anymore. She's had enough bullshit tonight, or ever for that matter.

I turn to look at Brad in disgust. I take a step towards him before I speak slowly in a cold and demanding voice, "Stay...the...fuck...away...from...Sara."

He sneers at me. "What're you gonna' do when she comes back to me willingly? She always does," he taunts.

"Not this time," I practically spit in his face. "You don't deserve to even be near a woman like her. You will never have the chance to treat her like shit again. I won't let it happen. Ever," I declare confidently.

"She's going to marry me soon. When that happens, she won't even remember the asshole she fucked a few times," he claims, his voice dripping with menace. My arms flex and my fists clench so tight if I don't walk away now, I will punch him so hard, he'll be lucky to be breathing. Being with Sara is all I need. I don't need to waste my time and end up in jail because of this asshole I tell myself repeatedly, trying to convince myself to back off. I have no idea how I do it, but I close my eyes and take a deep breath as I turn and walk away towards my life.

I step up close to Sara talking to her brother and immediately put my arm around her. She turns to me with a cautious smile. "You're shaking," she observes, whispering. I just nod my head and swallow hard. "Maybe we can wrap this up sooner rather than later." I nod my head again. There's no way in hell I can open my mouth to speak right now.

"Why don't you guys sneak out," Stephen suggests, "you said hi to almost everyone you need to anyway. I'll cover for you."

Sara looks relieved as she reaches up to hug her brother. "Thanks Stephen. I owe you one," she declares, smiling.

He laughs and teases, "You owe me a lot more than that!" He turns to me and offers his hand. "It really was great to meet you, Jason. Next time, hopefully we'll get a chance to hang out more. Take care of my sister." I give him a small smile and a nod of my head in acknowledgement, still not daring to speak.

"Bye Stephen," Sara calls as her brother disappears again with a quick wave over his shoulder.

As soon as he's gone, Sara looks up at me nervously, but I just quietly guide her out the back door of the ballroom. We grab our coats and stride to my truck. I help her inside before I jump in and start up my truck, swiftly backing out and driving to Sara's apartment. When I park the car, I stare out the window, still trying to calm myself down.

"Are you even going to talk to me?" Sara questions on a choked sob immediately catching my attention. My eyes fly to her tear-streaked face making my heart and body physically ache for her.

Chapter 23

Sara

The twenty-minute drive back to my apartment, Jason doesn't even glance over at me once. He doesn't open his mouth to say anything or ask me anything. He just remains quiet, silently seething. I can see how mad he is just by looking at him. His strong jaw is still twitching, his nostrils are flaring from taking several deep breaths, his broad shoulders are tense. I can even see the muscles in his arms rippling under his button-down shirt since he tossed his coat behind him while he white knuckles the steering wheel. His whole body has been shaking with anger since he saw Brad.

I didn't handle that well at all and now I ruined everything with Jason. It's really no surprise. I don't deserve someone as wonderful as him. I knew I wouldn't be able to keep him, I just hoped we would last a little longer. I need the memories of him to last me a lifetime.

We pull into the parking lot at my apartment building and he puts his car in park before he drops his head back and twists away from me. At this point, I can no longer stop the tears from streaming down my face as I watch him stare out the window. There's tension still rolling off him in waves. I finally grab onto my courage deep inside to open my mouth asking, "Are you ever going to speak to me."

At that he immediately turns towards me. "Sara," he murmurs. The reverent way he says my name sends chills down my spine and completely warms me to my soul. It's almost too much to hope for.

He reaches up with both hands and wipes away my tears with his thumbs, but they keep falling. "Sara," he whispers again cradling my face in his hands like I'm something precious.

He slowly moves towards me and gently presses his lips to mine. His mouth moves delicately over mine, barely breathing, barely kissing, barely touching, like I might break if he's not careful. Then again, I feel like I'm already broken. Maybe he's just trying not to get hurt on all my sharp edges. I sob at the thought, breaking our sensual kiss making him sigh softly.

"I'm sorry," I whimper. "I'm so sorry, Jason."

He shakes his head, insisting, "It's not your fault." He reaches for his keys and puts them in his pocket before gesturing to my building behind us. "Come on, Sara," he urges, "let's go inside and talk."

I nod numbly and reach for the handle to climb out of the truck. Might as well get this over with so I can cry myself to sleep.

Before I get all the way out of the truck, Jason is by my side helping me. He guides me into my quiet apartment and into my room where he closes the door and locks it even though Liz obviously isn't home. I flop down on my bed and take off my coat, tossing it on the floor. I then kick my shoes off before curling up on my side. "Do you want to change before we get comfortable?" he prods with a small grin.

I shake my head, mumbling, "No, thanks." I just don't have the energy to bother with changing right now.

Jason takes off his coat, jacket and tie, tossing all of it on the chair by my desk. He walks slowly over to my bed and kicks his own shoes off before he lies down on the mattress facing me with his head propped up on his arm. "Are you okay?" he prompts.

I shrug my shoulders in response, not really wanting to say no out loud.

He sighs regretfully. "Sorry, stupid question." He reaches for me and wipes away more tears. "I hate seeing you hurt so much. It fucking kills me to see you like this, Sara, especially when I feel like I can't do anything about it," he confesses.

With his admission, I look up into his blue eyes and I'm nearly floored with what I see reflected in them. I can see the concern he has for me, for my pain. I see warmth, caring and so much more, but I'm not sure what all of it is. The thing I don't see anymore, is the anger I saw before. "You're not mad at me?" I question with disbelief clear in my voice.

His eyes widen in surprise. His gaze holds mine as he declares, "No! No, I'm not mad at you! I'm mad at your father! I'm mad at your ex-boyfriend! I'm mad at your ex-boyfriend's parents! I'm livid at the situation you're in! I'm pissed at the situation we're in! But no, I'm not mad at you. You did nothing wrong."

His jaw twitches as he adds under his breath, "I wanted to beat the shit out of your ex though. I'm glad we got out of there before I did something he deserves and ended up getting arrested because I guarantee that asshole would press charges."

I ignore his last comment and breathe a sigh of relief as I dive into his chest wrapping my arms tightly around him. My tears continue to fall soaking his shirt, but this time it's because I'm happy. "Thank you," I whisper.

He chuckles lightly in response. "Sara," he says running his fingers through my hair, "you don't need to thank me. Tonight, I wanted to do everything I could to protect you and I felt helpless because I know you feel you need to be there. I don't want to do anything that will piss you off, but..." he trails off before starting again another way. "I understand you wanting to be there for your brother and I even understand feeling like you have to be there for your dad since he's paying for your school, but I don't like it. I'm sure you already know what I think of your father," he admits, grimacing.

He tucks a lock of hair behind my ear as he holds my gaze. "I will say I don't understand why your ex has to be a part of any of it. I know he's your brother's friend, but your brother is a good guy. If he knew," he begins.

I immediately cut him off, "I already told you I can't be the reason my brother loses his best friend."

"You wouldn't be the reason. Brad would be the reason," he insists. "Don't you get it?" he prompts with vehemence. "None of it is your fault. When he treats you like shit, it's on him! When he's an asshole, it's on him! From what I can tell of your brother, he would probably punch Brad himself if he knew how he treated you."

"Jason," I mumble, shaking my head in denial. "I just can't. Besides being my brother's friend, our parents work together."

"Sara," he begs.

"Please, I don't want to talk about Brad," I plead. His jaw twitches again and he sighs in frustration.

After a few minutes of complete silence, I hold my breath wondering if he's going to push this more. Thankfully he changes the subject back to my college education causing me to exhale in relief. "I think we need to look into any other options to finish paying for school," he suggests. "The sooner the better," he insists.

I laugh humorlessly. "What do you mean we? You're finished with school and you're just trying to figure out what you want to do. I'm the one that has the rest of this year and all of next year left."

He pinches his lips together before proclaiming, "Yeah, but I'm not going anywhere and I want to help you."

"It's not your problem," I answer reflexively.

"It is my problem if it involves you and your future. Let me help you figure this out," he pleads quietly.

I shake my head not knowing what to say to his offer. I've never had anyone want to do something like this for me. I can't help but wonder why he would want to. My dad always treats everything he does for me as more of an obligation than something he wants to do.

"Why?" I ask confused, searching his face and eyes for an honest answer from him.

A small smile softens his face and his eyes sparkle as he answers, "Well that one's easy, Sara, you. You're my reason for just about everything lately."

My breath catches and my heart instantly begins pounding hard. My body feels warm and tingly everywhere at the thought of Jason being my happily ever after. I've never wanted something or someone so bad in all my life. Could I really be this lucky? Is it really my chance to have someone like Jason in my life? It just feels too good to be true. Everything about him feels too good to be true.

I attempt to calm my anxiousness. I take a deep breath and give myself a shake, knowing I have to apologize again for my father. I don't want to lose this. I don't want to lose him. I begin rambling, "I'm so sorry about tonight, Jason. I always hate my father's events and I knew it would be crazy, but I was hoping to have a nice night with you despite my dad and Brad and..." I trail off.

He shakes his head. "I told you not to apologize to me. You have no reason to be sorry for anything. You don't need to apologize because of something someone else did or because of who someone else is. Sharing blood or even knowing someone doesn't put you at fault. As for tonight, we can still have a nice night," he adds sweetly making me melt. I smile up at him, feeling my face warm. I've never blushed easily, but with Jason I do.

I nod in acceptance, letting him get away with the change in subject. "What do you want to do?" I ask somewhat shyly.

"Nothing really," he reveals, shrugging his shoulders. "I think we should get comfortable and you should let me hold you for a while before you fall asleep," he suggests.

"Really? That's it?" I prod, smirking.

He grins playfully. "Well, if you want to do something else, I'm sure you could find some way to persuade me."

"Is that how it is?" I prod raising my eyebrows in challenge. His grin just grows in response causing my heart to skip a beat. "Ok, you asked for it," I threaten.

He reaches for me and pokes me in the side before I have a chance to follow through on my threat making me squeal. He tickles me and pulls me closer at the same time, but I'm so ticklish I can't stop trying to wiggle away from him. "Jason, stop," I screech, laughing. Suddenly he stops tickling me and his mouth is on my neck giving me a different kind of chill. I sigh melting into him.

"I think it's time to get you more comfortable," he whispers kissing me up my neck. As he makes his way to my mouth, I realize my dress is nearly bunched up to my waist and I'm already wrapping my right leg around Jason.

Whimpering as his mouth finally makes its way to mine, I kiss him like I'm ready to climb inside of him. I push my tongue inside his mouth wanting to taste every bit of him. He groans into my mouth urging me on. I roll him over onto his back and throw my leg all the way over him, straddling him at the waist. I tear my mouth away from his to sit up and I feel him getting hard underneath me heating me at my core. I reach down with both hands and pull my dress off, quickly tossing it to the floor.

"Fuck," Jason groans, staring at me with lust in my black lace bra and matching boy shorts making me grin. I lean back down and kiss him as his hands start to trail down my sides and then curve around my ass before pulling me into him with a squeeze. I start to unbutton his dress shirt when I hear banging around in the kitchen. I break our kiss, both of us gasping for breath as I try to hear what's going on, while Jason drops his head back to my bed with a sigh.

"Sara, are you here?" Liz calls.

187

Glancing at Jason, I whisper, "I'm sorry," before I give him a quick kiss and climb off him and off my bed. I step up to my dresser and grab a pair of pale blue and white flannel pants and a matching blue tank top and quickly pull them on.

There's a knock on my door. Before Liz can speak, I yell, "I'm here, I'll be right out!" I run my fingers through my hair as I make my way to the door and pull it open.

Liz looks over at me as I walk out of my room with her eyebrows pinched together in concern.

"Is everything okay?" I ask her quickly before she can think too much about what I must look like with my bloodshot eyes and swollen face.

She grimaces, "Um, yeah. Blake's sister Aubrey is sick and he's worried about her. We're going to drive down to Boston to check on her."

"Oh, I hope she's okay," I whisper. Blake and his family were in a bad car accident when he was a kid. Their car was hit by a drunk driver and pushed off the road into a tree. His sister, Aubrey, who's a couple years younger than him had permanent damage both physically and mentally from the accident and now lives in an adult home in Boston. Blake is understandably very protective of his sister, and Liz too if I'm honest.

"It sounds like she just has the flu, but Blake won't feel better until he checks on her himself and I can't let him go alone." I nod my head in understanding. "I'm just going to go pack a bag really quick, then I'll go sleep at Blake's apartment so we can get up early to leave. I think we'll miss Monday's classes, but I don't have a class until later on Tuesday, so hopefully we'll be back by then."

"Okay," I acknowledge. I walk over to her, giving her a quick hug. "Drive safe and let me know how Aubrey's doing," I request.

"Thank you," she murmurs appreciatively hugging me back. She starts to chuckle as she lets go. "I'm sorry. I didn't realize Jason was here." She smirks glancing towards my open door.

I wave her off with a small smile. "Goodnight, Liz!" I walk back into my room and shut the door with a sigh.

"Everything okay?" Jason prods.

"Yeah, Liz is heading to Boston with Blake to check on his sister. I guess she's not feeling well," I explain not wanting to go into details right now.

Jason nods his head in acknowledgement as he reaches for my hand. He grips my fingers and gently tugs me towards him. "I think we should go to sleep. It's been a long night." I sigh and nod my head in agreement, thinking it's been a rough night too. "Do you mind if I get a little more comfortable?" he questions. I shake my head and watch him as he removes his shirt the rest of the way, leaving only a plain white t-shirt, followed by his pants leaving black boxer-briefs over his thick muscular thighs. I gulp hard as he moves closer to me, getting a better glance of his legs that are nothing but lean, solid muscle.

I place my hand lightly on his chest as I struggle to breathe. "Holy crap," I mumble under my breath. I can't help but wonder how the hell a man built like Jason is here in my bed.

"Are you okay?" he prompts, chuckling. I nod my head in answer. I know I'll say something stupid if I open my mouth right now.

Taking a deep breath, he lets it go, moving on. "I've been wanting to ask you if you'd go with me up to my parents' place on the lake. I know you've already met them, but I'd like you to meet them as my girlfriend so they could really get to know you. So, what do you think?" he prompts to my surprise sounding incredibly nervous.

"I...I..." I stutter. My chest feels tight, overwhelmed with emotion.

"They're good people even when you get to know them," he adds. I blush looking away, embarrassed that he even has to say something like that to me. Of course, they are. Look at this man.

"I'd like that," I proclaim, releasing my breath. When are you going?" I question staring straight ahead at his chest, not wanting to look him in the eyes.

He touches two fingers to my chin and gently tilts it up until my gaze meets his. "Sometime in the next couple weeks. Probably a Sunday, so it's easier to get off work and I could get you back early Monday morning for your classes." I nod my head. "I could check with my brother too. Maybe him and Bree could go with us or just meet us there," he suggests. "They go a lot of weekends anyway." I nod my head again. "Are you sure?" he probes, eyeing me doubtfully.

I finally release the breath I didn't realize I was holding and give him a genuine smile. "I'm sure, Jason." He instantly relaxes and pulls me into his arms.

"Good," he declares. He grins and places a gentle kiss on my lips. "Goodnight, Sara."

"Goodnight, Jason," I whisper settling into the warmth of his embrace.

Chapter 24

Sara

4 years ago...

I walk down the steps towards our living room, excited to see my mom. She said she wanted to finally meet Brad. She said she would come early so we could go to get our nails done together before we met up with Brad for dinner. I don't remember the last time my mom and I did something together just the two of us. My happiness is more than obvious as I smile walking into the living room, but no one is there.

My confusion doesn't last long when I hear my father yelling at the front of the house and I run to stop my parents' confrontation.

"This asshole is not allowed near my house or my kids! I've told you that before!" my dad screams at my mother.

My mother gets right back in his face, screaming, "He's my husband and so much more of one than you ever were! And those kids are mine too!"

"Unfortunately, I see that every single day when I look at Sara," he declares eyeing her with disgust.

My mom's husband looks livid, his face red and hands fisted at his sides. Before anything worse happens, I step in front of my father. "Daddy, you know I have plans with mom today." I remind him, glancing over towards her husband, wondering why he's here.

"I only agreed for you to go with her. He was not included in this deal. You're staying home," he demands still glaring at my mother.

"Dad," I whine.

My mother shakes her head in resignation and takes a step away from me. "I'm sorry, Sara. This just isn't worth it."

I gasp as my mouth falls open and my heart drops down to my stomach like lead, making me nauseas. "What?" I cry.

She continues to shake her head as she backs away from me. "I just can't do this anymore, Sara. I'm sorry. I can't do it."

"Mom," I plead, crying.

She keeps moving to the passenger side of their Chevy Tahoe and mouths, "I'm sorry," again before she climbs in and blows me a kiss.

I don't know how long I'm standing on the sidewalk with tears streaming down my face before my father comes out to berate me. "Get in the house. You're being ridiculous. It's embarrassing." I turn towards the house and away from him to keep him from hearing my choked sob. "I'm going to take care of some business. Pull yourself together and go do something useful," he adds before stalking away.

Later that night, I'm doing everything I can to pretend I'm okay. I'm smiling and talking with Liz and a few other people at our friend May's party. I wasn't planning on going, but I asked Brad to meet me here when my mom cancelled. I thought it would be easier to forget and smile with a lot of people around. So, I called Liz and had to practically drag her here. She's not always big on parties, but she came for me.

I'm wearing a pair of blue leggings and a fitted short-sleeved pale blue knit shirt that hangs just above my butt with the boots Liz gave me a while ago. They are definitely my favorite. I wear them all the time. I want to look cute for Brad and hope he likes my outfit.

Liz and I both jump as a head pops up between us just as an arm swings around each of our necks. We turn, finding

Billy grinning broadly, one of Liz's brother's best friends. All three of us laugh at our startled reaction. "Hi, girls. Liz, I haven't seen Jax in a while. How's he doing?"

She grimaces at the question. "He's okay. You should give him a call," she quickly suggests.

"I'll do that," he concurs, nodding his head. Then he drops his arm from around Liz before directing his attention to me with a huge grin. "How have you been, Sara?"

I nod, mumbling, "I'm good."

"Are you still dating Brad?" he questions awkwardly.

I clear my throat and answer firmly, "Yes, I am."

His eyes narrow and he slowly lets his arm wrapped around me fall to his side. His mouth turns up slightly as he states, "That's too bad."

I laugh brushing off his comment with a shake of my head. Suddenly, I'm turned around roughly. Brad swiftly has me in his arms with a yank. Holding me tightly to him, he kisses me possessively in front of everyone. I barely kiss him back, hoping not to embarrass him as I try to gently push him away and catch my breath. I'm finally able to break the kiss and I quickly inhale, giving him my fake smile. "I'm really happy to see you, but why did you do that?"

"What? I can't kiss my girlfriend in front of her friends?" he prods, sounding like he's daring me. The way he's looking at me makes my stomach turn. I'm afraid to answer him, so I don't. "Besides, I needed to claim what was mine, you were acting like a slut flirting like that with him. I had to let him know only I touch you."

"I was just talking to him Brad," I defend myself.

"With his arm around you," he emphasizes, glaring at me.

My head drops in defeat. He's right. It was only for a second, but I should have pushed him away right away instead of just standing there and laughing. "I'm sorry," I confess. "I wasn't thinking Brad. I had a rough day."

He heaves a sigh. "Use your head next time," he insists.

Just then Kenni walks up and wraps her arms around Brad's waist giving him a squeeze. She whispers something in his ear, making him laugh. My heart clenches with hurt as he watches me and doesn't remove her hands right away. After a moment he grabs her hands and spins her around and away from him. He whispers something to her, then he slaps her on the ass as she struts away smiling like she just won something.

He turns back to me and places his hands on my hips. "How did that make you feel?" he asks me. I don't reply because he knows the answer to that question. "Do you want to be like her? Have people look at you like you're looking at her right now?" he questions accusingly. I shake my head like he's lost his mind. "Well, that's exactly how everyone here was looking at you before because they know you're my girlfriend and you were standing there with another asshole's arm around you. I'm not going to let you make a fool of me."

I flinch at his explanation. He's right. I'm just as bad. Except I'm worse, I'm the one with a boyfriend. "Brad, I'm sorry. You're all I want," I insist.

He raises his eyebrows in doubt. "Prove it to me, then."

I smile stiffly at him and gently place a kiss on his lips and he immediately pulls me closer. My mom doesn't want me. My dad doesn't want me. Brad wants me. I can't mess this up.

Present Day...

I wake up trembling in Jason's arms. He's rubbing my back in circles and whispering words of comfort, "It's okay, Sara. You're okay. I'm right here," he prompts causing my breath to catch.

I'm pressed to his chest and I realize I've soaked his shirt with my tears and who knows what else. "I'm so sorry," I sob brushing at his chest, desperate to wipe away the evidence of my tears.

He reaches for my hand, grasping it gently in attempt to stop my frantic brushing. "It's okay," he reiterates. I try to take a deep breath to calm myself down. "Does this happen a lot?" he inquires. I look up at him with confusion. My brain feels muddled from sleep. "Do you have bad dreams like this a lot?" he elaborates. I sigh heavily and bury my face back in his chest. I feel him tense. "I'll take that as a yes. Do you want to tell me about it?" he probes.

He doesn't ask anything else; he just waits patiently for my response. When I finally have myself under control, I whisper, "I don't know."

He runs his fingers through my hair a few times before leaving his fingers tangled in my hair and cradling my face in his hands. He tilts my face up to look at him again and holds my gaze before he speaks, "I want to be here for you. I want to know what's hurting you and support you. No judgment, Sara, if that's what you're worried about. Just you and me. I need to help you. When I wake up to find you shaking so bad and crying like that," trailing off, he gulps as if in pain. "Fuck, Sara, just please let me help you."

"Okay," I whisper my consent, still captured by his eyes.

"What was your dream about?" he prods again, pleading with his eyes for answers as he caresses my cheeks lightly with his thumbs.

I finally break away from his gaze. I can't look at him when I talk about this. I press myself tightly into his chest and he holds me just as tight, giving me exactly what I need to speak. "My mom, my dad and Brad," I admit. "My dreams kind of run together, but it's usually one particular time, like maybe a day. Sometimes it's different things and sometimes it's the same."

I pause and try to relax by enjoying the feel of being in Jason's arms, soaking up his comfort. I take a deep breath and try to explain. "I've never really been very lovable," I admit and I feel Jason's whole body harden at my comment. "It's true. I've made a lot of mistakes. My mom left and we would see her less and less until we didn't see her at all anymore. In one of my dreams, I was remembering one of the few times I saw my mom in the past five years. We had plans and her and my dad got in a fight because her husband came along. By the time they were done fighting, my mom decided I wasn't worth the trouble and my dad was embarrassed I was upset and yelled at me too."

I shake my head not wanting to remember it anymore, but also wanting to tell him to get it over with. "Then I went out with Liz, but I was supposed to meet Brad. We just went to a friend's party, but Liz never came with me to these parties because she hated running into this mean girl Tori. That night, she gave in to me because her boyfriend was going to be there. I always liked being around people. When I was, I could pretend everything was perfect, you know?" I prod, not really wanting an answer.

"Anyway, Brad showed up when I was talking to some guy. He was friends with Liz's brother. We were just talking, but he was pissed. He got possessive in front of everyone, kissing me.

He tried to show me what it felt like having me talk to another guy by flirting with other girls in front of me," I explain, grimacing. "I never meant to do anything wrong, but," I trail off, scrunching my nose up in disappointment. I shrug my shoulders and confess, "I always did and he punished me for it."

Jason delicately pries me away from his chest and tilts my chin up towards his face. His jaw is twitching and his nostrils are flaring when he opens his mouth. "First thing we are getting straight is you are so fucking lovable!" he proclaims before he snaps his mouth shut. My heart speeds

196

up with his declaration. He takes a few more deep breaths and I watch him attempt to calm himself down.

"It's obvious both your mom and dad have their own issues and they have absolutely nothing to do with you. They just use you to take out their anger and frustrations, which is such bullshit. It sounds to me like they never should have had kids, but I'm so thankful they did because that means I have you in my arms now. I'm going to do everything I can to help you move past the way they treated you. Just please know, you are worth it! You are always worth it, no matter what. I promise," he assures me.

I close my eyes in hope. "Jason," I whimper his name like a prayer.

"Sara, look at me," he insists. He waits until my eyes meet his again before he continues. "As for your ex. We both know he's an asshole, but you need to know he didn't treat you right and it was not your fault." I nod my head sadly in agreement, not really believing him. "No, Sara, look at me," he emphasizes. "It was not your fault!"

My breath catches in my throat and my heart skips a beat at the sincerity in his eyes. I know it's true, but I don't know how much I've really ever believed it. He can see that in me. How? I shake my head again feeling completely overwhelmed. "I can't talk about this anymore right now," I whisper. "I'm sorry."

He sighs, relenting, "It's fine. I understand it's a lot. Just please talk to me when you need me," he pleads. "Promise me!"

"Okay," I consent.

He gives me a squeeze before taking a deep breath and changing the subject. "I'm working a double today, so I should probably get more sleep since I'll be up for about the next 24 hours if I don't get a little more sleep. Maybe you can come down to visit me," he suggests.

I sigh in relief at the subject change and relax back into his chest. I'm thankful the conversation is over for now and grateful that he still wants me around. Maybe I will be lucky, maybe he will stick around.

He tilts my face back up to his. "Hey?" he prods making sure he has my attention. Looking at him, I give him a sleepy smile, waiting for him to speak. Instead of saying something, he gently tugs my mouth to his and kisses me, moving his mouth in a slow rhythm over mine until I whimper into his mouth, my insides tingling. He gently pulls away and guides me back to his chest, urging, "Now, I can get some sleep."

I chuckle softly as I quickly fall into a peaceful dreamless sleep feeling content and happy in his arms.

Chapter 25

Jason

I move around the bar cleaning glasses, stocking the refrigerator and the shelves, basically trying to get the bar back in order while the pub is slow. It always picks up later on Sunday nights with the college crowd who either doesn't have classes or doesn't care. Unfortunately, when it's slow like this, my mind has the opportunity to wander. I can't stop thinking about Sara's dreams or more realistically, her nightmares. It makes it even worse that they're actual memories. Waking up to her shaking and sobbing in her sleep like she did, cracked my heart in two.

I want to do everything in my power to protect her. I actually wanted to listen to every detail of her dreams and of her past so I could help her. I practically begged her to talk to me. The worst part of it all is I know she didn't tell me everything. I can tell she kind of skipped over things, not wanting to tell me all the particulars of her history. I hate not knowing if it's because she's embarrassed or if it's so bad she can't handle it or some other reason. I know anything she would tell me wouldn't change the way I feel about her. I just don't want her to have to deal with any of it alone. She should've never had to deal with it in the first place.

The *what if* scenarios run through my head constantly like I'm watching a horrible movie I can't turn away from. I'm sick thinking about all the things her father and especially her ex might have done to her. How the fuck could anyone treat her so badly and how can I fix it? I sigh in exasperation and glance at the clock knowing the night is going to drag.

A couple hours later there is standing room only at the bar. I wipe my hands on the towel at my waist and step up to ask a group of loud and slightly drunk college girls what they want to drink. A big chested redhead steps up to speak for the group with a sly smile on her face. "Tequila Body shots off of you," she answers confidently.

I shake my head, announcing, "Tequila shots I can do, but it won't be including me." She stands on the rungs of the bar stool and leans across the bar pushing her chest towards me. I take a half step back and raise my eyebrows in challenge. "So, would you like those shots?"

She grimaces and grumbles, "Fine. Then I'll go find someone who appreciates these," causing her friends to laugh. I try not to roll my eyes. I'm so sick of women like this. I need to figure out what I want to do with my life. I line up the shot glasses and begin to poor giving them the saltshaker and lime wedges. The redhead goes to place her money on the bar and doesn't let go when I reach for it. "Are you sure you don't want to make mine a body shot?" she prods suggestively.

I begin to politely tell her no again when Sara squeezes in next to her. She's so tiny she climbs onto her knees on the barstool before she leans over the bar, pulling my head to hers and kissing me hard. She pulls away and looks at the redhead with a grin. "He's sure." I can't help the huge smile that covers my face at her antics. She gives me one more quick kiss before she places her ass on the stool and grins mischievously at me. "Hi," she murmurs shyly. I can't stop my laughter as the redhead and her friends glare at Sara and stalk away after taking their shots.

When I finally catch my breath I tell her, "I'm so glad you're here." She grins and blushes slightly making me chuckle. "How the hell do I make a girl who walked in here with that confidence blush like you are now?" She turns an even deeper shade of red making me want to touch her. I quickly reach across the bar and give her hand a squeeze.

"What would you like to drink?" I inquire, not letting go of her hand.

Someone down at the other end of the bar calls for a drink, letting me know I need to get back to work. "Just a beer. Do you have any Maine Beer Company on tap?" she asks.

"Zoe," I answer.

"Perfect, my favorite," she claims, smiling.

I grab her beer and quickly hand it to her, refusing her money. "I'll pay for you. I need to take care of a few more customers though. Don't go anywhere." She smiles in answer.

As I'm serving beers and making drinks, I take every chance I can to glance over at Sara who appears to be just taking everything in while she sips her beer. A few guys approach her throughout the night, looking like they're trying to talk to her, but before I even react, she's blowing them off making me beam at her. When her beer is almost gone, I quickly make my way back over to her. "Want another one?" I inquire.

She shakes her head. "No, I really have to get some homework done," she admits.

"Are you headed home then?" I prod with obvious disappointment.

She shakes her head again and I raise my eyebrows in question. "I brought some things with me." I glance behind her and notice her backpack for the first time. "It was too quiet at my apartment with Liz gone. I thought I could find a table in a corner somewhere and..." she trails off suddenly looking unsure.

"How about I grab you a coke then and I'll come over on my break?" I offer quickly. I don't want her to change her mind and decide to leave. I'm probably being selfish because there's no way in hell, she's getting anything done here, but I want her to stay anyway.

She smiles, agreeing, "Okay. Thanks, Jason. I wasn't sure if you'd want me down here," she confesses hesitantly.

I get that sick feeling in my stomach again when I hear her comment. I hand her the coke and reach for her hand. "I always want you wherever I am," I insist. I know we haven't been dating long, but it's true. "There's a table back there," I state, gesturing over her shoulder.

Joey steps up behind me, joking, "Hey, slacker."

I don't even glance over at him as I introduce them. "Joey, this is my girlfriend, Sara."

He reaches across the bar to shake her hand. "Nice to meet you."

"Help me keep an eye on her?" I ask.

"I'll be fine, Jason. I'm a big girl," Sara teases, shaking her head at me I amusement.

"Hey, I remember you now," Joey declares pointing at her. "You're the girl he was too stupid to ask for your phone number." Sara laughs and I grimace, letting them have their moment. "Glad he found you. He flipped out after you left and realized what he did," he proclaims, griming and making Sara blush.

"I'm going to try to get something done. You guys need to get back to work." She grabs her backpack off the back of the barstool and quickly weaves through the crowd to find her way to the corner booth.

Joey laughs and slaps me on the back. "Come on man, back to work."

It finally starts to slow down at the bar and I'm able to glance over towards the corner booth to find Sara. She's sitting there with some books open, but I see April standing at the end talking to her making me cringe. Since our last encounter, we've been civil with each other, but I definitely don't trust her.

I call over to Joey, "Hey man, I'm going to take my break." He nods his head in acknowledgement, smirking at me knowingly.

I wipe my hands on a towel before tossing it under the bar and quickly making my way over to Sara. I try to decipher the look on her face as I approach to figure out what I'm walking into. I swiftly slide in next to her, pushing her into the booth in the process.

"I'll take care of her, April. Thanks," I quickly acknowledge her hoping she'll just turn and walk away.

Unfortunately, I'm not quite that lucky. "So, you do know her?" she probes sounding irritated. "You're not just kissing another one of your girls?"

I take a deep steadying breath keeping my eyes on Sara who's staring straight ahead, her face neutral. "I don't have any girls besides Sara. This is my girlfriend, April," I emphasize in warning.

I hear her gasp of surprise behind me. "You said you didn't do girlfriends."

"April, go back to work and leave my girl alone," I urge. Turning towards her, I level her with my glare so she knows how serious I am. She pinches her lips tightly together and spins on her heel, stomping towards another table. I turn back towards Sara, trying to read her. "You, okay?" I prod.

She won't look at me as she asks, "Have you ever gone out with her?"

"No," I answer instantly.

"Have you ever slept with her?" she asks cringing.

I take a deep breath when I recognize the wall she's trying to rebuild right in front of me. "Sara, look at me," I urge pulling her chin gently until she meets my gaze. "I've never done anything with April. She's tried, but it will never happen," I insist begging her to see the truth in my eyes. "What did she say to you?"

She swallows hard and shakes her head looking back at the books in front of her. "Nothing," she claims, sighing.

I don't know if I believe that, but I drop it anyway. "Are you getting anything done?" I ask instead.

"No, not really," she admits, grimacing. "It's too loud in here."

I laugh, loving the way she wrinkles her nose in displeasure. "Why don't you go back to your apartment and get some work done while I finish out the night," I suggest. She looks at me with disappointment, but nods her head, resigned. "Would it be okay if I came by after I finished tonight?" I prompt, hopefully. Her beautiful hazel eyes spark at my suggestion. "Maybe I could stay with you," I offer. "I don't want you alone if I can help it," I add playfully.

"Okay," she agrees, smiling and melting my heart. She turns and reaches into her backpack coming back out with her keys. She quickly pulls off one and hands it to me. "Here, it's the key to my apartment. I'll use the spare one when I get home."

My grin grows and my chest tightens with her offer. I immediately pocket the key before she has a chance to change her mind. I lean down towards her and press my lips to hers, tasting a mix of beer, coke and my sweet girl. I let my fingers linger on the soft skin of her cheek as I pull away with a crooked grin. "Okay, I'll be done around two tonight as long as all goes well." I give her another kiss and take a deep breath as I pull away, inhaling as much of her as I can. "I have to get back to work." She nods her head in understanding. "I'll see you tonight," I reiterate.

"Bye, Jason." She smiles and begins to gather up her things as I walk back to the bar. I give her a wave as she leaves and pray the rest of the night flies by.

I arrive at her apartment just before 2 a.m. I left work at 1:30 since Joey offered to finish up alone, but I wanted to run home to grab some fresh clothes. I don't want to climb into Sara's bed smelling like a bar and grease.

After I let myself in, I lock up behind me. I take a couple steps towards her room when I hear her scream, "No!'

My heart races as I sprint the last few steps towards her room slamming the door into the wall behind it

204

desperately seeking her out. "Sara, it's me," I call immediately, not wanting to scare her more. She's sitting up in bed, alone, eyes wide, looking terrified. I put my hands up cautiously, reiterating, "Sara, it's me, it's Jason, it's okay." I kneel on the floor at the side of her bed and put my hands, palms down on the mattress on either side of her. "Are you okay?" She swallows hard and shakes her head slightly. I start to panic. "What happened? Are you alright?" I ask again as I begin to scan her body from head to toe for any damage.

She finally catches her breath. "I'm...I'm fine," she stutters. "I just...I just had a bad dream," she confesses. "I'm sorry."

I sigh in both relief and fury as I sit on her bed so I can wrap her in my arms. "Don't be sorry," I insist, wishing I could do so much more.

Chapter 26

Sara

I try to pull myself together as Jason holds me tightly, rubbing comforting circles on my back and continuously telling me it's okay. "Will you tell me what your dream was about?" he prods. I gulp down the lump of fear in my throat trying to stop me from speaking. "Please," he begs.

For the first time I really want someone to know what really happened between Brad and me. Not just anyone either, I really want Jason to know. Maybe it will help. I'm a little overwhelmed thinking I actually have feelings for someone other than just a mild interest, or just someone to keep my mind off everything else. I would give almost anything to have a real relationship with him. Maybe it's true and he'll actually stick around after I tell him everything. Maybe he won't hate me. I don't know if I have the courage to tell him though. "Please talk to me Sara," he pleads sounding desperate.

I attempt to swallow the lump in my throat again and glance at his face out of the corner of my eye, trying to read him. I just can't pull away to look him in the eyes. It would be too much for me right now. I close my eyes and try to concentrate on the feel of being in Jason's arms to calm me down. "I..." my voice cracks and I clear my throat before I try again. "I'll try. My dream was about Brad," I confess. His arms instantly tighten around me. "I'm going to do my best Jason, but this is really hard for me," I admit.

"I know. Just remember I'm here for you, no judging. I just want you to talk to me. I want to help you Sara," he implores anxiously.

I really hope that's true. I take another deep breath to give myself the courage to begin. "Okay, maybe it would be easier to just tell you about our history?" I question, not quite sure where to begin. He gives a slight nod of his head as if to say whatever you can give me. I link my fingers together and stare at them fidgeting. It's almost easier to pretend I'm talking about someone else, so that's what I'll do.

"Brad and my brother were always good friends. Brad is an only child and he's expected to work for his father's company and his dad is very strict with him. His dad also respects my father when it comes to business. They have worked closely together on a few different business projects. Before my mom left things were different. My dad treated me like a princess and Brad treated me the same as Stephen, like his annoying little sister, but he wouldn't let anything happen to me." I need to refocus on the beginning of my end. There's no point in talking about the few good times before.

"When my mom cheated on my dad and then up and left, my dad started treating me differently and he expected perfection. The biggest problem was he couldn't stand to look at me because I look so much like my mother. He pushed me harder and expected more, but it didn't matter what I did. I was never good enough for him. When he looked at me, he saw my mother every single time. I kept trying to please him anyway. I just wanted to do the right thing, I wanted everything to go back to the way it used to be." I pause taking a shaky breath.

"When Brad and I started dating, I really liked him and he was good to me. That didn't last long though. He started to become jealous and possessive. But my life became unbearable when my dad decided Brad would be good for me or I should say good for him and his business. He would encourage Brad to help me grow up," I mutter sarcastically. "What that means to me is he encouraged Brad to control me, especially where he couldn't. Brad told me what to wear, what and how much to eat, where to be, what to do, who to talk to and who I could be friends with. Liz is the only friend I didn't let them take away from me," I ramble.

I feel a hand on my shoulder and I stop talking, but I can't look over at him. If I do, I might break. "Does Liz know about your dad or your ex?" he asks gently.

I shake my head, replying, "No, I didn't want her to see the weak person I was when they were around me. Besides it was nice to feel normal when I was with her. I learned how to paste a smile on and be the happy, fun friend. In fact, everyone at school would say I always had a smile on my face." I heave a sigh and shrug my shoulders. "Nobody could know it wasn't real or I would have to lie about what was wrong and I didn't want to do that."

"Why?" he whispers.

I swallow, admitting, "My dad became angrier and angrier whenever my mom came around, or when she was even mentioned. He got mad if I didn't put on my social face in public or anytime I didn't do something right according to him." I shake my head, wishing none of this was real. "He never hit me or anything but making him mad wasn't worth it. Then, when it started coming from both my dad and my boyfriend, I started believing more and more of what they told me. Why wouldn't I? Stephen would stick up for me if he was around, but my dad and Brad were both careful about what they said around him. Liz is really the only one who contradicted them. I just always thought that's what best friends are for."

Taking a deep breath, I continue, "Well, when Brad went away to college, I started to think of him as my ticket to get away from everything." I blush, completely embarrassed by my admission. "I didn't want him to stop loving me because I thought he could help me escape and at the same time it would make my dad happy if I was with him. So, I did whatever I could to do what they would tell me." I feel Jason tense behind me even more and I let the tears fall down my cheeks. I know I don't have any chance of fighting them now, so I don't try. All I can do is hope Jason will give me a chance after I'm done talking. "I was afraid if I didn't, I would be left behind with nothing but my father."

I take another deep breath, exhaling slowly, trying to calm myself down. "After Brad went away to college, he became more and more controlling and cruel. If he came home for the weekend and he didn't like the skirt I had on, he would tell me I looked like a whore. If I talked to a guy that wasn't him or my brother, I was a slut. If I had a cheeseburger when we went out to eat, I was fat. My dad would tell him I got a B- on a test and I was fucking stupid. When I was sick with the flu, I was irresponsible because I wasn't at school. When I got asked to go on a date with another guy it was only because they wanted one thing from me. After all, that's all I'm good for." I spit out bitterly. Sighing, I'm consumed with sadness. "Stephen was away at school too, so Liz was my only reprieve. I just wanted to be normal around her, so I pretended to be."

"When Liz decided she was coming here for school, I immediately applied too. I figured it was the only school I would be allowed to attend that my dad would still help pay that wasn't the same as Brad. My dad wanted to make sure someone would watch over me and since this way I'm close to home, I could get away with it. I convinced Brad it would be better to let him date other people while he was in college. When he finally agreed, he told me he would still marry me one day." I shudder at the thought and Jason gives me a comforting squeeze.

"The guys I've dated since we broke up have been someone who was interested in me and someone who has been a distraction for me. I never really cared if they even wanted to see me again. I just didn't want Liz or Stephen to get involved. I figured at least if I was dating, they'd believe I was making an effort and I wasn't crazy. I keep hoping Brad will find someone else and he won't bother me anymore. I don't want him to want me. Then it wouldn't be my fault we weren't together," I explain.

"Am I just a distraction?" Jason asks, his voice raspy.

"No!" I screech instantly. "I've never felt about anyone the way I feel about you," I quietly confess. I look up and his stormy gaze catches mine for the first time since I started talking, causing me to lose my breath. The pain in his eyes is evident. My heart clenches tightly inside my chest as I pray for his pain to be for me and for him to forgive me. "I'm sorry," I choke out the words almost inaudibly.

His hands stiffly move to my cheeks, cradling my face in his hands. He attempts to wipe my tears away as he holds me firmly in his grip. He struggles to take a breath just before he vehemently whispers, "Don't ever be fucking sorry for those assholes again!" He clenches his jaw and I can practically feel his body vibrating in anger. "I can't even comprehend how anyone could treat you like..." His hands drop away from my cheeks and clench into fists, while his head drops back and he glares at the ceiling.

"Jason," I whisper hesitantly causing his head to snap back to meet my gaze. I try to gulp down the nerves attempting to make their way up my throat. "Does that mean you forgive me?" I force out the question, needing an answer.

His eyes turn a darker shade of blue as they alone consume me. "There is nothing to forgive. You didn't do anything wrong. Like I've said before, you can't take responsibility for someone else's actions. Your family should support you and encourage you. They should be there for you and love you unconditionally." He shakes his head in disgust, insisting, "You can't believe anything they have ever told you."

"I don't," I say looking away from him. I can't look him in the eyes when we both know I'm lying.

He touches two fingers to my chin and directs it back towards his gaze. "You are beautiful Sara. Everything about you inside and out is beautiful. Your blonde hair is always so shiny and soft, your hazel eyes are the most incredible thing I've ever seen, I could just stare into them for hours. I love your full lips and when you let them truly smile," he pauses grinning appreciatively, "You light up the whole damn world. There's nothing I'd rather see. And when your lips kiss me, I'm fucking done for."

As he continues, I feel my heartbeat pound, feeling it all the way to my fingertips and toes surrounded by a million butterflies. "I love how tiny you are, you fit with my body perfectly, right under my arm. But you are also incredibly smart. It doesn't matter that you don't know what to do with your life, you'll figure it out when you're ready. When I'm talking with you, I never want our conversations to end. You make me laugh like nobody ever has and I know I'm going to have fun when we're together. Just being with you is a gift to me."

"How do you do it?" I ask in awe. His eyebrows draw together as he stares at me with confusion. "How do you make me feel so special? How do you see me? How do you see the me I don't share with anyone?" He takes a deep breath relaxing further into my bed. "You do see me, don't you?" I repeat, overwhelmed with the realization.

"I do, Sara. I see the sadness and doubt in your eyes. I notice the smiles you give nearly everyone that make me cringe because I know they're fake. But how I do it?" he raises his eyebrows and waits until he catches my eyes. He tucks a lock of hair behind my ear, and I nod slightly waiting for him to answer. He shakes his head lightly and confesses, "I haven't really done anything difficult. I just simply fell in love with you."

My mouth drops slightly open in shock as my breath catches in my throat. My heart feels like it's growing inside my chest and about to burst. Did he just tell me he loves me? "Wh...What?" I finally stammer.

"I love you, Sara," he repeats, his grin growing as he keeps talking. "I love watching you when you play like

211

you're a kid again and when you give me one of your real smiles, one of those genuine ones." He takes a deep breath and taps his chest near his heart, mumbling, "Holy shit, what you do to me." I think I've completely stopped breathing as he reaches towards me and wipes another tear off my cheek I didn't know had fallen. "And did I mention how beautiful you are?" he asks again with a playful grin. I finally release my breath laughing.

"I think I love you too," I confess quietly just as Jason presses his lips to mine.

"You think?" Jason challenges playfully as we fall into each other's arms. A smile tugs at my lips as I'm almost instantly completely lost in his kiss.

Chapter 27

Sara

It's Tuesday night and since Jason didn't have to work, we grabbed a pizza with Christian and Bree. Afterwards, we decided to go back to Jason's house to watch a movie. "I'm so tired lately with everything going on in my classes, then trying to spend time with you with your hours. I'm really glad we decided to come back here and just do this," I admit snuggling into Jason's arms. I love just lying together on his couch.

Jason brushes my hair back from my face and kisses me on the corner of my mouth. "It's not like I'm about to pass up time like this with you," he claims, smirking. He moves to my neck and takes a deep breath in before pressing his lips to my skin giving me goose bumps everywhere. He chuckles softly. "I love that I can do that to you," he confesses running his fingers gently along my arms.

I take a deep breath in attempt to stop myself from jumping him right this second. I want to ask him something I've been curious about for a while. "So, it was good to hang out with Christian and Bree tonight." Jason nods his head but doesn't respond. "How close are you with your brothers and sister? I mean you and Christian seem to get along fine, but I don't know…" I hesitate, afraid I'll say something to make him mad. "I guess you seem more like casual friends than brothers. Don't get me wrong, its…" Jason leans away from me with a sigh and I instantly snap my mouth shut.

I open my mouth to try to backtrack, but he puts his hand up to stop me, gesturing for me to give him a minute. "I will do anything for both of my brothers and my sister and I know they would do the same for me," he confesses.

"Theresa and I get along great, and Matt and Christian have always been closer to each other than either of them are to me, but Christian and I have had our problems in the past," he concedes.

He grinds his jaw and looks like he's thinking hard about what he wants to say. "I guess you could say, Christian and I have always been a lot alike and we're both like our father. As the oldest, I've always been expected to follow in my dad's footsteps in a way and I always felt like the pressure was on me. I had to get the grades, play football and play it well, go to West Point..." he trails off and I wait for him to continue. "I guess Christian felt like he not only had the same expectations as me, but he also thought he was living in my shadow, and he hated it. What I think pushed him over the edge is when one of his high school girlfriends started hitting on me. I didn't do anything about it at the time, but it didn't matter."

I quickly cover my mouth, trying to keep my reflexive gasp quiet. Jason cringes slightly at my reaction, but I can't help it. My heart feels instant sympathy for Christian, knowing what it feels like to not feel wanted or loved. I know it's not Jason's fault and as long as he didn't do anything about it, it's fine.

He sighs heavily. "Anyway, Christian and I are working on it. He's been great since he's been back with Bree." He glances at me, adding, "He had a rough couple of years when they broke up. I wasn't around a lot, but when I was," he shakes his head, "let's just say I'm really fucking glad he has her." He pauses, "And now that we're both living in the same area, we'll figure it out. He's my brother," he adds as if that's all they need as he shrugs his shoulders.

I nod my head and try to explain my inquiry, "I know it's none of my business. I didn't mean anything by it. I was just curious."

He laughs humorlessly, declaring, "I hope I'm your business."

"I didn't mean," I begin, blushing.

He waves it off chuckling, "It's fine. I like that you want to know about my family, and I am your business," he reiterates.

I smile reluctantly and search my brain for a change of topic. My mind is completely blank except for questions about his family, so I reiterate, "I had a lot of fun with Christian and Bree tonight. We should hang out with them more often."

"We will," Jason easily agrees. "They're meeting us at my parents on Sunday." He closes the distance between us, requesting, "Can we not talk about my brother anymore? Please?" he begs his eyes boring into mine.

With just one look, he knows my answer. My eyes go wide and heat spreads throughout my whole body. He slides one hand behind my neck and the other hooks at my waist. He pulls me into him and holds my gaze before his mouth crashes into mine like he can't wait another second. I can't help but moan in pleasure as he pushes his tongue inside, exploring and tasting me.

"I need you Jason," I whimper wanting to get as close to him as possible. This just isn't close enough!

I squeal when he stands up taking me with him. "Wrap your legs around my waist," he instructs. He slides his hands under my ass and continues to kiss me as he walks to his room. He tears his mouth away as he tosses me on the bed. I prop myself on my elbows so I can look at him. His eyes roam my body causing my breath to speed up. "You are so fucking beautiful, Sara," he murmurs in awe. I can't even open my mouth to speak as I watch him climb on the bed. He slowly crawls over me, kissing me as he goes, on my hip, my belly, my neck and finally my lips. He pulls away and looks into my eyes when he asks, "Are you sure you're ready?"

I don't even have to think about my answer. "I'm positive, Jason. I've never felt like this with anyone. You know the real me and you still want me." My voice cracks as I add, "I love you, Jason."

He kisses me gently and whispers against my lips, "Of course I want you. You're all I want. I love you too, Sara."

I pull him the last inch to me and kiss him hard. I want him to know how happy he makes me. I pull at his shirt and he pulls back, swiftly pulling it over his head. My hands run over the muscles in his shoulders, down his arms and back to his hard chest and abs, muscles like his I didn't think existed in my world. Every part of him I touch, makes me crave more.

I need him to touch me. I push him back slightly, so I can pull my navy sweater over my head. I go to reach back to release my bra and Jason reaches towards me, stopping me. I look up at him confused. He caresses my cheek and stares into my eyes.

"Are you with me?" he prompts softly. My heart gets caught in my throat as I nod my head in confirmation.

This man!

"Let me?" he prods. His hand moves to my back and he releases my breasts with a flick of his fingers. He slides the straps down my arms and tosses it to the side. His eyes move down to my chest and just as my anxiety begins to surface, he pushes it away when he cups my breast and runs his thumb gently over my nipple while he kisses my neck, slowly moving down. His hand moves to my other breast as his tongue shoots out to circle my nipple and take as much of it as he can into his mouth, licking and massaging. He groans and gives my other breast the same attention.

My hands move to his waist and I flick the button of his jeans open. "Off," I demand.

Jason pushes my hands away, refusing, "Not yet." He quickly tugs my jeans off, letting his hands slide lightly along the inside of my legs on the way back up, giving me goosebumps.

As he passes right by my panties and gently digs into my hips with his fingers, I break away from his kiss, begging, "Jason." I have never wanted someone so much in my life. My body is vibrating with heat and need for him. I've never felt this way before. "Please," I plead.

His lips come back to mine as he releases his grip on my hips and his hand slides back down to my bright pink panties lightly passing over me before curling his fingers in the sides and swiftly tugging them off. He touches my core and groans. I can feel how hot and wet I am. I pull away from his lips to catch my breath. He pushes a finger inside of me, but I want him this time. "Jason, I want you now. Please, I need to be close to you."

He looks me in the eyes still pushing his finger in and out of me with my insides on fire. He presses his lips to mine and jumps away from me in one agile movement. He shoves his jeans and boxer briefs off, his eyes never leaving mine. He reaches in his nightstand and pinches a condom between his fingers. He crawls over me, kissing me hungrily. He pulls back to find my gaze again. "Sara, are you with me?" he repeats. I nod my head slowly, my heart beating fast at how much he's caring for me. "I need you to tell me this time, not just nod your head. Are you with me?"

My voice cracks when I answer him, "Yes."

He opens the condom and slides it on as I look at him for the first time. My breath catches at his size, but I quickly focus back on this moment as he places himself between my legs. I feel him at my entrance. I gasp, having trouble catching my breath. He stops, demanding, "Sara, look at me." I look into his eyes and wait. "I need you with me. If you need to stop, tell me. You and I are what matter. Okay?"

"Okay," I whisper throatily.

"I love you, Sara," he declares staring at me intently. His words and the truth of it portrayed in his eyes causes me to melt completely and I truly relax.

He must see it in me too. "I love you, too," I murmur just as he pushes inside me with one quick thrust. He pauses, letting my body adjust to him. "I need you to move," I plead. Doing as I request, he moves slowly at first, but picks up the pace as my breathing gets heavier and faster. I gasp as he changes the angle, hitting my g-spot all the way inside me over and over again and driving me to the brink. "Jason," I breathe his name, wanting to tell him what he's doing to me, but not able to speak.

He begins groaning along with me, still looking into my eyes. His hands roam my arms, my chest, my hips before settling on my ass and pulling me to him. I cling to his shoulders and try to bury my face in his chest, but he won't let me. "I need to see you. I need to know you're with me," he tells me. I press my head back into his pillows and stare at his mouth, the corners turning up slightly. He leans in close, pressing his lips to mine, licking and sucking my tongue and my lips, tasting me and letting me taste him. He breaks our kiss and insists, "Eyes on me." I happily concede to his wishes.

His thrusts become faster and more urgent. "I need you to come, Sara. Please come for me," he pleads. My body can't refuse him. My eyes refuse to stay open as I easily fall over the top into oblivion, my insides throbbing around him over and over again. Just as I start to relax, I feel Jason tense. I force my eyes open, wanting to watch his climax as he thrusts into me a few more times. My body begins coming down from its high as Jason grips me tightly, releasing while his eyes remain on me. After one final grunt, he drops to the mattress as he rolls me over so I'm lying on top of him.

He stays inside of me while we both catch our breath. Tucking my hair behind my ears, he asks, "Are you okay?"

I grin down at him, mumbling, "I'm better than okay."

"Good," he grins back giving my ass a light tap and making me giggle.

"I should get cleaned up," he announces, rolling me to my side. He slowly slides out of me causing me to gasp with the loss. "I'll be right back," he states. He smiles and brushes his lips over mine, before jumping out of bed. I watch his bare ass walk away feeling like I'm in someone else's life right now. Everything feels so surreal. I'm not supposed to have this, have him.

I startle as he climbs back in bed with me, making him chuckle. "I wasn't gone that long," he teases. "Here, I brought this to help clean you up." I look up and see he's holding a wet washcloth in his hands. My throat clogs with what feels like rocks, but I know it's my emotions getting the better of me again. He lifts the sheet and wipes between my legs. I feel my eyes welling up and I take a deep breath trying to keep myself from crying. He tosses the washcloth into his laundry basket, easily sinking it then bringing his focus back to me.

His face immediately clouds with concern. He reaches his hand up to my cheek and brushes it lightly. "Sara, what's wrong? Was that too much too soon?" he prods anxiously.

I shake my head in denial. "No, no." I take a deep breath and my tears inevitably spill over. "That was perfect," I whimper.

"Then, what is it?" he prompts brushing away my tears.

I try to gulp down the rocks in my throat so I can tell him. "I…I've never…nothing has ever been like that. I didn't know sex could be like that." His face changes to one of understanding as well as concern. "I've never even had an orgasm during sex before," I admit embarrassed. "And I've never had someone care for me the way you are showing me you care by everything you do," I confess.

Jason releases a long sigh filled with regret. "Fuck." He takes a couple deep breaths and cradles my face in his hands. "I hate hearing you say that, but I hate it because I don't even like the idea of things being like that for you. You should always be cared for. You should always be cherished. You should always be loved. I hate that you've never really had any of it, but I'm honored to be able to be the one to give it to you as long as you'll let me." His lips meet mine in a slow, sensual kiss, his way of sealing his promise to me.

Chapter 28

Jason

"Thank you for coming with me," I tell Sara earnestly pulling her hand to my lips to give her a kiss. I glance over at her and notice she's fidgeting with her fingers and staring out the window again. "You, okay?" I prompt.

She heaves a sigh and looks at me. "I'm just a little nervous," she confesses.

I chuckle softly. "You've already met them and they already love you. There's no reason to be nervous." She nods her head in acknowledgement. "I just wanted you to be with my family as my girl so they can really get to know you," I try to explain. "My family is important to me and you're important to me. Besides, it won't be all bad, Bree and Christian will be there later for dinner."

She nods, mumbling, "I know. I'm being a little ridiculous."

I shake my head and give her hand a squeeze in support. "You're not being ridiculous. I understand, but you're going to be fine," I encourage her.

As I turn down our road, I can't help but think what a great week we've had together. I'm so happy she's finally opening up to me and she finally seems relaxed with me. I know she trusts me now. I've never had sex as fantastic as it is with her. My body heats just thinking about it. My mind always goes a little haywire at what I want to do with her, but I just pinch my lips together and try not to let my hands wander until I can get her alone. I have no idea how I got so lucky.

I park my truck and grab her face in my hands pulling her to me. I cover her mouth with my own and devour her.

When my heart begins pounding out of control and she starts to whimper I reluctantly break our kiss. I look into her eyes while we both catch our breath.

Smirking, I mumble, "That should get me by for a few minutes."

She laughs and I can see her shoulders relax slightly, which is exactly what I want. I grab my keys and step out of my truck, noticing an old blue Chevy Blazer parked in the driveway. I look at it curiously as I walk around to Sara's side of the car. It looks familiar, but I have no idea who it belongs to. When I get to Sara's door she's halfway out and I pull her the rest of the way down and into my arms giving her one more chaste kiss. "It will be fine," I reiterate.

I take Sara to the back door so we can throw our things in the mudroom. I pull the door open and guide Sara in before me. We take off our coats and pull our boots off as I yell to my parents to let them know we're here. "Mom, Dad?"

"In here, Jason!" my dad yells. I cringe slightly at the tone of his voice. It sounds like something might be wrong, but I don't want to alarm Sara, so I keep it to myself. Maybe it has to do with whoever's Blazer that is out there.

I grab Sara's hand and hold on tightly, guiding her towards our kitchen and living room. We find my dad standing in the living room with his arms crossed over his chest and a slight scowl on his face. He's facing my mom and a blonde woman whom she looks like she's comforting for some reason. With what happened with Theresa this past year, I worry someone we know might be hurt or worse and my steps slow, my entire body filling with tension.

When we're almost upon the living room, my father catches my eye, deepening his scowl. He looks full of disappointment directed at me causing my gut to instantly fill with dread. "Dad?" I prod hesitantly. He glances down at the woman, nodding his head.

She stands and turns to me. My heart stops the moment I recognize Christian's ex-girlfriend, Lexi. I glance down at her very pregnant belly. I don't think I can breathe. "What the fuck are you doing here?" I barely rasp out.

"Jason," my mom berates me. I don't apologize though. I can't.

Tears are streaming down her face, but she doesn't bother to wipe them away. She cries, "I'm sorry. I changed my mind. I couldn't do it." She drops back down on the couch, sobbing with her head in her hands.

It's then I realize that Sara has pulled away from me and has started backing away. My chest tightens, not caring about anything in this room except for her. I look to her pleading with my eyes for her to stay, "Sara." She shakes her head in refusal, looking paler by the second. I reach for her, desperate to hold on, but she turns and flees towards the bathroom.

I step in the same direction to follow her, but my dad steps in front of me stopping me in my tracks. "You need to handle this now, Jason. I know you want to go after her, but I'll call Christian and Bree to see if they can come early to help Sara. They're just down the street at her house." I feel sick, my head having trouble catching up with reality, but I nod my head in defeat. My dad turns to leave the room heading down the hall to his office.

I run my hands through my hair and grip them tightly behind my neck staring at the ceiling. What the fuck am I going to do? "I'm going to leave you to talk with Jason," my mom murmurs before she gives her one more hug and stands. She walks by me giving my arm a squeeze in support before she heads upstairs, but I can't even look at her, not wanting to see the disappointment on her face.

"You're pregnant," I state the obvious. She doesn't say a word, but her sobbing begins to slow down. "You lied to me," I accuse her.

"No, when I told you I wasn't going to keep it, I meant it," she insists. "I said you couldn't change my mind and that's true too. You couldn't do anything."

"So, what changed and why didn't you tell me?" I ask her through my teeth.

She takes a few calming breaths before she finally speaks. "When Axel found out I was pregnant, we got back together. He wanted me to keep the baby. But he just found out it might not be his, so..." she trails off and wipes her tears away.

"So, were you ever going to tell me?" I challenge. "What were you going to do when you have the baby?" I yell at her.

She shrugs her shoulders. "I don't know. I was hoping when I had the baby, I would just know it was his and I would never have to tell you!"

I grind my jaw and breathe through my nose trying to control my breathing. I need to go check on Sara. I can't deal with this shit. Just then, the front door flies open and Christian runs in followed by Bree. "What's wrong?" he screams. I don't know what my dad said when he called him, but he obviously didn't tell him very much. With everything Christian has been through, when there's something wrong, he'll jump to the worst-case scenario more often than not.

That's when he notices Lexi and his eyes go wide in shock. "What the fuck are you doing here?" he repeats my original question, his voice strained. "You're pregnant," he states just like me. His eyes go back and forth between her and me a few times before realization hits. "No, no, no, no, no!" he yells slowly getting louder. "Bree, go find Sara, please," he urges.

"Where is she?" she asks me quietly.

I try to speak through the thick wall of poison tearing up my insides, "She's down the hall in the bathroom. Please take care of her. I'll be there as soon as I can." She nods her head in acknowledgement and rushes out of the room.

224

"Christian it's not what you think," she begins but he puts his hand up towards her shaking his head to stop her from continuing. He doesn't want to hear a word she has to say, but I don't really blame him.

"This..." he seethes with barely controlled anger. "This is why I knew... I fucking knew she should stay away from you!"

"You don't know what you're talking about Christian!" I tell him quietly, barely getting the words out and not quite believing them myself.

"Don't I? Everyone always thinks you're so fucking perfect," he grumbles, shaking his head in disappointment. "I wanted you to prove me wrong, Jason! You're my brother, but this?" He shakes his head again before turning his back to me. He stops just before leaving the room and mumbles quietly over his shoulder, "Bree and I are going to get Sara out of here and drive her home. She doesn't need to be here to witness anymore of this shit."

"I need to talk to her," I beg. "She's everything to me."

He nods in understanding but continues to stand up for her. "If she wants to talk to you now, that's her choice. I wouldn't stop her. Honestly though, maybe talking to Sara should wait. You have other things you need to take care of and she might need some time to process," he suggests. "I know I do."

I clear my throat and try to ignore the pain consuming me, clawing at me from the inside out. "Christian?" He halts waiting for me to speak. I step towards him, so Lexi doesn't hear me and speak quietly, "I'm sorry. I know you haven't thought about her in years, but she should've been off-limits and I'm sorry. I made a mistake. One that will be with me for the rest of my life," I admit. I feel a stabbing pain in my chest with the truth of that statement. Whether or not that baby is mine, I will never forget this.

He nods his head in acknowledgement before he asks, "You never touched her back then?" His question feels like a punch in the gut, but it's exactly what I deserve.

"No! Never, it just happened once. We were..." I attempt to explain.

He shakes his head letting me know he doesn't need or want to hear more. "I'm not the one that needs to hear this. She hasn't been my girlfriend since high school. I'm with the love of my life now. I don't give a shit who she dates, but I do care what happens to her if she's carrying my niece or nephew." I cringe at the thought. "You need to figure it out and then decide what you're going to do."

He pauses like he's unsure if he should say anything. He grimaces and finally speaks, "I know I'm your younger brother, but just some friendly advice. If you are half as crazy about Sara as I think you are, talk to her. Be honest. She needs to know what's going on. Include her in your decisions if she's willing to after she has a chance to wrap her head around it all. Trust me, I speak from experience." He opens his mouth then closes it again before turning and walking out of the room.

Standing here with Lexi behind me on the couch I feel completely alone. I feel as if my whole life just crashed and burned around me. What makes it even worse is knowing that even when I get all the answers I need, I don't know if I'll be able to put the pieces of the life I want back together again. That scares the shit out of me. My chest tightens at the thought of losing Sara and I struggle to breathe.

What the fuck am I going to do?

I slowly turn and trudge back towards Lexi when all I want to do is barge into the bathroom and make Sara talk to me. I sit down opposite her in one of the chairs facing the couch. I rest my elbows on my knees and drop my head, gripping the back of my neck tightly. We sit in silence both waiting for the other to speak, but I don't even know where to begin. I'm not able to get my mind or my heart off Sara.

A few minutes later, I hear a door open and my head snaps up, hoping to see Sara. Christian walks in front of her and Bree, blocking my view. As I move, he comes to stand in front of me, while Bree rushes Sara past. "Sara," I call hopefully, but she won't even glance in my direction. She walks towards the back of the house with Bree, ripping my heart right out of my chest in the process.

"We're leaving," Christian informs me. "We're headed to Bree's for a little while, then we'll drive back to Portland a little later. We'll take care of her," he proclaims, attempting to reassure me as he grips my shoulder. Although, I think he already knows nothing he says will help. I nod my head numbly and drop it again as they all leave, taking my heart with them.

"I'm sorry," Lexi whispers hoarsely. I shrug in response with tears clouding my vision.

What can I even say? This is my fault.

Chapter 29

Sara

I'm a mess. I can't believe I let myself fall for him. Obviously, she got pregnant before I even met him, but she can't exactly be a one-night stand either. She knew where he lived and she knew his family. He said he hadn't had a girlfriend in a long time, so what does that make her? I threw up in the bathroom at Jason's parents' house. I threw up a few more times at Bree's house. Every time I think about Jason with that girl, I feel like I'm going to throw up again and again.

We stayed at Bree's house until she deemed me well enough to ride in the back of Christian's truck back to Portland with them. When I got home, I was thankful to find a note from Liz telling me she was staying at Blake's and she would see me after classes tomorrow. There's no way I was going to class, but no one needed to know that except me. When she walked in last night, I told her I didn't feel well right before I locked myself in my room for the rest of the night. I know she didn't really believe me, but since I wasn't eating and I've been throwing up, what choice did she have?

Today, she's done pretending. Liz pounds on my bedroom door relentlessly. "Sara, let me in! I'm done with your sulking I want to know what's wrong." I sigh, staring at my door as she continues knocking relentlessly. "I'm not going anywhere. I'm done for the day and Blake is working at the outlets. You're stuck with me, even if I have to annoy the crap out of you!"

"Ugh, fine!" I groan. I roll off my bed and stomp to my door, unlock it and let her in. Relieved to hear the pounding stop, I trudge back to my bed and flop down with a defeated sigh. "What? Why are you so obsessed to get into my room to talk to me?" I inquire with exasperation. "I'm not much fun when I'm sick," I add as my last shot attempt to maintain my lie.

Liz raises her eyebrows at me in challenge, telling me she knows I'm lying. "What's wrong? I have never seen you this visibly upset, not even when you and Brad broke up." I cringe at the sound of his name. "Did something happen with Jason?"

I gulp and reply throatily, "Yeah."

She sits on the corner of my bed and puts her hand on my ankle in comfort. "What happened, Sara? Please talk to me," she pleads when I don't respond. I sigh in resignation and scoot myself back to make more room for her. She arranges herself more comfortably on my bed and waits for me to say something.

I close my eyes and take a deep breath to gather my courage to speak. "I never meant to like him so much, Liz," I confess brokenly.

"Oh sweetie, it's okay," she claims. She leans towards me trying to encourage me.

I shake my head, insisting, "Not really. I really fell for him, Liz. I've never fallen that hard for anyone. Not even Brad."

Liz bites her lip before she tells me, "I understand, Sara. That's how I feel about Blake."

I look her in the eyes and I see the truth in them. Now I finally get it. I really understand what they have. The only difference is with them, Blake feels the same way. "I'm not meant to have something like you guys have," I whisper painfully.

Liz's mouth drops open in shock. "What? Why?"

I shake off her surprise, having never said anything like this to her in all our years as friends. "I'm meant to have a relationship that will help our family business," I state and shrug like it doesn't matter.

I didn't think Liz's eyes could go any wider, but they do. "You can't possibly mean that!" Liz screams at me.

I nod my head in affirmation. "I do, but it doesn't matter."

"It does matter," she insists. "You deserve to be happy and have something wonderful like what I have with Blake. Something I don't think I would have if it wasn't for you, so yeah, you deserve to have that! What happened with Jason to make you say these things?" she questions incredulously.

I shake my head again in denial. "I'm saying these things because that's the way things are for me," I claim, sighing in defeat. "As for what happened with Jason," I flinch as his name passes over my lips, "he has responsibilities that have nothing to do with me and I don't think I can be around for any of it." Her eyes scrunch together in confusion and I further explain, "We went to his parents' house for a quick visit and there was a very pregnant gorgeous girl there waiting for him." A few tears slip out and I quickly wipe them away as I notice Liz's attempt to hold back her gasp. "Bree and Christian brought me back," I enlighten her.

Liz takes a few moments to gather her thoughts and composure before speaking. "Have you talked to Jason?" she finally asks cautiously. I shake my head in response. "He hasn't tried to call you?" she prods appearing surprised.

I wince. "He has, I just can't answer. I don't want to talk to him," I admit as I begin to cry full force again. "I...I can't hear him tell me about another girl. A girl it seems is going to have his child soon," I gasp brokenly. "How am I supposed to do that?"

"Oh Sara, I'm so sorry," she murmurs and wraps her arms around me. She rubs my back just like Jason does when he tries to comfort me making me squeeze my eyes shut even tighter.

"Why does every little thing remind me of him?" I prod practically begging her for an answer. "You're right, Liz, nothing about Jason and me has been anything like Brad and I ever were, but maybe that's my problem. It hurts so much," I cry, attempting to rub the ache away in my chest.

When I calm down enough, I pull away from her. She grabs onto my hands and tries to look me in the eyes when she advises, "I know you're not quite ready yet, but you need to talk to Jason. You don't know the story. You can't just ignore him. Start by listening to him. I'm not saying let him tell you anything and take him back, I'm saying get the truth out of him and then make your decisions. You deserve that. Only you can decide what you want and what's best for you, but how can you do that without hearing all the facts?" she prompts.

I push my hands into my face to relieve some of the pressure from crying. "I know you're right, but I'm scared Liz. I keep fretting over every little possibility. I don't know if I can handle the truth. What's going to happen? If he's going to be a dad and it's someone else's kid," I gulp down the painful lump in my throat, "I just can't," I sob.

Liz squeezes my hand in support. "I know you're scared Sara, but you have to at least talk to him. You're making yourself sick over this!" She lets me cry in her arms continuing to comfort me and attempt to calm me down.

Eventually, I sigh in defeat. "Fine, I know you're right. I'll talk to him." Liz gives me a small smile of encouragement before I add, "I can't today. I'll answer him tomorrow."

Liz nods in acceptance. "Okay. Can I get you something to eat?" she offers. I groan and shake my head in disgust. The thought of eating makes my stomach turn. She grimaces but accepts my answer. "Do you want to watch a movie with me then?" I shrug my shoulders and she jump at my reluctant response. "I'll go pick one out and make some popcorn. Just bring your blanket and a pillow," she instructs before running out of the room.

I do as she says, slowly trudging to the couch and curling myself up into a ball, attempting to protect myself. I mindlessly stare at the TV screen, barely even seeing the images that pass in front of me. The movie ends in what feels like seconds as well as days if that's even possible. She puts a second movie in before she drops back to the opposite end of the couch.

The doorbell rings causing my whole body to go rigid. Liz takes one look at me and offers, "I'll get it," swiftly pushing herself off the couch.

"No," I yell instinctively reaching for her arm. Her eyebrows shoot to her hairline as she looks at me like I've lost my mind.

"Sara, it's me, Jason. I know you're home. Please talk to me," he begs agonizingly through the door. If possible, my heart breaks a little more the moment I hear his voice sounding so broken.

I shake my head, begging, "I can't Liz. Not yet." I look at her pleading with my eyes.

She nods in acknowledgement. "Okay, Sara, just let me answer the door." I let her go and watch her as she strides away. I hold my breath, close my eyes and attempt to listen for his voice over the pounding of my heart.

"Hey Liz, I need to talk to Sara," he demands.

"She doesn't want to see you, Jason," she tells him honestly.

"Please, I just need time to tell her, to explain. She has to give me the time." He sounds incredibly insistent, even desperate. All I want to do is jump off this couch and into his arms, but I can't.

"Try calling her tomorrow, maybe she'll pick up," she suggests.

I hear his groan of frustration and defeat. "Tell her," I hear him pause and I strain to hear his last words, "No, I'll tell her when I see her. Just tell her I'm thinking about her. I'm not giving up on us," he proclaims.

I hear Liz mumble, "Bye, Jason," just before I hear the click of our door. I listen to her footsteps approaching me, inhaling a shaky breath. "You sure you don't want to see him today?" she prods cautiously. I shrug my shoulders in response keeping my eyes closed. "Okay," she concurs, thankfully giving me the quiet I need right now.

I wake up, my entire body aching with tension. I try moving my head from side to side to get the kinks out before stretching my stiff legs and arms out in front of me. I finally pry open my eyes to a view of my living room. "I fell asleep on the couch," I groan in pain.

"Yup," I hear from somewhere close. I peak over the back of the couch and find Liz standing over me with a bowl of cereal in her hands. "I didn't want to wake you. I was afraid you wouldn't go back to sleep and you really needed the rest."

I whine, "But now my body hurts."

"That's not completely from sleeping on the couch," she states reminding me of why I'm curled so tightly in a ball, Jason. Even the thought of his name makes my stomach flip.

I hear my cell phone ringing from my bedroom and I pull my covers over my head. "Ugh!" I still don't want to face reality.

"It's been ringing for the past three hours. Maybe you should answer it," she suggests. I pull the covers down, glaring at her. She responds by prompting me, "You promised."

I grunt, "Fine!"

As soon as the words leave my mouth, I watch as Liz runs to the table in the kitchen, sets her bowl down, runs into my room and quickly back out. Stepping up to me, she holds my phone out to me with her eyebrows raised in challenge.

I glare at her again when I jerk it away from her. "Who was calling all morning anyway?" she asks innocently.

"Jason," I grumble even though we both know what the answer to that question was without looking. Just whispering his name makes my heart ache.

"Call him," she encourages me again.

I look at her and then back to my phone. Instead of calling him back, I hit my messages and type out a quick text without reading any of the ones he sent in the last few days and there are a lot.

If you still want to talk, I'll come to you. What time?

I'm not surprised he immediately texts me back.

As soon as you can get here.
I'll be waiting for you.

Ok.

I answer not giving him a time. I have to shower and clean myself up, but he said he'd wait for me. I'll be there before he has to leave for his shift at the pub. If I remember correctly, he goes in at 4 today. I hear another text come through, but I don't even bother looking. I drop my phone on the couch instead.

"So?" Liz prods inquisitively.

"I'm going to his place to talk to him," I respond quietly, my stomach twisting into knots.

"Good! I can make you something to eat while you shower," she offers.

I shake my head, refusing, "That's okay, I'm not really hungry." I shove myself up off the couch and stretch my sore body. I stiffly walk towards the bathroom to clean myself up.

"You have to eat something," Liz pleads with me. "You've barely eaten anything in three days!"

She's right, so instead of worrying her more, I accept her offer. "Fine, make me something. But keep it light. My stomach is still really queasy," I admit.

I step into the bathroom and close the door quickly behind me. I turn on the shower and strip down before assessing myself critically in the mirror. I don't like what I see reflected back at me. "Brad is right," I whisper as a tear escapes. I turn towards the shower feeling completely hollow inside. I don't want to hear what Jason has to say because I know I'll have to give him up when our conversation is over.

I just know it! That's the last thing I want.

I always knew I never deserved something good like this.

Chapter 30

Jason

I pace my small apartment waiting for her. It's been three fucking days and she's finally coming to talk to me. I swear these have been the longest three days of my life. I glance at the clock for the tenth time in the past hour and a half. She said she was coming, so I'm assuming she will.

I can't help but ask myself, what if she doesn't?

At that thought, there's a knock at my door and I rush to take the last couple strides to the door. I throw it open and I completely stop breathing at the sight of her. She's standing in my doorway looking tired, nervous and so fucking beautiful. I catch my breath and grumble, "Hi," with a relieved smile. I flinch when she gives me one of her fake smiles in return. I gesture for her to come inside and she stiffly walks past me. I close my eyes and take in her smell, crowding her as she passes.

When she has a little room, she spins on her heal to glare at me. "Let's just get this over with," she snaps. I cringe and quickly turn to shut my door, so she doesn't see my reaction. "Where are we doing this?" she prods nonchalantly, breaking my heart even more.

She's acting like she's already made her decision, like it's already over between us and I can't let that happen. I grind my jaw holding in my temper with her attitude. I have to remind myself she has every right to have an attitude with me right now. It's my job to change her mind. I step up to her and feel her body tense even more as I gently guide her to my couch. She sits all the way in one corner. "Can I get you anything to drink?" I offer.

"I guess I could maybe use some water?" she softly requests as more of a question.

I nod my head in acknowledgement and turn towards the kitchen. Focusing on the job at hand, I try to pull myself together while I grab a glass of water for both of us and come back around the couch. I hand her a glass and set mine on the coffee table. Slowly, I sit in the middle of the couch, giving her some space, but not as much as I know she wants right now, but I'm desperate to be near her. "I'm glad you're here," I tell her honestly.

There's a slight change in her eyes, but it disappears as quickly as it came. "I need you to tell me about the girl, Jason," she urges uncomfortably.

I nod my head and grind my jaw. I run my hands over my short hair before gripping the back of my neck. I lean back on the couch so I can watch her reactions to everything I have to tell her and hope she understands. "First, I need you to know I didn't lie to you. I haven't had a relationship in a really long time. Lexi and I were never in a relationship."

She cringes when I say her name and turns her doubtful eyes on me. "I know how it must look, but Lexi was Christian's girlfriend back in high school," I explain. Her visible wince makes me pause.

"I thought you guys weren't originally from around here," she accuses looking hurt and confused.

"We aren't. We know her from when we lived in Maryland. Christian was in high school at the time. She goes to college in upstate New York now, not far from West Point," I elaborate.

I see understanding covering her features, but it's not what she thinks. "After I graduated West Point, as you know, I wasn't really sure what I wanted to do with my life. I'm still trying to figure that out," I mumble. "Anyway, I stayed there and eventually started working as a bartender at a local bar. She came in a few times with her friends or with her boyfriend and we caught up a little when she recognized me."

"I'm sure you did," she mumbles under her breath.

"It wasn't like that," I argue, trying to help her understand. "Lexi was Christian's ex-girlfriend and there was some bad history between all of us, so I wasn't going to do a fucking thing. For me it was just nice to see someone I knew. Besides the fact that half the time she came she was with her boyfriend."

I pause taking a sip of my water and Sara asks hesitantly, "What do you mean bad history?"

I grimace not wanting to tell her, but I know I have to be completely honest. "When she was dating Christian, she would make a point for their dates to be at our house when she knew I was home from college for the weekend. When Christian wasn't looking or when he was not in the room, she would flirt with me. At first, I thought it was harmless, but she started getting more forward, like walking into the bathroom on me after a shower. Well, at one of Christian's pool parties she asked me where she could get a towel. I should've known she knew, but I didn't even think. Christian was inside the house grabbing more snacks, so I went back to the cabana to grab her a towel. She followed me in, shut the door and dropped her top. Christian walked in with her standing in just her bikini bottoms. I didn't do anything, but it didn't matter. He blamed me for a long time." I grind my jaw, hating the pain that caused my brother.

"She was the one you told me about," Sara whispers almost inaudibly looking pained. My breath catches at her meaning. I forgot I ever mentioned her. I told her she was part of the problem with Christian and I, now she might be having my baby. I'm such an asshole. I try to breathe through the pain when I realize at least part of her agony at this realization is for my brother, not me.

I take another deep breath and try to continue, "Anyway, I hadn't seen her for years when she showed up at the bar I worked at. She seemed to have grown up. She said she'd been dating Axel for a couple years and they were happy. So, I forgave her for her bullshit and we talked when she came around with him or her friends. Well, one night right when I was finishing up my shift she came in crying. Her boyfriend broke up with her and she was really upset, so I stayed and had a few drinks with her."

I pause taking in Sara's features, which have returned to looking like stone, giving nothing away. I wish she would give me something. I take deep breath before continuing, "When it was time for the bar to close, she was too drunk to drive. I asked her where she lived so I could get her a cab, but she wouldn't tell me. I checked her license, but all she had was the one from her hometown and a college ID. I eventually gave up and said she could sleep it off at my place. When we got there though, she wanted to drink more, so we both did. The next morning, we woke up naked in my bed," I confess, a wave of regret washing over me again.

With my last comment, a small noise escapes Sara. I reach for her wanting desperately to comfort her, but she flinches away further into the corner of my couch making me cringe as my chest tightens. "I knew I'd made a mistake and I knew then I was done with one-night stands. It never should've happened, but it was a long time ago, long before I ever met you," I tell her in hopes it means something. She stares at me blankly waiting for me to continue.

"I didn't see her again for a while after that night. When she did show up again at the bar, it was to tell me she was pregnant. She admitted she didn't know if it was Axel's or mine, but she told me she wasn't going to keep it and no one would change her mind." I laugh humorlessly. "Obviously that's not true since she's still pregnant. When she told Axel she was pregnant, they got back together. She however, didn't tell him it might not be his. Recently, someone they know who was at the bar the night she went home with me told him. He confronted her right before kicking her out." I need to finish and get her to look at me. "When she first told me she was pregnant, Theresa had recently had her accident. I knew I would be moving here, but I didn't have a place yet, so I gave her my parents' address and phone number in case things changed, but I never heard from her."

"Until now," she mutters irritably. I nod my head stiffly, hoping she'll look my way for her answer. "What are you going to do?" she rasps out continuing to stare at her lap.

"I honestly don't know, Sara. I need to know if this child is mine," I admit warily. "For everyone's sake, I hope its Axel's. I'll do right for that child if it's mine, but I want a family some day with the woman I'm in love with and I want my kids to have that too." I cautiously scoot closer to her. "No matter what, I don't want to do any of this without you."

She looks up at me and meets my gaze for the first time, her agony obvious. "Jason," she rasps. Shaking her head slightly, she stammers, "I...I don't...I don't know if I can do that." I watch her Adam's apple bob up and down, pleading with her through my eyes. "I'm not ready for that, for..." she trails off and tears her eyes from mine making my heart drop into my gut.

I shake my head. "I'm not ready either, especially with someone who's not you, but I'm the one who fucked up. I know it's a lot to ask of you Sara and maybe even selfish, but I want you with me, no matter what happens with Lexi."

Sara flinches when I say Lexi's name, squeezing my heart. "So, when will you find out?" she asks so quietly I almost miss it as a couple tears slide down her cheeks.

"Soon," I choke out. "She's due in a few weeks. She said her doctor said she could have the baby any day now. After the baby is born, they can do a DNA test."

She nods her head rigidly in understanding. "So, what happens until then?" I look at her confused. "Do you go to the doctor with her? Will you be with her when the baby is born?" she questions, her voice breaking and she quickly looks away from me.

"I'm so sorry, Sara. I hate that you're hurting and I hate even more that it's my fault!" I scoot behind her and wrap my arms around her. She flinches and doesn't look at me, but she doesn't push me away either, so I'll take it. "Please," I beg her, a tear escaping out of the corner of my eye. I just pray I'm not asking for more than she's ready to give. I know she has a lot of her own problems with her family and I'm afraid she'll think adding mine to all of that will be too much for her to handle. I wouldn't blame her, it's too much for anyone, but I don't want to let her go.

My cell phone rings, but I don't move. As soon as the ringing stops, it picks back up again and Sara whispers, "You better answer it."

I sigh and give her one more squeeze from behind. I reluctantly let her go to reach for my phone. Lexi's name flashes on the screen and my heart plummets. Fuck, I have to answer this. I glance over at Sara warily as I do. "Uh, hello?"

"Jason, I'm having pains. Your parents are taking me to the hospital. You have to meet us there," she gasps sounding frantic.

"Okay, okay. I'll be there," I answer and quickly hang up. Sara glances at me and waits for me to say something. "Um, that was Lexi," I reveal uncomfortably. "She's having some pains and my parents are taking her to the hospital."

Raw fear passes over me at the look Sara gives me after I speak. It starts at my chest and spreads to my limbs like tiny knifes stabbing me over and over again. "Your parents are taking her to the hospital?" she asks brokenly.

"Um, yeah. Like I said, Axel kicked her out and she said she couldn't go to her parents, so she's staying with my family," I ramble. With each word that comes out of my mouth I watch her heart shattering through her eyes. I rush to fix it, only making it worse, "I have to help her. It's the right thing to do. If she's carrying my baby, she has a part of me I have to protect."

Sara fumbles reaching for her things and getting to her feet with tears streaming down her face now. "Um, I better get going," she stammers.

I reach for her needing to wrap her in my arms and comfort her. She steps around me and cringes away from me, breaking my heart even more. "Sara, please. Don't go," I implore desperately.

"You need to go to your family, Jason and I need to go," she cries backing towards the door before spinning on her heel and running out.

The slam of the door makes me flinch. I grab the thing closest to me, which happens to be a throw pillow and whip it across the room. "Fuck!" I scream. I run my hands over the top of my head to the back of my neck and grip tightly. I stare at the ceiling wondering how the fuck I could be so stupid. Forcing myself to move, I grind my jaw and drop my hands stomping over to grab my coat and keys before following her out the door.

As I reach the back parking lot, the only thing left of Sara is the tracks from her car in the snow. My whole chest feels like a bulldozer is compressing it. I don't blame her, but I'm not giving up on her. I can't lose her. I'm supposed to be protecting her, not hurting her. I squeeze my eyes shut tight trying to forget the pain I saw in her and this time, knowing it's my fault destroys me.

"Fuck!" I scream again, feeling helpless and completely defeated. I take a few calming breaths before I jump in my truck and drive to the hospital.

Chapter 31

Sara

For the first time in my life, I'm truly struggling with putting on my happy face. My body aches, but I feel completely hollowed out inside. Or maybe I'm trying not to acknowledge any of my feelings. It's just too painful.

I keep telling myself this is for the better. Jason wants to have a family and Lexi is already giving it to him. I get that the baby might not be his, but she's already moved in with his family. Jason and his family are already taking care of her as if she's one of them. It might be the right thing to do, but if the baby is his...being so close to all of that and knowing her for so many years, how could he not fall in love with the mother of his child? He could love her, although she's his brother's ex. I wonder how Christian is taking all of this.

But what if the baby is the other guy's baby? It might not even matter. Jason's the one going through everything with her now. He's the one who's there for her. All she has to do is call and he drops everything for her, even me. I groan, feeling slightly irrational, but I can't help it. How can anyone be rational in a situation like this?

It's been just over a week since I've seen him and Jason has called every day until yesterday. I didn't ever answer, but I've listened to every single message he's left for me. Lexi was just having Braxton Hicks, which are basically contractions attempting to prep your body for when the real thing happens. Besides, he's just been saying he's sorry, he loves me and asks me to call him. His last message sounded defeated. He said he understands and he hopes for the best for me.

243

So, I guess that's it.

I pushed him away and he's completely given up on me. Jason's gone and so is my heart. I'm probably better off without it for a while anyway. I'm not crying anymore, but I've been going through the motions of my life. Doing what I have to do and no more, feeling completely hopeless. Liz says I look like a zombie. She keeps trying to get me to go out with her and Blake, but I know I'd just ruin their night.

My phone rings and my eyes jump to the screen, with a slight irrational flare of hope. My dad's name immediately squashes my unconscious dream. I answer the phone with a sigh, "Hi, Dad."

"Sara, pick up your attitude. There's an event tomorrow night at the Portland Science Center. I need you there with your date for an 8 p.m. ribbon cutting of a new exhibit. Formal dress and suit or tux for your date," he quickly spits out the information to me. "Got it?" he prompts.

"Um, Dad, I can't make it," I mumble.

He clears his throat, emphasizing, "You will. Your brother can't be there this time. He has an exam. I need you to be there. There's a reason I let you stay close to home."

"Um, I won't have a date," I whisper even quieter.

"That's good news. Brad will escort you. He'll pick you up at seven," he states happily right before he hangs up on me, giving me no chance to argue.

I close my eyes feeling defeated. Of course, that's what he would do. I really don't know why I'm at all surprised.

My phone beeps with a text from Brad.

I knew you'd come back to me.

I groan with disgust, not knowing what the hell I'm going to do, but I don't know if I really care.

The next night I walk out of my room in a long black dress with spaghetti straps and a black sequined wrap to keep me warm. I have black strappy shoes with a two-inch heal on my feet. I figure, I can use them for protection if necessary. Liz whistles, looking me up and down. "You look good, Sara. Are you going out with Jason?" she asks looking relieved.

I flinch, my heart squeezing at the sound of his name. "No, I have an event for my dad at the Science Museum. Brad's picking me up," I confess.

Her eyebrows unsurprisingly shoot up into her hairline. "Brad?" she repeats.

I sigh in defeat. "It's not a date. It doesn't matter anyway."

"Are you sure he knows it's not a date?" she questions, but I don't answer. "If Jason finds out, this will really hurt him," she advises. I cringe but remain quiet. She steps closer to me, assessing me, making me slightly uncomfortable. Her eyebrows draw in, looking more and more concerned the closer she gets. "Are you okay?" she asks cautiously.

I try to give her a smile, mumbling, "Yeah, I'm great."

She shakes her head. "You're looking a little pale and actually kinda' thin. Are you *really*, okay?"

I shrug off her comments. "I'm fine. I'm just a little tired with everything," I tell her vaguely. "I'll leave tonight as soon as the speech is over and I'll be back in bed. No worries."

Liz looks like she doesn't believe me, but she's not sure how to get the truth out of me. She opens her mouth to say something else just as the doorbell rings. I grab my coat and purse rushing to answer it.

"Bye, Liz," I call over my shoulder as I shove past Brad and out the door. I'm not ready to give her a chance to say any more.

"Boy, you're anxious to see me," he grins.

"Don't get your hopes up," I declare stomping over to his car. He chuckles following right behind me.

We arrive at the event and I flinch away from Brad every time he attempts to even guide me with his hand. I know he's getting frustrated with me, but I don't care. He looks like he's about to confront me when my dad steps over to us with a broad smile. "Sara," he formally greets me. I give him my obligatory kiss on the cheek. "Brad," he states, smiling as they shake hands. "Glad you made it."

"Good to see you, Sir," Brad answers back and I fight to roll my eyes.

My father's eyes come back to me critically. I grimace, waiting for his bite. He finally nods his head with a smile directed at me. "Looks like you're finally listening to me," he claims with satisfaction. I can't help but look at him with confusion. "You're finally losing some weight, although you could still lose a little more off the back, but you have a nice dress and the perfect date."

He looks proud of himself while I'm struggling to keep my mouth closed and not cause a scene. "What the fuck," I mumble just as he turns away. Brad must see the look on my face because he tries to pull me back to stop me, but no one can hold me back anymore. I'm done with being treated like this. At this point I have absolutely nothing more to lose that means anything to me.

"Dad!" I grit out poking him hard in the arm.

He turns to me with a warning glare, "Easy, Sara. Whatever you want to say, now is not the time."

"Now is the perfect time! I'm done catering to what you want. You're so concerned about my weight?" I ask accusingly. "Maybe that's because I've barely eaten anything in nearly two weeks and when I do choke anything down, I throw it right back up. But you probably think that's a good thing cause I gotta' look the part, right Dad?" I throw out bitterly. "And Brad isn't my date. He was just my ride to get here." I notice Brad flinch, but I don't care. "I don't give a shit about the dress or the shoes or whatever the hell we're here for! I don't want to be a trophy daughter or wife!" I glare at my dad.

"Calm down, young lady. Go home and tomorrow you will fix the mess you made," my dad insists with barely controlled anger. "I didn't raise you to cause a scene. You're acting like your mother again," he sneers.

"There's nothing to fix," I state truthfully. "I'm standing up for me for once. I don't give a crap what you think."

"Keep it up and I won't be funding your last year of college," he threatens. I still don't care and continue to glare at him as he turns to Brad. I glance over and am a little surprised when I notice he seems to be frozen in shock. My dad pokes him in the chest and demands gruffly, "Take her home, now!"

I gladly take him up on this, spinning on my heel towards the exit. I'm halfway out the door when Brad appears behind me trying to put my arms in my coat. I let him help me and escort me out to his truck. Luckily, he remains silent on the ride home. I'm just not in the mood for any more arguments tonight from anyone.

Before I open my door, he stops me and says, "I know you had a stressful night, so I'm going to give you time, but we need to fix us. I really do miss you, Sara." I stare at him blankly, not answering. He finally lets me go with a sigh and a kiss on the corner of my mouth. I can't even react to that. I'm done giving him anything.

I step into my apartment and pull the door closed behind me, feeling relieved the night is over. "You're home early," Liz mumbles from the couch as soon as I walk in the door.

"Yeah," I grumble.

"You, okay?" she asks looking concerned.

I take a step towards her when the bathroom door opens and Blake steps out. "Hi, Sara. You look nice tonight," he compliments striding towards the couch and Liz.

I give him a fake smile, proclaiming, "Thanks. I'm exhausted. I'm going to bed early. Pretend like I'm not even here."

"You don't have to go," Liz states. "You can watch a movie with us," she offers.

I keep side stepping towards my bedroom and respond, "Thanks Liz, but I think I need to get some sleep."

She looks me over before slowly nodding her head, probably agreeing I need sleep. "Okay, goodnight, Sara."

"Goodnight, Liz. Goodnight, Blake," I call over my shoulder as I step into my room and shut the door.

I kick off my shoes and quickly shimmy out of the dress. I pull on a pair of fuzzy black pajama pants and a long sleeved thermal red tee before climbing into bed. I don't care that I didn't brush my teeth or wash my face. I just want to get in bed.

My phone pings with a text right as I pull up the covers. I roll over and snatch it off the nightstand and bring it up to my face. It's from Jason. My heart begins pounding again for what feels like the first time in forever with just the sight of his name. I hesitantly move to open the text and hold my breath while I read.

I don't know if I should be sending this, but some part of me needs to be with you today. Lexi had a baby boy today. I stayed in the waiting room until after she delivered. He's beautiful. Axel showed up too. They're going to do the DNA test tomorrow and try to put a rush on it, so it only takes a few days. There's so much more I want to say, but for now I just need you to know I miss you. I wish you were here with me. I haven't stopped loving you.

I drop my phone to my bed feeling so much. I curl into a ball and wrap my arms around myself and squeeze as tightly as I can, trying to hold myself together. Jason might be a father now. The thought of him holding a baby, his baby, consumes me and I can't help but wish the baby were mine. I'm not ready for something like that, but I'm selfish. I don't want Jason to have that without me. I hate where he is right now and the feelings, he's experiencing that he may never experience again for the first time. I don't want the baby to be his, but I think I want that more for me than for him and that just makes me hate myself even more.

I miss him so much that everything physically hurts inside and out. I don't deserve him anyway. I can't handle this kind of pain. Maybe it's better I find out now because I know eventually, he'd realize I'm not the woman he thinks I am.

Then, he would leave me, just like everyone else.

Chapter 32

Jason

I'm pacing my small apartment like a lunatic. Sara won't answer my calls and she won't return any messages or texts since Lexi had the baby over a week ago. I guess I can't blame her, but this really fucking sucks! My hands are shaking and I can't slow the beat of my heart back down to normal. I swear I'm having constant palpitations. I know just the sound of her voice would help calm me down, but I can't expect that from her. I do realize it's unfair, but I need her right now.

"Fuck," I mumble impatiently. I'm supposed to receive the paternity test results today from the hospital. Due to the situation, Lexi, Axel and I all asked to receive a direct phone call regarding the information instead of waiting even more time for the mail. In my heart I don't believe the child is mine. When he was born, I thought, "What a beautiful little boy. I want a family like this someday with Sara." I felt like I was an outsider intruding on this family's first moments with their baby.

No matter what I thought, I couldn't make my feet walk out the door. I kept asking myself, "What if you're wrong? Do you want to miss this?" I just couldn't take the chance of missing those parts of his life, just in case he's mine. I want to do the right thing. I want to be a good father. I want to make sure both Lexi and him are taken care of. So, I've been at the hospital every single day. I spend time there before my shift and longer if I don't work. Most of my time though, I'm sitting in the cafeteria or the waiting room trying to figure out what I'm supposed to be doing.

Now that Lexi and her son have been discharged, it's even worse. She's staying with her parents in a temporary condo here since they still live in Maryland. When she went into labor, they finally decided to get over the issues with her having this baby and came to the hospital. Axel came down when she went into labor too and he's even staying here in a hotel until everything is resolved. The awkward levels hit an ultimate high with all of us every time I walk into the room, but I have to continue to suck up every minute of it until I know. When I do...well, when I do, then I'll decide what I'm going to do.

As I cautiously act like he may be mine, at the same time, I don't want that reality and pray for it constantly. I feel selfish for even thinking it. If he's mine, I'll love him no matter what, but I don't want to be reminded of my fuck-up every day.

I know Christian said we would be fine, but the tension Lexi always held between us sucks. I want Christian and me to be closer and even though this would mean he has a nephew, I think it would be hard on him. Unfortunately, the baby doesn't come alone, Lexi will always be a part of him and she would be around. I can't imagine what Bree would feel like with all of this. I don't ever need to be the cause of another problem for my brother.

Most of all, I don't want my child to be a reminder of what could have been. No matter what, I want Sara back, but I need her to give me that chance. It may be selfish, but if the baby isn't mine, I think my chances with her might increase. At least it would be one less thing standing between the two of us. I want a baby. I want a family. I just want it all with Sara. My heart clenches again with the realization I might never have what I want. I need to get my shit together.

The phone rings, startling me out of my thoughts. I jump to answer it without even glancing at the caller ID, "Hello!"

251

"Is this Jason Emory?" a women's voice asks through the phone.

"Yes, it is," I retort anxiously.

"Hi, Jason, this is Janet from Maine Medical Center. I'm calling in regards to paternity test results for the baby boy of Alexandria Covey."

"Yes," I impatiently encourage her to keep going.

"First, I need you to verify your identity with the last four digits of your social security number and your mother's maiden name," she requests. I immediately spit out the answers. "Thank you. Okay, the results show that you are not this baby's father," she finishes.

I groan a sigh of relief and feel my whole body instantly relax. I have no idea what the woman says after that, but I disconnect with her soon after feeling overwhelming relief. The phone rings again almost instantly, the screen showing Lexi. I hit answer and close my eyes as I mumble, "Hi Lexi." My voice comes out sounding hoarse from the emotions coursing through me. I clear my throat and wait for her to speak.

"Axel and I just got the results," she gasps.

"Me too," I tell her, feeling even lighter. "Congratulations."

"Thank you, Jason," she cries. "I just wanted to say I'm sorry for all the problems I caused you with Christian and your girlfriend," she whimpers through the phone.

I cringe hearing her cry. We've all done enough of that in the last few weeks. I sigh into the phone, "Lexi, don't take on the blame. What happened with us was not your fault. I was there too," I remind her. "Is Axel with you?" I ask hesitantly changing the subject.

I hear another small whimper before she answers, "He's putting Ryder down for a nap. We're going to move near my parents and we're going to try."

"Ryder, huh?" I prod. Lexi didn't want to name him until she knew who his father was. They had to get special

252

permission because of the birth certificate, but they discharged him as baby boy Carver. They told her she would need to file as soon as the paternity results came through. I continue, not needing a response. "I'm happy for you, Lexi. I really am," I tell her honestly. "I hope everything works out for you and Axel."

"Thank you, Jason," she whispers and then hangs up without another word. It's strange to think I will probably never hear from her again, but I sincerely do hope for the best for her and her new family.

I stare at my phone for a few minutes before dialing Sara. I don't think she'll pick up since she hasn't taken my calls in a while, but I need to tell her first anyway. After the fourth ring her voicemail picks up. I close my eyes and let the sound of her voice wash over me. I try to swallow the lump in my throat, but I end up having to speak through my emotions. "Hi, Sara. I just heard from the hospital and I needed you to be the first to know...the baby...he's not mine. I'm sorry for what I put you through. I miss you. Please call me." I end the call knowing my voice sounded broken. I hope she doesn't think it's for the wrong reasons.

I sigh again before dialing my parents. With both of them listening in, I quickly tell them the results. After I get another brief lecture from both of them, I hang up and move to dial Christian. When he answers instead of telling him I ask, "Are you home?"

"Yeah man, what's up?" he prompts.

"I'll be over in a few," I tell him and hang up my phone without waiting for a response. I quickly stride out the door pulling my coat on as I make my way to my truck. I'm at Christian's place in minutes.

He's pulling the door open even before I make it up the walk. "What's wrong?" he questions frantically, instantly making me feel guilty.

"Nothing's wrong," I insist. "I'm sorry. I didn't mean to make you panic. I just needed to talk to you face to face." I notice his sigh of relief as he lets me inside and he shuts the door behind me. "Sorry, Christian. I should know better by now," I add regretfully.

He pats me on the back telling me he forgives me. He gestures to their couch and chairs in his living room before heading that way. "In here, okay? Joe and Dean aren't around and Bree is at class."

"Yeah, fine," I mumble my voice cracking. "He's not mine," I blurt out as soon as we sit down across from each other. I watch him intently for his reaction.

Christian stays quiet for a minute, processing, before responding to me. "How do you feel about that?" he asks guardedly.

"Relieved," I answer honestly. "I was struggling to find the good in the situation if he was mine and I hated myself for that. If he was mine, I would've loved him no matter what, but I really didn't want that. I kept thinking how it would affect everything else, everyone else. Mom and Dad, Lexi and her boyfriend, you and Bree, you and me," I pause shaking my head, "me and Sara."

"Jason," Christian begins.

"Christian, this wasn't just a little mistake and I hate that it ever happened. I know it's over, but I'm so fucking sorry," I emphasize.

Christian sighs. "Jason, what you need to remember right now is that it really is over. We're good. Like I said, it had been years since I even thought of Lexi. You and I are good," he emphasizes. "Bree and I are fan-fucking-tastic," his lips twitch up at the mention of her name. "As for everything and everyone else, they will figure their own shit out and it will eventually be as it should be." He pauses and watches me carefully as he continues, "I think what you need to do is concentrate on yourself for a while and stop worrying about everyone else. What I mean by that is you need to figure out what you want."

"I know what I want," I answer instantly, thinking of Sara.

Christian nods his head. "Does she know what you want?" he probes knowingly.

I grimace, grumbling, "I've tried. She won't talk to me. Last time she talked to me I told her about everything with Lexi, including your history. Then I had to leave in the middle of our conversation to go to the hospital. Lexi has great timing. That's when she called for those pains." I shake my head, complaining, "She hasn't talked to me since. I had to leave her a message to tell her about the results that I pray she'll listen to. I hope it actually helps, but I don't really know if it will," I admit.

Christian narrows his eyes and assesses me again. "I know how you feel," he empathizes with me before he inquires, "Do you remember when Bree and I were broken up?"

"Which time?" I ask sarcastically.

He chooses to ignore my comment. "You told me it was obvious how much we wanted to be together. You told me she deserved to have me fight for her to show her how much she means to me. You were right. I'm also a much better man with her." He pauses, emphasizing, "Sara deserves to have you for her. Show her how important she is to you. It's obvious the two of you want to be together. And I'll tell you something else that you only had the guts to say to Bree," he smirks. "You're an asshole without her."

I chuckle and give him a light shove. "She told you, huh?" He smiles in response. I groan clasping my hands behind my neck, "You're right, Christian."

"About you being an asshole?" he jokes.

I shake my head. "I just hope my advice works as well for me as it did for you," I tease the corners of my mouth turning up. He stands and playfully shoves me back. I jump up and quickly wrap my arm around his neck and we begin wrestling. I ultimately pin him before mumbling, "Thanks."

He pushes me off laughing. "Just go get your girl."

I nod my head. "Yeah, I'm on it. Tell Bree hi for me." I stand up and walk to the front door pulling my coat on as I go.

"I will. Hey, have you told Matt or Theresa yet?" he asks.

"Not yet, but I'll take care of that when I get home. Thanks, Christian," I add sincerely, "for everything." I turn and walk out the door knowing what I have to do. I just have to figure out a way to make it happen.

"Later, Jason," he calls nonchalantly. I give my brother a quick wave and climb into my truck, already forming a plan to try to win Sara back.

Chapter 33

Sara

"Are you okay?" Liz asks me from my doorway.

I'm lying on my bed with my ethics and accounting books spread out in front of me, but not getting anywhere. I grimace hearing those same words again. "I'm okay. Just trying to study and not doing too well with it," I confess giving her half the truth.

Her eyes narrow on me, but I keep my mouth pinched shut. She finally nods in acknowledgment and informs me, "I'm supposed to meet Blake at the pub for a burger later."

"Why isn't he picking you up?" I ask her surprised. "He wouldn't want you to walk into a bar alone."

A funny look crosses her face. "Well, his roommates are going with him since he hasn't seen much of them lately. So, I told him I'd bring you with me. We're leaving in an hour," she spits out as quickly as she can before spinning on her heel trying to make her escape.

"Wait, what?" I yell scrambling off my bed after her. Liz turns slowly back around towards me. Just as I get to my feet my vision quickly becomes blurry and I begin to lose my balance. I'm really lightheaded and whisper, "Whoa," as I focus on a spot on the floor trying to regain control. My knees buckle and I attempt to put my ass back on my bed, but I slide down the edge of it instead.

Moments later everything begins to brighten again, my head slowly clearing. I look to my right and find Liz sitting next to me staring at me, her eyes full of concern. "Are you okay?"

"Yeah, just got a little dizzy for second. I think I just got up too fast," I suggest. "I've been sitting down for a while."

"Have you been eating okay? I know I'm gone a lot, but I never see you eat anymore," she tells me. Sometimes I don't like how much she notices.

I shrug my shoulders trying to push her towards another explanation, "I've just been feeling a little off lately. I'm fine."

"You're coming to eat with me," she insists.

I shake my head, "No, I'm not. I don't want to see Jason." I panic, not ready to talk about his phone message from yesterday telling me the baby isn't his. I don't know what to do and I don't want anyone to decide for me.

"Isn't it his day off?" she prods.

"What if he's working anyway?" I ask nervously. "He switches shifts all the time."

"I'll be with you. It will be fine," she encourages. "I want to see some actual food go in your mouth."

I sigh in defeat, knowing she won't relent on this one, especially now. "Fine!" I concede.

She squeals and gives me a hug. She stands and helps me to my feet. "It will be good for you to get out of here to go somewhere besides classes or the library!"

I don't believe that, but I'm good at pretending. I groan, but this time I stay steady on my feet. "Go, I'll be ready. I promise." She gives my hand one last squeeze before she turns to go.

An hour later, I'm sitting in the passenger seat of Liz's car and I'm gripping my hands tightly trying to make them stop shaking. I'm wearing black leggings, a black turtleneck and a long, baggy gray sweater with my tall black lined boots. I'm not feeling very colorful today. "I'm so nervous. What if Jason's there?"

"Stop, you're going to make yourself sick again. Don't torture yourself with what if's. Whatever happens,

258

happens and we'll deal with it. Besides, maybe it would be good for you to see him." I glare at her making her chuckle. "I'm just saying."

I sigh and stare out the window as she pulls up to a parking lot near the pub. We climb out of her car and she links her arm through mine. We huddle close walking down the street quickly to keep warm.

As soon as we step inside, I put my head down, afraid to even scan the crowd or look behind the bar. I don't even want to know if he's here. "There he is," Liz exclaims. My heart skips a beat before I'm reminded, she's talking about Blake. "Come on," she urges grabbing me by the hand and pulling me through the small crowd. When she stops, I do the same, dropping her hand and finally lifting my head.

"Hi Lizzie," Blake says sweetly before placing a chaste kiss to her lips. He glances at me with a small smile. "Hi, Sara, it's good to see you."

I give him my fake smile. That's all I've got. "Hi Blake," I reply.

"Do you remember my roommates?" he asks.

"Yup," I respond. I give his three roommates the same smile and a small wave.

"Talkative tonight, huh?" his roommate Thad asks cheerily. I shrug in response making him chuckle. "I thought you were always the one smiling and talking," he teases. I raise my eyebrows in response making him shake his head and turn back to his beer.

I sit down next to Liz at their table. After we all order burgers and fries, I finally let my eyes wander carefully to the bar. I immediately notice the pretty girl I remember from last time that kept asking me questions about Jason. I see one of the guys Jason works with, I think his name is Joey. I breathe a sigh of relief, assuming he's not here.

I remain quiet, watching everyone interact, while Liz keeps trying to pull me into the conversation. I'm grateful when the waitress sets all our burgers on the table, giving me a reason to stay quiet. I nibble on a French fry at the same time assessing the burger. I pick it up and get one tiny bite in my mouth when Liz's eyes suddenly go wide. I'm about to ask her what's going on when I feel hands grip my shoulders making me tense.

Brad leans down to my ear, whispering, "What's my girl doing here with all these boys?"

I turn to glare at him, "I'm not your girl, Brad."

He kisses me on the cheek and smiles at me. His eyes move to Liz, "Hey, Liz. Good to see you."

"Hi, Brad," she responds watching me carefully. He turns and walks away. I breathe a sigh of relief grateful he didn't push it any further. Liz asks, "Are you okay?"

I swallow hard before answering, "Yeah. I'm going to run to the bathroom though. I'll be right back," I tell her even hearing the anxiety in my own voice. I quickly jump up and walk away before she has a chance to offer to come with me.

I step into the bathroom feeling nauseous. I hate seeing him. I'm not about to let him back in. I make it to the toilet just in time, as I get sick, throwing up the couple bites in my stomach. I flush the toilet and trudge to the sink to wash my hands, thankful for the extremely rare occurrence of an empty girls' bathroom.

I look up into the mirror, not liking what I see. I'm pale, my eyes are red and my face looks tired. I rinse my mouth out with water to get the awful acidic taste out of my mouth. I splash my face a couple times before drying it with a paper towel. I toss the towel in the garbage and turn away from the mirror in disgust.

Just as I step out of the bathroom someone immediately grabs my arm, roughly pulling me back and pinning me against the wall. "I've had enough of this bullshit, Sara!" Brad yells irritably. "First, you're dating that asshole, now you show up to a bar with a bunch of guys?" he accuses me like I'm doing something wrong.

I struggle to keep myself calm. "I'm not your girl, Brad. It's none of your business who I date. But tonight, I came here with Liz. Those guys are her boyfriend and his roommates," I add even though I don't think I should have to. I just need him to calm down.

"You're acting like a slut again and my girl does not act like a slut," he states glaring at me and making me nervous.

"Brad, you're hurting me," I tell him hoping he'll let go of my arms.

He barely loosens his grip before he continues, "Let's get something straight, Sara, you're mine and you will always be mine. No one will ever want you like I do. No one will ever love you like I do. Just like that asshole you were dating, guys will use you for sex and throw you away, but I'll always be there."

In an instant, Brad no longer has me pinned to the wall. I take a breath in shock as I watch the scene unfold. Jason throws Brad up against the wall hard. He shoves up against him with one hand gripping his jaw and the other arm compressing his chest, holding him there.

He quickly gets in his face. "Don't ever fucking touch her again. Don't talk to her. Don't even look at her," he demands fiercely, giving Brad a deathly glare. "She is not yours and she will never be yours again! Do you understand me?" he challenges. Brad doesn't respond, he just glares back at Jason. Jason regroups and shoves him hard and further into the wall before asking again, "Do you fucking understand me?" He nods his head so slightly you'd miss it if you weren't watching carefully. "The words asshole," he commands.

"Yes," he gasps. "Now, fucking let me go!"

Jason gives him one more shove before hitting him in the jaw with what looks like barely a flip of his wrist. Brad groans in pain as Jason tosses him to the bouncer standing right behind him. I didn't even notice the guy was standing

261

there. "Kick him out of here," Jason instructs the bouncer without even glancing his way. He nods his head in confirmation before he turns and walks away, escorting Brad to the exit.

The whole time, Jason's eyes remain on me. "Are you okay?" he asks softly taking a cautious step towards me.

I nod. "I'm okay," I croak. I clear my throat still staring at him.

"Are you sure? Did he hurt you?" he prods now assessing me from head to toe with his eyes. "You look really pale and your eyes are red." I nod my head and his eyes grow more concerned. "Are you sure you're alright?" he asks again.

I finally shake myself out of my stupor. "I'm fine, he just grabbed my arms," I shake my head like it's not a big deal, but I don't believe it for a second.

He looks at me doubtfully and takes a step closer, grimacing slightly. "Okay, forget about the asshole for a minute. Is something else going on? Your face looks really thin." He cradles my face in his hands and my voice gets caught in my throat at the feel of him touching me. "Are you sick?" he prompts with a slight quiver in his voice.

"I'm not sick," I rasp.

"Are you eating, then?" he questions.

I grimace. "Yeah, my burger is getting cold right now. I should go," I proclaim moving to step around him.

"Sara, wait," he prods placing his hand tenderly at my waist to stop me. I have to force myself to slow down my breathing and my heart by breathing in through my nose and out through my mouth. "Please, we need to talk," he requests gently.

I lightly shake my head. "Thank you for helping me, Jason," my voice cracks when I say his name. I move to step around him again and this time he lets me go.

Although I freeze briefly as I hear him say, "I miss you," just loud enough for me to hear. His gravelly voice saying those words makes me want to throw myself into his arms. Instead, I force myself to walk back towards Liz.

Liz jumps up as soon as she sees me striding towards her. "Are you okay?" I'm so fucking sick of that question I want to scream. She continues to blabber on, "You were taking so long. I was just about to come after you to check on you when I saw the bouncer throw Brad out..." she trails off as she glances behind me and her eyes go wide again. I don't even have to turn around to know Jason is standing behind me. She brings her eyes back to me, now alight with amusement. She gives me a small grin and mutters, "Oh."

It's probably not what she thinks, but I'm not about to explain anything to her right now. I just need to get out of here before I completely freak out. "I'm not feeling well. Do you mind if I take your car home?" I request.

Her eyes fill with worry and she reminds me, "But you didn't really eat anything."

"I'll eat something at home. Blake?" I question to get his attention. "Do you have room for Liz in whatever vehicle you guys brought?"

"Always. I'd make one of the boys walk if I didn't," he smirks. He earns a small smile from Liz and me and an elbow in the gut from one of his roommates for his comment. "I drove, so I'll bring her home safe. I promise," he adds.

"Thanks." I turn back to Liz, begging, "Can I please have your keys?"

She reluctantly reaches into her bag and pulls them out handing them to me. "Fine. Text me when you get home and I'll be checking on you when I get there." I try to hand her some money for my burger, but she refuses. "You didn't even eat anything," she glares at me pushing my hand back. I relent and turn to grab my things to leave. Her eyes go wide and she grabs my hand to stop me, "Wait, Blake will walk you out to the car."

He starts to stand, but Jason slides in next to him, obviously listening to the whole conversation. "Enjoy your burger. I'll walk her."

Blake sits back down and I pull my coat on, grab my bag and stride quickly towards the door. I shiver as the cold hits my face but pick up my pace. Warmth fills my gut when I hear his chuckle right next to me and my eyes reflexively go to him. "You're not wearing a coat! It's freezing!" I scold him.

He grins with his hands jammed deep into his pockets. "Don't care. Wasn't about to let you walk out the door without me." My mouth drops open, but I quickly snap it shut, not having a reply. "I wouldn't complain if you wanted to help keep me warm on the way," he taunts, smirking and making me melt. He cautiously puts his arm around me and surprisingly, I let him. I feel his sigh of relief as he pulls me close.

My steps slow to match his leisurely pace, but it still feels like no time before we arrive at Liz's car. "This is her car. Thank you for walking me."

Jason looks past me to Liz's car. "Are you sure that's alright in the snow?"

"It's fine," I assure him. "Besides, I'm not far."

He doesn't look so sure when he questions, "Why don't I bring you home in my truck?" I shake my head making him visibly cringe. He relents offering, "I'll follow you, then."

"Don't you have to get back to work?" I probe.

"You're more important," he declares causing my already queasy stomach to go into overdrive. "I'll make sure you get home safe and I'll be back soon."

I nod my head in acceptance and move to get in the car when he stops me by pulling me to him. He wraps his arms around me with his cheek resting lightly on the top of my head. I push my face into his chest and take a deep breath, searching for the scents of Jason underneath the smells of the pub. "Thank you, I needed that," he tells the top of my head. He squeezes me tight before loosening his hold and kissing my cheek. "Warm up the car for a few minutes and when you're ready I'll follow. Drive safe, I'll be right behind you."

I just nod my head, continuing to try to control my breath, knowing I'll completely lose it if I try to speak. He taps my ass as I slide into the car pulling the door shut swiftly. I feel the blush cover my face as I start the car.

Jason follows me home and he doesn't leave until I'm locked inside my apartment. I give him a small wave as he backs out. I've never had someone watch over me like he does, even though we're not together. My stomach flips and warmth spreads throughout my whole body just thinking about it.

About ten minutes later when I'm curled up on my bed, I receive a text from him.

I really fucking miss you.

My chest physically aches as I think about how much I miss him too. Another text soon follows.

Please give us another chance!

Maybe.

I finally answer holding my breath.

*You just made my night.
When can I see you?*

I'm not ready yet.

Ok, whatever you need. I
want to see you soon
though. Please!

Can I really do this with him again? I honestly don't know if I can, but I'm going to have to at least talk to him eventually. He deserves at least that much. I don't know if I could handle losing him again though. My biggest fear with him is that's exactly what would happen.

Chapter 34

Sara

"Still missing you. Love, Jason," I read the simple card accompanying the beautiful bouquet of white lilies, blue delphiniums and a couple pale yellow roses in a tall glass vase with a rounded bottom and ice blue ribbon to tie it all together. I put my face to the flowers and take a deep whiff of the wonderful scent.

"It's been over a week since he got the test results back and since you saw him. You have received something from him every single day. He's obviously not giving up on you. How much longer are you going to torture the guy?" Liz challenges me with a smirk.

I roll my eyes. "I'm not trying to torture him, I'm just..." I trail off, pinching my lips together while I try to organize all the thoughts in my head. "If I go there with Jason again, I just need it to be right. I need to fix myself," I lamely explain. That's the closest I can get to telling her my truth; my truth that I'm not good enough, but I want to try to be. A long time ago I stopped caring what happened to me. Jason makes me care and want what he's offering. But I'm also terrified he's going to hurt me again if I do take a chance.

"Why don't you let Jason help you? I'm really worried about you, Sara. I've never seen you like this before," she expresses her concern.

I grimace. What am I supposed to say? Tell her I just used to be much better at hiding myself? Tell her I'm done trying to be someone I'm not? I'm freed from saying anything when my cell phone rings. I quickly grab it, barely flinching when I see my father's name and answer it with an odd sense of confidence, "Hello, Dad."

"Sara," he states as his only greeting. "We have another event this weekend I need you to attend and the shit you pulled last time is not going to happen," he commands leaving no room for argument.

"You're right, Dad. It won't happen because I can't go," I refuse his demand anyway and wait for his wrath.

"What did you just say to me?" he asks in shock.

I take a deep breath to try to gain more courage before I answer. "I can't go to your event this weekend."

"Whatever you have planned Sara, change it. You will be there. Brad will pick you up on Saturday at 6 p.m.," he commands.

"Dad, I'm not going to your thing this weekend and I'm never going anywhere with Brad again," I insist.

"If this is about that boy again, bring him, but you will be there!" he nearly screams through the phone.

"No Dad, I won't. It's not about any boy. For once it's actually about me. It's about how Brad treats me, but most of all it's about how you treat me," I force myself to tell him, standing up for myself. My stomach is roiling, but I have to make it through this conversation and I'd rather not face him when I do. "I'm not going to let you do it anymore."

"How dare you! You think you can talk to me this way? I'm your father! I'll disown you! You'll have nothing! You won't survive without me! You won't finish school and you'll become a loser whore just like your mother! You need me!" he screams through the phone. I cringe at his words and watch as Liz's mouth drops nearly to the table and tears fall freely from her eyes.

I swallow down my emotions as I watch the shock, horror and finally sadness cross her face and I know all of it is because she loves me. I think about my brother and how he stands up for me with the small amount of things he has actually witnessed. I think about Jason and everything he does for me to show me how much he cares, even when he's not here because I'm pushing him away. I hold all of them in my heart to give me the strength to finish this with my father. "I'll figure it out. I may not know how I'm going to do it, but I do know I'm not doing this with you anymore. If you decide you want to be a real father, call me. Otherwise, I'm done, Dad," I insist, telling him what I've dreamed of telling him since my mom left, my heart breaking just like it did the day she left.

"You..." he begins, but I'm done listening to anything he has to say. I end the call and drop my phone on the table staring at it with my eyes wide. I can't believe I just did that.

I'm suddenly tackled and engulfed by Liz's arms. "I'm so sorry, Sara. I'm so, so, sorry! I'm the worst friend ever! I didn't know. I swear I didn't know," she rambles.

I nod numbly. "I know. I didn't want you to know," I confess. "Even my brother didn't exactly know."

"How?" she questions shocked and confused, shaking her head in disbelief. She squeezes me harder, crying, "I'm so sorry."

My stomach can't handle my emotions much longer and begins churning faster and faster. I hastily shove her away and run to the bathroom slamming the door behind me. I bend over the toilet and heave, but there's nothing to throw up except stomach acid. I continue to gag involuntarily over the toilet anyway. When I finally calm my nerves and get my body to follow suit, I lean against the sink and splash my face with cold water. I stretch my aching sides and rinse out my mouth, first with water followed by mouthwash.

"Ugh, my throat hurts," I complain to my reflection.

I sigh and walk out of the bathroom, tripping over Liz sitting on the floor right outside the door. "I'm sorry," she repeats. "I didn't want to leave you."

I sigh. "I know you're not going anywhere, Liz. It's fine. I'm fine."

She shakes her head. "No, no you're not."

"Liz," I start, sliding down the wall to sit next to her. I cross my legs under me, finally ready to really talk.

She immediately interrupts me, "Sara, you should have talked to me about your dad years ago." She gulps hard, "And Brad?" she prods sounding pained, maybe even betrayed and that hurts. "Please, talk to me," she pleads with me.

I squeeze my eyes shut tight before taking a deep calming breath, then slowly opening my eyes again. "I can't go over everything right now. It's just too much. But I'll start by telling you this; after my mom left us, things changed. My mom only cared about her new family. The little effort she made wasn't enough. She left us to my father's mercy. Stephen was okay, but my father would just look at me and you could feel his hatred."

"Because you look so much like her," she murmurs in disturbed understanding.

"He treated me like I was left with him only to taunt him after his wife cheated on him." I grimace and attempt to end the story of my father. He's just not worth any more of my time.

I block out Liz, not wanting to see her reactions to my pain and rapidly blurt out the rest of my story. "My dad decided I should at least help him with his business since I wasn't good for anything else. Well, since I was dating Brad and he wanted to work on some projects with his dad, he moved to take Brad under his wing. The only problem with that is my relationship with Brad was already rocky, so my father just pushed him over the edge. They always say girls date their fathers, while my ex-boyfriend became that nightmare. Both of them constantly made me feel worthless and told me Brad would be my life," I recoil at the thought of that fate.

Liz scoots even closer to me and puts her hand on my back as I continue, "When we left for college, I did what I could to change that outcome. I got away with coming here with you to college because my dad is here. He thought he could still control me if I was close to either him or Brad. Then Brad said he would let us go on a break. I think it was so he wouldn't feel guilty about screwing other girls. He tried to make me believe I wouldn't be worth it for anyone else," I shrug. "They honestly succeeded in making me feel very insecure. Brad just wanted to be sure I would go back to him when he wanted me to. I compensated by dating guys I thought were nice guys, but I didn't care if we stayed together. They couldn't hurt me." I sigh, "Until Jason."

"Sara, I'm so sorry," she repeats again.

I shake my head. "Please don't Liz. I can't have you feel sorry for me. I didn't tell you because with you I just wanted to be normal. I wanted to be happy. I love my brother, but you were my only real escape."

Liz winces and looks away. After a few minutes she turns back to me completely changing the subject and I love her for it until I realize where she's taking it. "I think you should call Jason. I'm really worried about you and I think you could use all the support you can get right about now. You're not eating, you've lost a ridiculous amount of weight, I hear you throwing up anytime something upsets you, which is all the time lately," she glares at me. "Please, Sara, it's not healthy and I know he would do anything to help you. It's obvious he loves you," she pleads.

My heart pounds hard hearing someone else say Jason loves me, giving me hope it might be true. I give myself a mental shake and try to focus on the other part. I suck in a shaky breath and confess to Liz something I never thought I'd have the guts to tell anyone, but if I can tell my father no, I can do this. "I've had problems with an eating disorder on and off since middle school. My father and Brad," I stammer my excuse with a grimace. "Stress and depression both bring it out in me. When the pregnant girl showed up at Jason's parents, my heart broke like it did when my mom left and I started really falling back into it. I knew then I needed help," my voice cracks. "I can't go back to my father. I can't go back to Brad. Not after having Jason in my life. For the first time in my life, I know I don't deserve the shit they've been giving me," I whimper. "But I want to be better for him, for me too, but he made me want it." My eyes drop to my lap, "I guess what I'm saying is I'm ready to ask for help," I add watching the tears drop onto my trembling clasped hands.

"I…I…I hate that you went through all this without talking to anyone," Liz sobs. "I…I hate that you went through all this alone!"

"I was never alone, I've always had you," I whisper hoarsely.

Liz wraps her arms around me and I let my arms go around her, feeling completely relieved to have shared my burden. "I'll help you. I'll do everything I can to help you. We'll figure it out, but you need more than me, Sara."

"I'll talk to Stephen," I reply quietly. "I just can't tell him everything. I don't want to ruin his future."

"He's a smart man, Sara. You won't ruin anything. He'll do well no matter where he ends up. You know he will," she reiterates, trying to convince me. "You need to tell him and you have to tell Jason."

I shake my head. "He knows about my dad and Brad. He's the reason I know I can do this," I admit. "I just don't know if I'm ready to tell him about this. I want to get better."

"He can help you do that. Let him," she pleads.

"I don't know," I mumble, knowing my fear of losing him is holding me back. "Will you go with me to talk to my doctor? I don't want to go by myself."

Liz nods her head vehemently, "Of course I will. I still think you should talk to Jason about this."

I drop my head to her shoulder. I know I should and I will. I need to be strong first. Without responding to her comment, I whisper, "Thank you, Lizzie. I don't know what I'd do without you." She hugs me tighter. "And Liz?"

"Yeah?" she prods letting go and looking at me compassionately.

"I need a job, like now," I emphasize. She chuckles and I relax into the wall. I'll figure it out, but I'm done pretending.

Chapter 35

Jason

It's been two weeks since I saw Sara at the pub and I'm still waiting for her to be ready. I send her texts every day to let her know I'm thinking of her, even though she hasn't responded to a single one. I've sent her flowers, chocolates, snack and fruit baskets or cards trying to tell her how I feel about her, but still nothing. I need to see her. I'm done with her pushing me away. I grab my coat and head for my door ready to go find her when there's a soft knock. I fling open my door to find Liz, hand still poised to knock on my door.

"Um, Hi Jason," she stammers. She glances down and sees my coat in my hands. "I'm sorry, are you headed out right now? I can come back later."

I take a step back, needing to know why she's here. I shake my head. "I'm not in a hurry. What's up Liz?" I ask curiously. A horrible thought suddenly crosses my mind and my heart drops into my stomach with dread. "Is Sara, okay?" I ask shakily.

Liz's eyes go wide as she takes in my sudden stiff appearance. "She's fine, she's fine," she swiftly insists. She steps awkwardly inside and turns slightly away mumbling hesitantly, "Well, sort of."

I can feel my face pale at her words. I ball my hands into fists as my heart begins to race in panic. I growl, "What the fuck do you mean sort of?"

She sighs in defeat, shaking her head. "She won't be happy I'm here, but she needs you and I love her too much to let her stubbornness win out on this one."

I clench my jaw, regretting I didn't do more damage when I had the chance. "Is it Brad?" She shakes her head, but I don't feel any relief from her answer. "Her father?" I ask.

"No," she answers straightaway causing me to relax marginally. Her lips twitch slightly as she proudly proclaims, "You should've heard her tell her father off. She was truly amazing," she confesses. "She's really doing everything she can to keep both him and Brad out of her life. Thanks to you," she adds giving me a small appreciative smile. Tilting my head to the side, I look at her slightly confused by her comment. Before I can question it, she adds, "She may be pushing you away right now so you don't get to see her, but you're inside her head and her heart with every single thing she does."

Gasping, my heart warms at her words. I take a deep breath wanting to believe they're true and soak it all in, but it's really fucking difficult. My voice cracks as I prompt, "Then, why won't she see me?"

Liz's eyes go soft with understanding, seeing my obvious pain. "Do you mind if I sit?" she inquires, telling me she has a lot to say.

My heart races with anxiety, wondering if that's a good or bad thing. I gesture towards the couch and chairs behind her in my living room. "Have a seat," I offer.

She sits on one end of the couch, unzipping her coat, but leaving it on. I stiffly sit down in a chair across from her, impatiently waiting for her to tell me what's going on with Sara, needing her to be okay. Taking a deep breath, she finally blurts out, "She's scared, Jason. She won't say it, but she is scared. She's never had what she has with you. I believe she has convinced herself she needs to make herself better for you first, then maybe she'll have a chance at deserving you."

"That's bullshit!" I yell.

"Ridiculous, yes, but not bullshit," she emphasizes. I know that's what she thinks. Sara has even hinted to me that

275

she doesn't deserve you, even though she won't come right out and say it," she admits regretfully.

"She's already too good for me. If anyone needs to work at being deserving, it's me," I insist. "Especially after everything I just put her through."

She shakes her head and sighs heavily. "You know the kind of damage her dad and Brad did to her. Her mom too for that matter, just not quite as directly."

I look at her in both surprise and relief. "She told you?"

"Yeah," she divulges. "She finally shared all of that with me. I wish she would have done it a long time ago, but I do understand why she didn't want to. Doesn't mean I have to like it," she grumbles, scrunching her nose up in displeasure. "I have to admit, I'm thankful she at least told you, but I hate that she hid it from everyone for so long."

I nod in understanding and agreement. She gives me a hard look like she's preparing me for something huge and my muscles clench in anticipation. "Well, they did more damage than you know," she confesses. I instantly freeze, my heart stops and breathing ceases, fearing the words about to come out of her mouth. I feel the panic taking root deep inside, wondering how it could it get any worse. She grimaces faintly and confesses, "She has an eating disorder."

"What?" I gasp, stunned by her words. That is definitely not what I was expecting. Wouldn't I have noticed something? Or did I notice and not realize what I was seeing? I question myself trying to process her words. I should've known!

"Her dad and Brad have made her feel like she's always too fat," she states. My mouth drops open even further in reaction. I didn't think I could hate them anymore, but I do. Liz continues, "Whenever she's stressed or depressed things seem to get worse. That's when she doesn't really eat at all and she gets sick. Sometimes it's the anxiety that makes her throw up, but sometimes she does it on purpose. With what happened with you," she pauses blushing, "she has lost a lot of weight."

I flinch, guilt consuming me knowing I caused her even more pain. "Fuck," I mumble.

Liz continues to explain what I've been forced to miss. "I went with her to the doctor a few days ago and she's getting help. There's a treatment center right at Mercy Hospital, including a support group. She wants this, Jason. She wants to get better," she emphasizes. "She asked for help. She's fighting to push all the bad out of her life because she wants to be strong. She wants to be herself and feel good about it again. I just think she'll be so much stronger if she has you supporting her from close up instead of far away."

I gulp down the anger I feel for her family and her ex and attempt to focus on Sara. "How am I supposed to do that Liz if she won't let me?" I probe desperately, feeling my jaw tick. "She won't even fucking text me!" I yell with growing anxiety and frustration.

Liz's expression changes to one of hope as she proclaims, "That's where I think you're wrong. I believe if you shoved yourself in her face, she would cave." My eyebrows draw together in confusion and doubt, waiting for her to continue. "If you show up at our place and do something nice for her, she won't be able to resist. I think she's only been successful in keeping you at bay because you've been doing nice things for her, but she hasn't actually seen you. If you're face to face, she won't be able to block you out anymore. I'm sure of it."

I place my elbows on my knees and put my head down. I run my hands over my head and clasp them tightly behind my neck. I hate that she's fucking dealing with this at all!

"Jason, I wouldn't be here if I didn't believe you two should be together. She's in love with you, she's just afraid she's not good enough and you are the only one who can convince her otherwise," she insists causing my chest to tighten.

"Sara's my best friend and she has always been there for me. It's my turn to be there for her. One of the things I've learned already about helping her with this, is she needs as much support as possible from the people who love and care for her the most. If you're the man I think you are, you're one of those people for her. She really needs you, Jason," she reiterates, spreading the ache throughout my whole body, camouflaged as tiny pinpricks.

"If she needs me," I croak, "I'll be there. I'll find a way in and I'll find it now," I declare emphatically.

There's no other option!

Liz's lips turn up into a huge smile. "Thank you, Jason," she whispers on an exhale sounding completely relieved.

I shake my head. "You don't ever have to thank me when I'm doing something to help Sara." Her smile grows even more. I tell her candidly, "Thank you for coming to me. I should have pushed it sooner, but with everything that happened," I pause breathing through the painful memory of her leaving me, "I thought she was done with me. I thought I'd have a better chance of earning her back if I took everything slowly."

"I get that, but at the rate Sara's moving, if you don't do something a little more in her face, I don't know if you guys will ever get back together," she pushes. She needs you now," she reiterates.

I nod my head in complete agreement. I will do whatever it takes for her. "Okay," I concur. Now I'm absolutely determined to be there for her. "Well, she's not going to have a chance to push me away anymore. I won't let her," I promise.

Liz stands up and zips up her coat, pulling her purse over her shoulder. "Let me know if you need my help with anything," she proposes.

I stand and follow her to the door. "I will and I'm sure I'll be taking you up on your offer. Thanks, Liz," I reiterate. "Actually, I have off tonight and I'm not waiting any longer than I already have. In fact, I was actually about to go look for her when I found you at my door," I admit with a smile. Liz grins up at me, her eyes sparkling with amusement. "Do you know if she'll be around tonight?" I ask hopefully.

Her grin grows as she answers, "Yeah, I think she gets done with work at five, so she should be home a little bit after that."

My face scrunches up in confusion and I prod, "Work?"

She grimaces. "Yeah, she no longer has her dad's help with paying for anything," she explains. Even the words feel like a punch to the gut. How can he take that away from his own daughter? "She had to get a job to help pay rent, bills and try to save to pay for school for next year. She's looking into getting a student loan, too." I cringe, my mind already running with how I can help her with everything. That is if she'll let me, but I won't stop until she does.

"Where is she working?" I ask.

"At the coffee shop around the corner from our house. She does okay. They get some tips and she likes the free coffee," she concedes with a slight grimace.

I nod my head in acknowledgement. If this helps get rid of her father, it's a step in the right direction. I glance at the clock and think about what I want to do for her tonight and assess how much time I have to do it. "Okay, I think I'm going to do some shopping. Then, do you think I can get into your place before she gets home? Like around 4:30?" I request, an idea forming in my head.

She smiles and instantly agrees, "Yeah. Blake and I will be there to let you in and we can help you with whatever before we get out of your hair."

"Thanks. I'll see you then," I assure her. "I'm really glad she has you," I express to her with as much honesty as I can portray with my eyes. I pull the door open for her and wave goodbye.

"I'm glad she has you too, Jason," she whispers earnestly. Spinning on her heel, she turns and walks out the door.

"I have to get to work!" I exclaim.

I feel like I have a purpose again, that being Sara, helping her and bringing her back to me. I want to see her smile genuinely. I want to see her laugh so hard she can't stop. I want to see her hazel eyes sparkle with pure happiness.

And, I want to be the one to give that to her now and forever.

Chapter 36

Sara

I trudge into my kitchen after work and inhale something that smells delicious. "Mm," I moan in appreciation. "Liz, something smells good. Are you making dinner for Blake?" I prompt, pulling my boots off my sore feet.

"No, I'm making dinner for you," a gravelly male voice responds. I freeze, my breath catching in my throat. "Need help?" he prods as I slowly straighten up.

I gasp at the sight of Jason coming towards me. He looks better than in my dreams. He's wearing a navy-blue Henley ribbed long-sleeved shirt, fitting tightly along his muscled arms with a pair of faded old blue jeans and white socks. He unzips my coat and tugs it off for me, tossing it over the back of a chair all while I stare at him, wondering if he's real. He chuckles softly and prods, "You, okay?"

I shake myself out of my stupor and stammer, "Wh…What are you doing here?"

He grins at me, causing me to melt into his mischievous blue eyes. "I told you. I'm making dinner for you." His hand comes up under my chin and gently closes my mouth before resting along my jaw. My heart begins pounding so hard and fast I'm sure he can feel the vibrations in his hands. He looks deep into my eyes, opening himself up to let me see everything inside of him. "I can't wait anymore. I needed to see you. I needed to hear your voice. We need to start talking everything out," he demands, giving me no choice but to let him in.

I exhale a shaky breath and reply without thought, "Okay, Jason." His smile grows even more and his eyes sparkle, showing his happiness with my answer. My stomach churns like the beginnings of a hurricane, sending vibrations out to every limb. Although I'm terrified, I know this is right where I belong. I glance down at my coffee-stained wine-colored work t-shirt with a grimace. "I need to go change first though. I'm a complete mess!" I exclaim.

"You look absolutely beautiful," he proclaims sincerely, his eyes never once leaving my face. I swallow the lump in my throat, trying to get myself to move. "Dinner is about ready. Why don't you sit?" he suggests. "You must be tired."

I nod my head and allow him to guide me to a chair at my own kitchen table. I sit down, turning to watch him move around my kitchen pulling the last of our dinner together before he brings it to the table. He serves me and sits in the chair across from me. "How did you do all this?" I prod. He chuckles and I feel a blush cover my face. "I mean…" I trail off, biting my lower lip.

Jason continues to grin at me while I take in the salad, garlic bread and linguini covered with a clam sauce that smells so delectable. I haven't liked the smell of any food in quite a while, but this, smells delicious. "Liz let me in and showed me where to find everything in your kitchen. She also told me when you'd be home from work," he enlightens me.

I nod my head in understanding, glancing down at my plate. I wonder what else she told him. "How do you like your job?" he asks cautiously.

I shrug my shoulders. "It's good, I guess. I love the smell of the coffee and it kinda' pushes you to keep going. We get paid okay and there is a tip jar we all share at the end of the day. It's hard though," I admit. He nods his head in understanding and gives me a look I don't quite comprehend as I take my first bite of linguini. "Mm," I groan appreciation. "Jason, this is sooo good!" I emphasize.

"I'm glad you like it," he answers modestly, watching me closely as I take another bite. "So, I have to say Sara, I'm really proud of you with the new job and all."

"Thank you, but it's nothing," I tell him, attempting to brush it off.

He shakes his head not letting me. "It's something and we both know it," he insists. "Does this mean you're not talking to your dad?" he inquires.

"Wow, jumping right into it, huh?" I ask, setting my fork down with a heavy sigh. His eyebrows raise in question causing me to instantly cave as I drop my eyes to my plate. "I got into it with my dad. He wanted me to go to another event to represent the family with Brad and I said no. I'm not letting him control me anymore. So, he disowned me," I explain simply.

Biting my lower lip as my insides begin brewing up a storm, I look up into his eyes preparing for his reaction and see nothing but concern. "Are you okay?" he prods. I nod my head in confirmation. "What about Brad? Have you heard from him at all?" he asks apprehensively.

I shake my head. "Not since you scared the crap out of him." Jason chuckles and the sound of it calms me at the same time warming me all the way to my soul. "God, I missed you," I whisper.

Jason's blue eyes turn darker as he reaches for my hand and squeezes. "I really fucking missed you too." Goosebumps spread throughout my whole body, even on my insides as I stare at him. "You need to know I want to be here with you, but whether I'm in your life or not, they can't be around. This is your chance to break away from them for good. They're toxic and I can't let them leave you with anymore scars. I just want you to be happy." He gives my hand one more squeeze, clears his throat and encourages me, "Eat some more, Sara, please."

The rest of dinner, we keep the conversation light and I eat more than I've eaten in what feels like forever, but in reality, wasn't all that much. We clean up together in comfortable silence before sitting down on the couch, my nerves instantly ratcheting back up to unhealthy levels. "Thank you for dinner," I mumble. He acknowledges me with a small smile, making my heart skip a beat. I begin fidgeting with my fingers, not sure where to go from here.

I'm thankful as Jason takes over the conversation again. "Sara, I'm sorry about what happened with Lexi, but I need you to know I would have wanted you with me no matter how that turned out. If it turned out differently, I know it would have been a lot to ask and maybe that makes me selfish, but I really didn't want to go through any of it without you," he confesses looking pained, making my own heart ache. "I may have known her when we had our one night, but that's all it was to me, one night that was a mistake. The first time she told me she was pregnant, after how it ended, I knew I was done with just one night with anyone. I needed to find my forever girl. With you, you fucking stunned me with all that you are. I felt it with everything in me that you were exactly that for me, my forever girl."

I concentrate on controlling my breathing before I speak. "I'm sorry I wasn't there for you. I should've been," I claim, wishing I could've been stronger for him.

He shakes his head. "I'm glad you concentrated on taking care of you, but now it's my turn to help take care of you. You just have to let me," he begs. "I want to be the one who's there for you. I want to be the one who protects you. I want to do everything I can so you don't hurt anymore and no one ever hurts you again," he emphasizes reaching into my soul and planting himself in the center of it.

I wipe away the tears streaming down my face as Jason reaches over to help me. "I…I have a problem Jason," I blurt out looking away from him. He needs to know. "I have an eating disorder. I'm getting help, but I'm struggling every single day right now. I wanted to make myself better before I talked to you. I wanted to be worthy of you. I know I have a long way to go, I just..." I trail off as I'm suddenly lifted off the couch and into Jason's lap as his arms wrap around me.

"Stop!" he insists, his eyes so intense the only thing I can do is listen. "You are incredible. Don't let the bullshit those assholes told you affect us. I'm the one who needs to work my ass off every day to prove to you how much I want to be in your life and keep showing you every day to earn the privilege of being with you. I want that and I hope like hell you want that too."

"I do," I confirm, whispering hoarsely into his chest.

"Sara, look at me," he gently urges. I continue breathing into his chest, loving the warmth and comfort I feel being right here. "Sara, please?" he prods his voice catching. Glancing up at him, he holds my gaze as he speaks. "I want to help you. Please, let me help you," he begs, his eyes watery. Suddenly, I can't get rid of the lump in my throat to speak, so I nod in agreement.

His eyes fill with relief. He moves his head slowly towards me, pressing his lips to mine. I whimper at the contact after not having it for so long and try to deepen the kiss, but he quickly pulls back. "I love you, Sara," he declares. My stomach flips and heart pounds thunderously in response. I know I feel the same. "I'm not going anywhere and I need you to understand that," he insists.

"I do," I murmur, nodding my head, but my brows draw together in confusion, not exactly sure what he's trying to say.

"I'm not going to let you push me away this time. If you push, I push back. If something is bothering you, I need you to talk to me. If you ignore my calls or texts, I will come find you. I need to know that you're okay. If you're struggling with anything, even if you think it's not a big deal, I need you to tell me and I promise I'll respect you by doing the same. I want to be all in together. You get me?" he prompts.

I nod my head in understanding. He will be there for me. He's not going to leave me. He can handle all of my bullshit. I answer him claiming, "You're already showing me what love really is and I need you to know I love you too, Jason."

He grins. His chest puffing up slightly. "As long as I get your genuine smile and I have you, I've got what I need. I love you," he reiterates, attempting to emphasize his point.

"I need you," I whimper pulling him closer and pressing my lips to his.

He deepens the kiss, tasting me and quickly stands with me in his arms. He strides towards my room holding me tight. He shuts and locks my bedroom door never taking his mouth away from mine. He steps over to my bed and gently lays me down. He pulls back, looking down at me. "You feel so small. I feel like I'm going to break you," he whispers his worries.

"I'm okay," I insist, trying to comfort him. "I'm doing better." His eyes are full of concern and doubt. "I ate more tonight with you than I have in a while," I confess, "and I know I'll keep getting better with you around. I'll even promise," I proclaim, the corners of my lips twitching up.

I must have said the right thing because the next second I'm staring at the most beautiful abs and arms I've ever laid eyes on. He reaches down to tug my shirt off as well and he tosses it on the floor. He then reaches for my khaki work pants and tugs them off too. With him staring at me in just my white lacey bra and panties, my hands move to cover myself up, suddenly feeling overwhelmingly self-conscious.

Jason immediately puts a stop to that by leaning over me, grabbing both of my hands and pinning them above my head. "Don't cover your gorgeous body. You are so beautiful and sexy," he gasps. He places soft kisses on my lips, trailing down to my neck and shoulder, before brushing his lips in the

286

opposite direction and moving towards my breasts. "So fucking beautiful," he rasps.

Sliding one hand behind my back, he unhooks my bra, pushing it up and away from my breasts, revealing me to him. He kisses each breast, moving to one, licking lightly around my nipple and ending with a kiss before moving to the other to do the same. Leaving my nipples taut he kisses down my stomach, over my belly button and down to my hips, letting my hands go so he can keep moving. I toss my bra off my arms and drop my hands to the bed gripping my comforter tightly in desperation. He places kisses on my inner thigh, breathing for a beat over my panties, igniting my core to an inferno.

I pant feeling myself get wet as he moves to the other thigh and down my leg with more kisses. "I love all the noises you make when my lips caress your skin. It drives me crazy; you drive me crazy," he emphasizes.

"I didn't know I was making any noises," I pant, my breathing erratic. He chuckles and begins to move back up my body, nibbling over my panties for a brief moment before he wraps his fingers in the sides and tugs them off, tossing them out of the way. He moves back to my core, digging his fingers into my thighs. He barely sticks his tongue out to lick, nibble and suck sending me into an instant tailspin. "Jason," I scream not able to contain myself. I gasp as I ride out my unexpectedly fast and hard orgasm.

As my body slows and I catch my breath, Jason begins trailing kisses back up my belly, between my breasts, to my neck and when he's close, I reach up, turning his face to mine and kiss him with everything that's in me. Flicking, licking and sucking, I tease him, attempting to taste every inch of his mouth with my tongue. My hands begin roaming down his torso and he breaks our kiss to catch his breath just as I meet his jeans. "Pants, off," I stammer. He kisses me again before he stands to tug off his jeans and boxer briefs. Reaching into his jeans pocket, he grabs a condom out of the back pocket before dropping everything to the floor in a heap.

He carefully climbs back over me and presses his mouth to mine before he rips open the condom, swiftly and carefully rolling it on. He settles himself between my legs and focuses on my eyes. "Are you ready?" he prompts.

"I've been ready for you my whole life," I divulge with as much emotion as I can muster into one sentence.

We both gasp as he instantly thrusts all the way into me. He stops, letting us both adjust. "Are you okay?" he asks, always watching out for me. I nod my head and try to pull him even closer. He relaxes into me and begins moving in and out, slow and methodical. He threads one hand into my hair and tucks the other one at the back of my neck, his weight on his elbows, just barely off me. I whimper as each thrust becomes faster and faster, pushing all the way in, my body feeling like a live wire as he reaches the spot to try to push me over the edge. He covers my mouth with his, kissing me deep and gentle. I love everything about this moment as we move together, each of us pushing closer. I move my knees up to his sides and hook them around his back. He thrusts so deep inside of me, stars begin to appear behind my eyelids as I feel my impending orgasm building deep inside me, burning me. "Sara, look at me, please. I need to know you're with me," he begs.

I instantly obey, looking into his eyes, now a dark blue filled with heat, desire and love for me as we move together and he drives me over the ledge without restraint. I whimper his name, "Jason" as my insides throb around him, squeezing him tight. He grips me tighter, his fingers digging in as I watch him come apart after a few more deep thrusts. He stills deep inside me and his head drops into the crook of my neck with a groan, both of us sweaty and breathing hard.

"I love you, Jason," I express needing to tell him in this moment.

He pulls back to look in my eyes. "I love you, Sara. I'm going to make sure you never doubt it for a second." I see the determination, love and pure devotion in his eyes making my heart fill with true happiness. He presses his lips to mine, kissing me sweetly, before pulling back with a broad smile. "I'm going to get us cleaned up." I nod my head, instantly feeling the loss of him as he pulls out. I watch as he pushes off the bed and retreats to my bathroom to toss the condom.

When he's gone, I pull his shirt on over my head. I want to be surrounded by his smell. He quickly returns with a washcloth and gently cleans me up before tossing it to the floor and helping me slip on my panties, caring for me. He tugs on his boxer briefs and lays down next to me, pulling me close to him with a low chuckle. "You like my shirt, huh?"

I just grin in response. Taking a deep breath, I settle into his embrace, finally knowing I'm right where I'm supposed to be.

Epilogue

Jason

Two months later...

"It's so different here when it's green and colorful!" Sara exclaims for I think the fifth time since we got here making me chuckle. I love seeing her eyes sparkle like they are now, causing her hazel eyes to appear golden.

"I heard you guys had fun here over the winter though?" my sister Theresa questions. Sara nods her head in confirmation. "I know my brothers are always doing something outside and it doesn't matter what time of year it is, so it's good he has you. You can help keep him in line too," she teases. I grin broadly at the two of them, enjoying their chatter.

I grip Sara's hand tightly as my eyes wander taking in everything around me. This barbecue to welcome Theresa home was really a great idea. She's been through so much and I'm thrilled she's finally back here where we can all help her out. My eyes wander to Matt standing next to our sister. I'm glad he made the effort to fly home to be here for Theresa. I have to admit, I wouldn't mind if he moved somewhere around here permanently. We all moved around so much growing up, it would be nice to have the whole family end up in one place, or at least in one area.

Christian and Bree stand talking with my parents over by my dad manning the grill. Christian has his arms wrapped around Bree from behind with a huge smile on his face while she looks up at him laughing. They both searched and fought so hard to find their happy together, no one deserves it more. My mom arranges the snacks along the table, her smile never seeming to waiver. I think she's just happy to have all of us together.

I focus my attention back to my girl. She hasn't had an easy few months, but we've worked through everything together. She attends a support group for her eating disorder and I'm thankful for their help, especially with things I don't understand. Although I always want to be there for her.

I'm even more grateful she entrusts me with everything that is her. She talks to me when she's struggling and she talks to me when she's happy, but she doesn't talk to her parents or her ex anymore at all. It sucks that she had to push her family out of her life, but no one deserves that kind of toxicity in their life, especially not my girl.

At least she still has her brother, Stephen. She only told him a little bit of how she was treated by both her dad and her ex and as I expected, her brother completely lost it. He left the family business and got a job with a big corporation in downtown Portland. He'll have to work his way up, but he's a smart man and we all know he'll prove himself quickly. Sara felt guilty, but he insists she did him a favor and constantly thanks her, fighting his own guilt and trying to do everything he can to make it up to her.

"Jason," Theresa calls, waving her hand in front of my face trying to get my attention. My eyes flash to her and she laughs. "You're so gone," she mumbles, grinning.

"Yup," I confirm, grinning with pride and love at Sara. I'm not about to argue when it comes to being gone for her. I'm happy to admit she holds my heart in her hands. Sara blushes deeply, glancing up at me from underneath her eyelashes and warming me from the inside. I pull her to me and place a chaste kiss on her lips. She melts into me causing my chest to tighten. I pull back, glancing down at her with both of us grinning like fools.

"Anyway, I was trying to find out when you were going to give Sara her birthday present?" she probes, wiggling her eyebrows.

Sara's eyes flit back and forth between Theresa and me. "My birthday present?" she questions. "But this party is for Theresa, not me! I thought we were celebrating with Liz next week?"

"We are, but we kinda' all went in together on a gift for you and the whole family wanted to be here to see you open it," I inform her with a nonchalant shrug.

Her eyes go wide in surprise. "What do you mean, all of you?"

"Well, me, my whole family, including Bree," I add glancing over towards her and Christian, "Liz and Blake and even your brother," I finish. Her mouth drops open in shock. "I feel bad your brother and Liz and Blake can't be here for this, but since you're part of our family too," I begin, trailing off.

"Jason," she whispers her breathing becoming labored. I know how much it means to her that my whole family already treats her like one of their own. We may not be engaged like my brother and Bree, but I have no doubt in my mind or my heart we will be one day soon and everyone knows it.

"I guess, I have to give it to you now," I tease. Tugging her by the hand towards the rest of my family now surrounding the outdoor table, I grin playfully.

As we step up to the table, my brother, Matt whistles loudly to get everyone's attention. "Hey, your eldest is ready to stand on his pedestal and speak. Everyone, listen up!"

I shove him in the arm, a bit harder than necessary for his comment making him laugh and quickly stepping out of my reach. I shake my head with amusement. "Well, I just wanted to give Sara her birthday present from everyone and we thought she should be with family who love her and those who gave her this gift when she opens it."

Sara blushes again as I reach into my back pocket for an envelope. I hand it to her grinning proudly. She smiles shyly, hesitantly taking it from me with all eyes on her.

"Thank you," she whispers. We all watch, as she opens the envelope and pulls out the paper inside, my mother already wiping tears out of the corners of her eyes. As Sara looks it over, her face scrunches up in confusion and a lone tear escapes. "I don't understand," she mumbles shakily, looking to me for an explanation.

"Well, we figured instead of all buying you a birthday present separately, we would all pitch in and help pay for your tuition. All of us together were able to pay for your fall semester," I explain wishing I could do more.

She shakes her head, insisting, "This is too much." Tears begin streaming freely down her cheeks.

I wipe a few away as I look into her eyes. "It's not enough," I tell her gruffly.

"But..." she begins.

I immediately interrupt her, "I love you. We all love you. You should have family and friends you can depend on to help you. You've worked hard to get where you are and you deserve to be able to finish your last year of school without having to wait. Use the money you've saved towards your last semester and your bills. Since you won't move in with me yet, you still have all of those," I tease her.

She wants to be done with college when we move in together. She wants to prove to herself that she can make it on her own first. I know she can, but I want her with me. Seventy-five percent of the time I'm at her place or she's at mine anyway. Working at the pub is the only thing that seems to get in the way, along with the occasional girls' night for her and Liz. I'm definitely happier though when I know she sleeps through the night without any of her horrible dreams. I can't guarantee that if she's not in my arms.

She laughs through her tears and buries herself in my chest. "Th...thank you," she stutters. Taking a deep breath, she attempts to pull herself together as she gently pushes herself away from my chest. She looks into my eyes and I can see her love shining in them before she turns her gaze on every other person surrounding us, repeating, "Thank you, thank you so much. I've never had so much…so much love," she whispers with awe.

We all grin back at her, everyone taking their turn hugging my girl. Matt goes last and when he lingers too long for my taste, I smack him in the back of the head. He chuckles softly and lets her go. "So, when are you and Christian going to tell me more about this business you're starting?" he prods.

Christian overhears and steps up with Bree in hand. "I know, can you believe it? Me teaming up with our big brother?" Everyone laughs except me.

I just shake my head at my brothers before adding sarcastically, "Yeah, don't know what I was thinking." I throw my free arm around Christian. "Do you want to explain?"

"Well, anyone who knows us knows we are always doing something outdoors, so we decided to make a business out of it. The plan is to offer different activities to people throughout the year like kayaking, paddle boarding, hiking, snowmobiling, fishing, cross-country skiing."

"I get the idea, keep going," Matt presses grinning.

"Well, we can do groups, families, individuals, but we'll offer limited instruction, training and education depending on the activity. Or we can act as a guide on trails or in the water since we know the area in all seasons," Christian explains.

"We both finished first aid and CPR training and we are working on a few additional certifications for the recreational side of things and we both have the business side already with our degrees and dad. If it goes well, we could always expand into other areas, hire more staff in different areas of expertise, things like that. In the meantime, we'll start basic and figure it out, but with just our local marketing we're already getting a lot of inquiries and have a few groups scheduled," I add feeling my excitement growing.

"That's really cool!" Matt exclaims.

"Maybe if you move your ass back here, you could work with us," I suggest.

"That's a fabulous idea," my mom exclaims squeezing in between all of us and focusing on Matt. "All my boys working together," she grins.

"Thanks a lot, big brother," Matt smirks at me.

I burst out laughing. "Good luck!" I wrap my arm around Sara and pull her with me as I retreat.

We slowly stroll towards the blue of the lake. The water is completely calm in the afternoon sun and quiet for a Sunday. It's still too cold to swim in, but I'm surprised there's not a few people out on their boats on a day like today. We stop a few feet from the rocky shore and Sara wraps her arms around my waist fitting perfectly snuggled under my arm. "It really is beautiful here," she murmurs reverently.

"Yeah, it is," I concur. Tipping my head down, I kiss her on the top of her head. I take a deep breath and exhale slowly, feeling completely relaxed for the first time in a while.

"I can't believe you did that," Sara mumbles into my chest.

I ignore her comment and tilt her chin up so I can look in those beautiful hazel eyes. "Are you happy, Sara?" I prod, hoping I already know the answer.

"Extremely," she whispers her confirmation. "Are you happy, Jason?" she echoes.

My lips twitch at the corners as I fight my grin. "Emphatically," I answer releasing my smile. I lean down and press my lips to her soft ones. I move slowly over her mouth and let my tongue slide along the edge of her sweet lips. I tuck my tongue back inside and nip at her bottom lip before brushing my lips back against hers.

A loud whistle, followed by my brother Matt's voice swiftly shatters the illusion of being alone. "Pull your face away from your girl so you can get your ass over here and feed her!" he yells. I pull away from a blushing Sara, just as I hear Matt yell, "Ow!" We turn towards my family making me chuckle at my mom's glare focused on Matt.

"Come on, Mom. Isn't it about time Jason actually gets harassed for once?" Christian asks innocently.

"Yeah, it's his turn," Matt adds, ganging up on me. "Ouch! Theresa, what was that for?" he prods.

"I was feeling a little left out," she claims defiantly and shrugs like it doesn't matter because she knows Matt won't do anything about it, especially since her accident.

Sara bursts out laughing, causing my head to reflexively turns towards her. I love that tinkling sound! I sit at the table pulling her down next to me. The happiness on her face appears all encompassing. I can't resist placing another chaste kiss on her mouth when her face lights up. She looks at me blushing and slightly surprised.

"I love you," I reiterate.

She smiles at me as we settle in for dinner with my family. I can truly say I've never been happier than I am in this moment, and I'll do everything I can to make sure the same is true for her from now on as long as she'll allow it.

The End

What's Next?

Are you looking for more? Find out what happens when Theresa wants to continue to heal closer to home and sets her sights on a man who doesn't want to be caught? Find out in book 4 of The Unforgettable Series, Unforgettable Memories. Each book in The Unforgettable Series is a stand-alone novel, but better read in order.

The Unforgettable Series in order includes:

The Unforgettable Summer

Unforgettable Nights

Unforgettable Dreams

Unforgettable Memories

The Unforgettable One

Unforgettable Mistakes

An Unforgettable Spin-Off:

Breaking Cycles

Acknowledgements

I want to take this opportunity to say thank you to my family. I know I wouldn't be able to be doing what I love if it wasn't for their love and support. I greatly appreciate all those extra "minutes" of quiet and patience you give me to make sure I'm able to get my thoughts down while I have them in my head. Most of all, Michael, Ty and Allie, thank you for being my happy ending.

Thank you again to Kelley for always being there for me. I'm grateful to have you in my life and it means so much to be able to share my books with you. Thank you for your encouragement and feedback with all of it!

Thank you to my other beta readers and editors, with special recognition to Nancy and Dina. Your honest opinions and assistance truly means a lot to me. I wouldn't have been able to release this book as quickly as I hoped without your help!

Thank you to all my readers from around the world! I really hope you enjoy reading my books as much as I love writing them! The Emory family, their friends and significant others have really become part of my own family. Please know, I love to hear from you!

Connect with the Author

For more Adult Contemporary Romance, read more by Nikki A. Lamers. Connect with her here:

Official Author Website
www.nikkialamersauthor.com

Linktree for All Nikki A Lamers Author Links
https://linktr.ee/NikkiALamersauthor

For Clean Contemporary Romance, read books by Nicole Mullaney. Connect with her here:

Official Author Website
www.nicolemullaneysauthor.com

Follow Her on Instagram
@nicolemullaney

Author Facebook Page
www.facebook.com/Nicole-Mullaney-Author-103006415283835/

BookBub
@NicoleMullaneyAuthor

About the Author

Nikki A Lamers has always had a passion for reading and writing, especially romance. She grew up in Wisconsin with her sister, mom and dad. She always loved reading romance books and watching romance movies with her dad, something they both enjoyed. After college she lived in Florida for a few years working for the "Happiest Place on Earth," where she met her husband. She now lives on Long Island in New York with her husband and two kids. She spends her free time reading or hanging out with friends and family. She would love to spend more time traveling, visiting new places and meeting new people.